MW01194455

# WIND OF ERUNA

Book Two: A Flight of Dragons

Kathy Hyatt Moore

Author's Tranquility Press
ATLANTA, GEORGIA

Kathy Moore/Author's Tranquility Press
3800 Camp Creek Parkway, SW building 1400-116, #1255
Atlanta, GA 30331
www.authorstranquilitypress.com

Publisher's Note: This is a work of fiction. Names, characters, places, and incidents are a product of the author's imagination. Locales and public names are sometimes used for atmospheric purposes. Any resemblance to actual people, living or dead, or to businesses, companies, events, institutions, or locales is completely coincidental.

Ordering Information:
Quantity sales. Special discounts are available on quantity purchases by corporations, associations, and others. For details, contact the "Special Sales Department" at the address above.

Winds of Eruna Book Two: A Flight of Dragons/Kathy Moore
Paperback: 978-1-961908-02-4
eBook: 978-1-961908-03-1

# Table of Contents

# PROLOGUE

Eruna was a planet where the majority of the inhabitants are winged and lived in giant trees, and where the wingless are in servitude to the winged population. In the Eight Realms, all young winglets attend Cliffside School where they prepare to study magic, but only if they pass the Wind Trials at the end of their eighth cycle at the school. The students then had the opportunity to not only study magic at Wind Dancers' Ledge, but also to become Wind Dancers themselves.

T'Algren Lynettelle and T'Ardis Joranaire, better known by their diminutives Lynette and Joran, had undergone the Desideratum and were life-mated. They each bore a unique mark over their hearts signifying their union. They also expected the birth of their winglet when they ran away from Cliffside School, where they were both eighth-level students. They had forgone the Wind Trials to escape the wrath of Lynette's mother, the High Matriarch of the Eight Realms. The High Matriarch, furious that her daughter had fallen in love with someone from Tree Ardis, sent her soldiers to apprehend the couple. Lynette and Joran travelled north with two of their friends, Hanoera and Kevar, into the Borderlands of the Northern Provinces where they discovered the entrance to the mythical city of Halalouma. But they were not alone.

Ooloo Noo'Loon, a young winglet, and her grandfather, Tavat, the Ema'Kame of the Clans of the Northern Plains and High Plateaus far to the north, also made their way to Halalouma. They were accompanied by several warriors of the

Clans and three Malakand, small reptilian creatures who were displaced from the Kahairnan desert, better known as the Wastelands. They escaped an attack by the evil wizard, T'Ardis Morrenaire, as they fought their way to the safety of the island city of Halalouma, located in an enormous cavern deep underneath the Wastelands. They had found their way to Halalouma in search of a southern passage through the cavern. Ooloo was determined to go to Cliffside School to learn the ways of the winged society living there. If she passed the Wind Trials she would be allowed to study Wind Dancers' magic, although she already learned to wield magic of her own. She was growing stronger and more powerful with every turn of Eruna.

Lynette's father, Mattern, better known as T'Algren Matternaire and lifemate of the High Matriarch, also searched for the runaways. He had finally made a break from his life-mate, the High Matriarch of the Eight Realms, only to discover that his daughter had left Cliffside. Traveling north toward the Wastelands, Mattern had acquired a blood-spell from a pair of witches to help him locate Lynette and her life-mate, Joran.

Also traveling north was a young wingless man named Lare, who had accidentally killed his winged master, Tree Ferndoren, in the woodshop where he had worked as a furniture maker and decorative carver. He had escaped the capture so far, but he was afraid it was only a matter of time before Master Ferndoren's family guards or the High Matriarch's soldiers apprehended him.

Meanwhile, Morren the wizard and former Wind Dancer, sought to capture Ooloo. Many cycles before and lost his wings in an ill-fated experiment with a spell of great power. As a result of the experiment, he had been trapped in a void inhabited by demons. A creature known as Saarnak ruled over the demons in the void. It took all of Saarnak's malignant energy to send Morren, along with a baby dragon, from the void back to Eruna. Morren was tasked with finding a way to open a portal of sufficient size to allow Saarnak and his hoard of demons to pass through. Only an innocent with superior magical abilities would be able to open the portal into Eruna through which Saarnak could pass. The winglet Ooloo, whose natural abilities could be perfected by Morren for Saarnak's purposes was the ideal innocent.

If Morren was successful, Saarnak promised to heal him and give him back his wings, which had been destroyed in the failed experiment. Morren was frustrated that he had failed so far to capture Ooloo, even with the aid of his now fully-grown black dragon, Death. He had tested his strength in magic against hers when he attacked at Halalouma, and Ooloo had come out ahead. The warriors with her had conquered the squad of undead soldiers Morren brought with him to capture her. Saarnak, furious with Morren for having failed to capture the young winglet, provided him with a special magical weapon with which to trap her the next time he attacked. Morren planned on returning to Halalouma with his entire army of undead to try once again to capture Ooloo.

Joran and Lynette had joined forces with Ooloo and her group in Halalouma. They planned to return to Cliffside School to warn the leaders, Mother Kerinelle and Father Libraenaire, about Morren's plan to attack the Eight Realms and destroy Cliffside.

Mother Kerinelle and Father Libraenaire had recently returned from the Northern Provinces where they had been staying in an old inn for over two octurns. No one at the inn knew their true identities as they had waited for a report from

Mother's agent, Hanoera, Lynette's friend who had accompanied her when she left Cliffside. They had awaited news of the birth of the offspring of their wayward students, Lynette and Joran. The message had indicated that they had a daughter and had named her T'Ardis Aerielle, facts which would further infuriate the High Matriarch.

The news of an impending attack on Cliffside School had come shortly after the first message delivered by Wing Guard Swen, Hanoera's contact. The news shocked Mother Kerinelle and Father Libraen to their very cores. Morren was alive and

set on revenge for what had happened to him. Mother Kerinelle and Father Libraen had destroyed the first message hoping to protect the newborn winglet from the wrath of the High Matriarch. The second message would not be destroyed, but would be shared, the sooner the better.

# CHAPTER 1
# HANOERA

Lynette, Joran, Kevar, and Hanoera sat around a large dining table at an inn in the mythical city of Halalouma with Ooloo and Tavat discussing the recent battle with the strange wizard and his golem.

The expansive cavern in which the ancient city was located, was lit by luminescent stalactites and stalagmites as well as the walls of the cavern. But inside the inn, fanciful lanterns placed on the dining table and throughout the room glowed brightly and shed a warm light over the group.

The six warriors accompanying Ooloo and Tavat were scattered in the dining room sharpening their blades and tending their other weapons. The Malakand, Gormon, Fessa, and Bicken, sat on the floor near the fireplace where a warm blaze burned, their scaled bodies reflecting the light. Wug, Gormon's short-furred pet bacanu cuddled against his side with his tail wrapped around one of Gormon's scaly arms, his large ears twitching. It was as if he could sense the danger they were in.

They had just finished a meal of gruel Fessa prepared for them, with travel bread, smoked oarao meat, and fish from the lake in the cavern, contributed by the warriors from the north. Joran sat at the head of the table as he held his new daughter, Aerielle, on his shoulder. He gently patted her back until she burped. He passed the winglet to Lynette who smiled with joy.

"I know we need to warn Mother Kerinelle and Father Libraen about the wizard's plan to attack the school and the Eight Realms. But how can we return to Cliffside while the High Matriarch's soldiers are surely still hunting us," Joran asked.

"We have been able to avoid them so far," said Lynette. "We must go back, Joran. We can't just stand aside and let the school be destroyed. Besides, Mother Kerinelle and Father Libraen will surely speak to my mother on our behalf, and now that the Eight Realms are in danger, she will have more important things to worry about than us."

"I wish we could stay here," said Ooloo. "There are many treasures throughout this cavern that we should investigate. We might even find something to help us against the wizard. Unfortunately, there isn't time because he will be back soon with more undead soldiers."

"And we must get word to Cliffside about the wizard and his army," said Lynette. "We should be there to help protect the school."

"You may as well tell them," said Kevar to Hanoera. He got up from the table, walked over to the fireplace, and folded his arms over his chest as he leaned against the mantel. The look on his face indicated he was not giving Hanoera a choice.

"Tell us what?" asked Lynette. "What is he talking about, Hanoera?"

"I...I may be able to get word to Mother and Father much sooner then all of us could return there," said Hanoera resignedly. She pushed her chair away from the table and rose to walk over to the fireplace as she looked guiltily at her friend, Lynette.

She stood next to Kevar, turned her back on the group, and sighed. She put an arm on the mantel and leaned her head against it, gazing into the flames.

"How?" asked Joran and Lynette at the same time, staring at Hanoera in suspicion and surprise.

"It's a long story," said Hanoera as she straightened up and turned to face Lynette. "You see, Mother Kerinelle assigned me to be your roommate to protect you and report on you..."

"She what? What are you talking about Hanoera? What do you mean 'report on me?'" Lynette asked angrily. She stared at her roommate in disappointment. "We've been friends since we were in our original octet together at the school. We chose to be roommates."

"I was supposed to keep you from harm and report on your progress," said Hanoera. "But our friendship is genuine," she assured Lynette.

"So Mother Kerinelle and Father Libraen know about Joran and me being life-mated," interrupted Lynette, "and that I was pregnant."

"Yes, by now she knows, but I didn't tell her everything. She somehow knew that you and Joran had undergone the Desideratum. But I didn't tell her. Apparently, Sister Fairenelle told her you were pregnant just after we left Cliffside," said Hanoera. "At least according to Swen."

"Who is Swen? I still don't understand how you can get word to Cliffside any sooner than we can return," said Joran.

"I have been keeping in touch with the leader of the Wing Guards whom Mother and Father sent after you, passing the word to him or one of his agents about our journey and how you were doing," said Hanoera. "They have been following us for some time now."

"If they know where we are then why haven't they apprehended us?" asked Joran. He rose from his chair and paced back and forth to the dining room as he glared at Hanoera. It did not go unnoticed that his hand was on the hilt of his sword.

"They haven't apprehended us because they were ordered not to interfere unless we were caught by the High Matriarch's soldiers," said Hanoera."I don't think they know where we are at the moment. I haven't communicated with Swen since before we found the entrance to this cavern and Halalouma.But more importantly, Mother and Father wanted to let things run their course, for you to have your winglet. They think she is important."

"She is important," said Ooloo. "She was foretold."

"Foretold?" asked Lynette. "What do you mean?"

"She is also Ans'Isna," said Ooloo."She will save her people in a time of great need. But her life is not going to be easy."

"Joran, I don't know what she is talking about, but I don't like the sound of it," said Lynette worriedly.Joran stopped pacing and stood behind Lynette. He placed his hands on her shoulders to calm her. He laid a hand gently on his baby's downy auburn head.

"Ooloo, have you had a vision involving this little winglet?" asked Tavat indicating Aerielle.

"Yes, I have, Paap. But it was not clear. I just know she is powerful or will be when she is my age," said Ooloo. She did not want to share the rest of what she knew. It was too painful. "I also sensed the wizard is not acting on his own. There is someone or something controlling him. I sensed a very evil presence in the wizard's mind."

"So, you can read minds too?" asked Joran as he turned to stare at Ooloo.

"No, I cannot read minds. I can just sense what someone is thinking sometimes," said Ooloo. "It's not the same as reading someone's mind. I can't control it very well."

"Let's not get off track here," said Lynette. "Hanoera, if you can get word to Mother and Father then that's what you should do. We need to find the guards from Cliffside. We can't stay here. We need to leave this place as soon as possible if that wizard is coming back."

"The wizard's name is Morren," said Ooloo. "T'Ardis Morrenaire."

"Oh, great winds, are you sure?" asked Joran. "He is from Tree Ardis? If he is, then we are related. But he disappeared many cycles ago, long before I was born. He was involved with some kind of experiment in dark magic that went terribly wrong. Mother Kerinelle and Father Libraen were somehow involved and saw the whole thing according to a rumor in our family. He disappeared as a result and no one has heard from him since. Are you sure that...that monster who attacked us is Morren?"

"I do not know if he is your relative. I just know that is his name," said Ooloo. "And I am certain he is returning with his army of undead. That much was clear in his mind. We must leave, soon. There are not enough of us to defeat his entire army."

"Yes, we should leave now," said Tavat as he stood. He spread his wings as he stretched. The rest of those sitting around the table also rose. They gathered their packs and weapons as they leave. Ooloo explained to the Malakand that they were leaving Halalouma and Bicken started to argue against the plan. Fessa soon set him straight with much barking and trilling.

"We are ready," said Conoc after a few moments. "It will be good to use my wings again." The rest of the warriors grunted their agreement.

"We cannot go back the way we came, across the lake," said Tavat. "That is where the wizard will probably return. We must continue our journey south. Is that not where you came from?" he asked Joran.

"Yes, we came through a long tunnel that exits into the forests of the Borderlands," said Kevar. "We can go back that way."

"There is a lift that will take us back up to the level of the city where the tunnels are located," said Joran. "It's how we came down to this level of the city and found you under attack by that giant and the wizard with his undead soldiers."

"I am reluctant to leave," said Ooloo wistfully. "There is so much here to see and explore. Bicken wants to stay here, too. But I know we must go."

"I also wish we had time to explore," said Joran. "Maybe we can return sometime in the future. But for now, we must go to the lift, quickly."

"Then lead the way," said Tavat, shaking out his wings again. The warriors gathered their weapons and packs and followed Joran and his group to the door and exited the inn.

They followed a winding road through the empty city, flying past beautiful buildings the use of which they could only imagine. They saw strange sculptures and carvings displayed artfully in parks and squares. Most of the statues were of winged beings, but there were also statues of the wingless. They flew past them all and eventually made their way back to the center of the city where the lift was located. The Malakand ran down the road and caught up with the rest of the group at the lift.

"We won't all fit in the lift at once," said Joran.He placed his hand on a panel outside the lift and the door opened. Bicken glared at him angrily, but Joran didn't notice. "Lynette you and the others wait here while Kevar, Hanoera, and I go up first to see if it's safe."

Bicken protested loudly to Ooloo. She translated for the others. "The Malakand, Bicken, wants to go with you first. He says he should be the one to control the lift as he is the one who led us here."

"Fine," said Joran impatiently. He stepped aside as Bicken, Fessa and Gormon went into the lift. Then he, Kevar, and Hanoera entered.

He turned to Tavat, "To get the lift to come back down you just put your hand in the indentation on this panel," Joran showed him how to call the lift back down and then stepped into the lift. The door closed as Bicken slapped his hand on the indentation with the up arrow. After a few moments, Tavat called the lift back down and ushered Lynette, who held her baby closely, Ooloo, and three of the warriors, Ingni, Samas, and Ramar into the lift.

"I will come last with Conoc, Kivik and Batab," he said. Suddenly they heard a loud boom and crash. The noise came from across the lake. Morren and his army of undead swooped into the cavern through a large hole in the rocks. He rode on a great black dragon that roared and spewed flame.

Tavat hurriedly sent the lift back up with its passengers. He called the lift back down after a few tense moments.

"Hurry," said Tavat to the remaining warriors. They all squeezed into the lift and Tavat slapped his hand on the indentation to go up. The lift shook as Morren threw balls of fire at the city wantonly. The door to the lift closed just as a ball of fire smashed against it. The lift shook as it rose to the top of the lift shaft. They found the others waiting for them when the door opened.

"What was that sound?" asked Lynette. "What happened?"

"It is the wizard, Morren, and his army of undead," said Tavat. "We must make haste to leave this place."

"Which tunnel did we come through?" asked Hanoera. There were three other tunnel entrances leading to the lift.

"I think it is this one," said Joran pointing to the tunnel to the left of the lift.

"Yes, that is the way," said Ooloo. "That one goes south."

Bicken stayed back and did something to the lift. He chattered and explained what he was doing to Ooloo.

"Bicken says now the lift will not work. He says there are a few other ways to get up here to these tunnels but he doesn't think the wizard can find them before we can get away," she said.

"Let's go now, before Morren figures out where we are and finds a way to get to us here," said Joran.

They all ran into the tunnel with Tavat bringing up the rear. But before they had gone a hundred wingspans they ran into a wild-looking winged man. His sword was drawn and he looked as though he had been traveling for a long time. He was gaunt and his eyes were bloodshot. He brandished his sword at the group menacingly.

"Father?Is that you? What are you doing here? How did you find us?" Lynette asked incredulously as she pushed through the group and made her way to the man. She barely recognized him. It was obvious he had not shaved for many turns.

"I have been looking for you since you left Cliffside," said Mattern, her father.

"But how did you find us?" asked Lynette. She passed the baby to Hanoera and threw herself into Mattern's arms.

"I used a blood spell," he replied wearily.

"Oh no, Father," said Lynette stepping away from him. "There are always consequences to using dark magic."

"I know. But I had to find you before your mother's soldiers did. I've had a terrible time staying ahead of them. She knows you have life-mated with an Ardis. Who is this? You had a girl?" Mattern asked indicating the baby in Hanoera's arms.

"We don't have time now for any more questions, sir," said Joran. "We must go...before we are discovered by the wizard and his army."

"Wizard? Army?" said Mattern eyeing Tavat and the warriors suspiciously.

"Not now, sir," said Joran. "We need to go back the way you came. We'll explain everything when we stop to rest. But now we need to go!" He grabbed Mattern and Lynette by their shoulders and prodded them into action.

"My warriors and I will bring up the rear. Take Ooloo with you and go ahead," said Tavat to Joran. They began flying down the tunnel. It was just large enough for them to fly single file while the Malakand ran just below their feet.

"Paap, wait, let me try to close this end of the tunnel so they can't follow us," pleaded Ooloo.

"What can you do, Ooloo, that won't collapse the tunnel on our heads?" asked Tavat.

"I will be careful, Paap. Please let me try," she beseeched.

"Wait," said Joran. "Wait until we get farther down the tunnel before you try anything."

"Alright," said Ooloo. As the others moved farther down the tunnel, she held out her hand and summoned a ball of blue fire. It grew in her hand until she was satisfied it was big enough. She threw it at the roof of the tunnel. Then she turned and flew toward the others. The roof at the end of the tunnel caved in, sealing the group off from the lift and Halalouma.

"That should hold them," said Tavat. He hugged Ooloo to his side while Bicken glared at her. He was not happy at the destruction she had wrought, even though Ooloo explained to him why it was necessary.

"At least it will buy us some time," said Joran. "Let Hanoera carry Aeri for a while," he said to Lynette. "At least until you are sure you are strong enough to fly. It has only been a turn since you gave birth."

"Alright, but I'm fine, really," she said as she took off into the air and flew down the tunnel. Hanoera and Kevar flew after her and then Joran.

"Wait," said Joran. "Let Kevar and me lead the way in case we run into trouble." He and Kevar flew ahead of Lynette and Hanoera. Ooloo and Tavat followed with the Malakand running behind them. The six warriors brought up the rear.

Soon the tunnel widened and they flew two abreast for most of the turn. Finally, they arrived at the large room where a fountain was located. It had only been two short turns since they had originally stopped there and filled their canteens on their way to the lift. This time though, they were running for their lives from a different foe, rather than the High Matriarch's soldiers, one far more dangerous and deadly.

When they landed Hanoera passed the baby to Lynette who sat down and immediately began to nurse her. Hanoera sighed and looked down at her friend with remorse.

"I'm sorry I couldn't tell you..." Hanoera said as she paced back and forth in front of Lynette.

"It's okay," interrupted Lynette. "I should have known Mother Kerinelle and Father Libraen would do something like that, considering who I am. I just wanted to be like everyone else, instead of the daughter of the High Matriarch. I guess you can never run from whom you really are. It always catches up with you."

"I'm still your friend, Lynette," said Hanoera. She stopped pacing and looked down at Lynette. "I always will be. I am sworn to give my life to protect you...and Aerielle."

"But I don't want you to give your life for me," protested Lynette. "I just want us to be like before I found out you were planted by Mother Kerinelle as my roommate."

"I would have chosen you for my roommate anyway," said Hanoera. "And we are still the same. It's just now you know you have a protector."

"I am her protector," said Joran. "I guess we are both her protectors." He sat down next to Lynette.

"I am thankful to have both of you as Aerielle's protectors," said Lynette.

"I will be her protector," said Ooloo solemnly. She knelt down in front of Lynette and placed her small hand on Aerielle's head. "I swear it." Her hand began to glow and Lynette snatched it away from the baby's head.

"It is alright, I am bound to her now," said Ooloo.

"What have you done, Ooloo?" asked Tavat.

"Yes, what have you done?" Lynette asked, concerned.

"Our paths were bound to cross. Now we are bound in spirit," she said. "We are Ans'Isna."

"What does that mean, exactly," asked Joran.

"Our people, the Clans of the High Plateaus, have a legend that in a time of great need, one will be born who will save her people. But it will be at a great price," answered Tavat. "The Ans'Isna is one who is gifted with the "sight" and is strong in other gifts. Ooloo was named "Ans'Isna" by my people before we left on this journey. She is very gifted," he said proudly.

"Where were you going?" asked Lynette.

"To the school by the cliffs," said Ooloo. "I have "seen" it. I saw three enormous Trees in the mountains, on a plateau by the cliffs, with many winged people living in the Trees. And wingless ones living among the roots."

"You are referring to Cliffside School," said Lynette. "How could you know about it other than hearing us talk about it?"

"Like I said, I saw the School over a cycle ago, before we left the High Plateaus," said Ooloo. "I will go to Cliffside to study and learn about magic."

"But you will have to pass the Wind Trials and become a Wind Dancer before you will be allowed to study magic," said Lynette. "However, you seem to know quite a few things about magic already."

"Yes, she is Ans'Isna," said Kivik. The other warriors added their assent.

Lynette finished nursing Aerielle. She stood and looked around for her father. She spotted him by the fountain.

Mattern finished filling his canteen with water from the fountain and walked over to her. He passed the canteen to her and held out his arms indicating he wanted to hold the little winglet.

"What is her name?" he asked as Lynette passed the winglet to him.

"Her name is Aerielle, T'Ardis Aerielle," said Lynette. "I want her to be known by her father's Tree."

"Hello, Aeri," said Mattern, using the diminutive of her name. He placed her on his shoulder and patted her on the back. After a few minutes, she let out a healthy burp. Mattern laughed happily.

"Father, where did you get a blood spell?" asked Lynette.

"I got the spell from a witch in the Esteryian Province. An old priest told me about her," he answered.

"Did her name happen to be Selene?" asked Joran.

"As a matter of fact, yes, her name was Selene, and her sister was Merium. How did you know?" asked Mattern.

"We went to her for a potion to prevent conception right after our life-mating ceremony. But as you can see she tricked us," said Lynette. "Her potion didn't work."

"Well, I have no regrets," said Joran. He laid a hand on his daughter's head and smiled down at her as Mattern cradled her in his arms. "Mattern, would you like to carry Aeri for a while? We've rested long enough."

"Yes, I would love to carry her," said Mattern.

"Lynette, are you strong enough to keep going?" asked Joran.

"Yes, I believe so," she assured him.

"Then Kevar, Hanoera and I will go first. Mattern, you and Lynette stay back with the others in case we run into trouble. Keep about twenty wingspans between us." Joran leapt into the air and flew down the tunnel. Kevar and Hanoera followed him while Mattern and Lynette waited a few moments before they followed. Ooloo and Tavat flew after them while the Malakand ran, and the six warriors brought up the rear again.

Almost half a turn later the tunnel began to curve upward and narrowed to a point where they could no longer fly. They walked the rest of the way back to the rocks where they had originally entered the tunnel three turns earlier.

"Let my warriors go through first," said Tavat. "You have put yourself at risk enough. They will scout around and find a good place to camp. Ooloo waits here with these people until we return."

"As you wish," said Joran. "Thank you."

Bicken pushed his way through the others and slapped his hand on the handprint and the rock pivoted open. Tavat, the six warriors, Bicken, and Gormon went through the opening. Fessa stayed back with Ooloo and the others. The sun had just risen and the ground was still damp with dew.

"Do not hesitate to hunt for something for us to eat as you scout around," said Tavat. "We have no oarao meat left and I don't care to eat more of the Malakand gruel."

The warriors flew off in different directions as Gormon and Bicken began foraging for greens and berries.

Still in the tunnel, Lynette took the baby from Mattern and sat down to nurse her while Joran and Kevar guarded the entrance. Fessa and Ooloo chattered and trilled in Malakand discussing the food situation. Hanoera stood protectively over Lynette and the baby.

Before mid-turn, several of the warriors returned. They reported that they had seen nothing to cause concern and had located a place to camp near a river.They also reported that two of them killed some kind of furry, long-legged creature none of them had ever seen before. Tavat went into the tunnel to fetch the others.

"You should come out now," he said to Joran. "We have a camp by a stream not far from here and fresh meat. My warriors are preparing it now.

"Thank you," said Joran. He helped Lynette to her feet. They all exited the tunnel and flew off in the direction indicated by Tavat. Fessa ran after them bringing up the rear. When they arrived at the camp they found Bicken and Gormon with Kivik and Batab, who were roasting a skinned animal on a spit over a welcoming fire.

"That smells delicious," said Ooloo. "What do you call this animal?"

"It is a tioldoer," said Joran. "They are plentiful in this region. The meat is delicious and the fur is very soft." Gormon offered some berries to everyone while they waited on the meat.

"Where are the rest of your warriors?" Joran asked Tavat.

"They are guard-keeping," said Tavat.

Soon the tioldoer meat was ready and Kivik cut strips of meat from the haunch and passed some to Ooloo. Wug hopped over to her and whined. He took the piece she offered him and scuttled back to Gormon to gobble it down.

After everyone had eaten their fill they laid out their blankets and bedrolls. They heard scuffling from the woods and shortly Conoc came into the camp pushing a wingman ahead of him. He had his knife at the stranger's throat.

"I found this one sneaking toward the camp," said Conoc. He threw the stranger's pack on the ground in front of the campfire.

"Swen!" said Hanoera. "It's alright, Conoc, he is the one I needed to find to send word to Cliffside about Morren."

Conoc grunted and shoved Swen toward the campfire. "Sit," he said. Swen did as he was told and plopped down next to Hanoera.

"Swen, it is vital that you get word to Mother and Father as soon as possible. It's a long story, but we believe there is going to be an attack on the School," said Hanoera.

"What kind of attack?" Swen asked.

"Do you remember hearing about T'Ardis Morrenaire?" asked Joran. "He was a former Wind Dancer who disappeared after a failed experiment with a powerful spell."

"Yes, I remember," said Swen. "He's dead, isn't he?"

"No, he's back and he has an army of undead with him. He is wingless and disfigured and also has a dragon. He's planning an attack on Cliffside School," said Joran.

"That's not all," said Hanoera. "You need to get word to Mother Kerinelle that Lynette and Joran have a daughter."

"Congratulations," said Swen to the happy couple.

Swen started to reach into his pack but Conoc stepped threateningly forward with his knife. Swen held his hands out to his sides and said, "I'm just going to get something from my pack for Hanoera to write a message." He moved his hands slowly and deliberately as he reached into his pack and brought out some paper, ink and a quill. He slowly passed them to Hanoera, who immediately started writing the message. She wrote for a while as she had much to tell Mother Kerinelle. Finally, she was finished and blew on the paper to dry the ink. She rolled up the message and passed it to Swen.

"Please allow him to leave immediately. The sooner he goes, the sooner Mother and Father will know about the attack," said Joran to Tavat.

Tavat nodded his assent to Conoc who stepped away from Swen.

"Let him eat something first," said Lynette, taking pity on the wingman.

"That would be nice," said Swen. Tavat cut some meat and passed it to Swen on his knife. Swen gratefully took the meat and tucked into it with vigor.

"Where are the rest of your wingmen?" asked Hanoera.

"I sent them ahead, into the Wastelands. When we saw no sign of you for several turns I decided to double back and see if I could find you," replied Swen. "This was the last place I saw you before you disappeared."

"Then your wingmen are most likely either dead or taken by Morren," said Joran. "The Wastelands are no longer safe for anyone."

When Swen was done, he drank from his canteen and stood slowly. He nodded to Lynette and the others and saluted Hanoera. Then he walked a short distance from the group. He leapt into the air and flew quickly away heading south to take the message to Mother Kerinelle and Father Libraen telling them of the birth of Aerielle and of the danger coming their way.

# CHAPTER 2
# HOMEWARD

Early the next turn, Lynette awakened to find Joran already up and cuddling Aeri. He and Mattern conversed quietly. She sat up, wiped the sleep from her eyes and yawned.

"I think she's hungry," Joran said as soon as he noticed Lynette was awake.

"Well, give her to me, then. Have you changed her yet?" she asked.

"Yes, I have and I washed the other diapers in the stream already. I hung them close to the fire so they should be dry soon. I'm really glad you had the foresight to purchase supplies in the Caverns before we left the Eight Realms. I'd hate to have to use my shirts for diapers," he laughed.

"Where is everyone," asked Lynette, noticing that only Mattern, Tavat and Ooloo were in the camp with them. Ooloo was still asleep with Wug snuggled up against her side. Tavat sat next to her sharpening his knife. He nodded his head toward Lynette in greeting. Mattern sat down beside her.

"The Malakand are away foraging for more berries and edible plants, and all of Tavat's warriors are on patrol or hunting for game," said Mattern. "In the meantime, we need to decide what we are going to do."

"We really don't have much of a choice, do we, Joran," said Lynette looking at her mate. "We can't go into the Wastelands now and risk getting caught by Morren.

There is really nowhere we can go except back to Cliffside. My mother's soldiers wouldn't expect us to go back."

"Don't count on that," said Mattern. "I would not put it past her to have used a blood spell on them. They could be out there right now just waiting for the right opportunity to attack."

"My warriors will warn us long before any soldiers could sneak up on us," said Tavat defensively.

"I meant no offense," said Mattern. "You have no idea how devious my former mate can be."

"Former?" said Lynette.

"Yes, I was going to tell you, I have left your mother for good," said Mattern. "I have much to tell you. She is more corrupt than ever."

"I'm glad you have left her, Father," said Lynette. "She has no love for either of us anymore. I don't remember her ever telling me she loved me and she was certainly never a mother to me. I couldn't wait to leave Tree Algren and go to Cliffside. The only regret I had was leaving you alone with her. I'm not afraid of her anymore, not with Joran and you by my side. We must go back to Cliffside and we would like you to go with us."

"I must take my granddaughter to the school by the cliffs," said Tavat entering the conversation. "I would welcome your company, and my warriors and I can keep you safe."

"Thank you," said Joran. "Lynette is right. We must go back. Mother Kerinelle and Father Libraen may be able to reason with the High Matriarch now that Aerielle is born. But more importantly, if there is going to be an attack on the School, we should be there to help protect it."

Ooloo was awake and listening to the conversation. She sat up and stretched. The Malakand returned and Fessa put the armload of leaves and freshly washed roots she carried into her cook pot. She added some water and put the pot over the fire. A pleasant aroma arose from the pot as she stirred the concoction. She chattered at Ooloo, who translated, "Fessa says first-meal will be ready soon." Gormon and Bicken each carried a large leaf full of berries. They spread the leaves out and offered some of the berries to the others.

Tavat leaned over Fessa's pot and sniffed suspiciously. "Well, it certainly smells edible," he said. He accepted a handful of berries from Gormon and ate them quickly.

"There is still some meat left from last night," said Conoc as he walked into the camp. He glanced at Fessa's pot of gruel and wrinkled his nose scornfully.

Tavat looked at him expectantly. "What have you to report," he asked.

"We have not spotted anything unusual other than a road running parallel to the river about five hundred wingspans to the east," Conoc replied. "We saw no one traveling the road, though."

"This is the Borderlands," commented Joran. "You won't see much traffic this far north."

Ooloo suddenly jumped to her feet and screamed, "He's coming! The wizard Morren is coming! He will be here soon."

"Oh, great Wind!" said Lynette. She gently pulled Aeri from her breast and passed her to Mattern as she closed her shirt. Aeri started crying in protest.

"We must go, now," said Tavat. Everyone grabbed their packs and leapt into the air to fly away. They could see a great cloud bearing down on them from the Wastelands to the north. It was Morren and his hoard of undead. Tavat whistled loudly and the warriors rose one by one into the air from the forest.They saw the others flying toward them from a long way off and didn't have to ask what was happening. They could see the hoard coming their way. They joined the group fleeing in the air. They flew south as fast as they could while the Malakand ran in the direction of the road.

"They are catching up with us," said Tavat. "We must fly faster." He grabbed Ooloo from the air and held her to his chest. "Wrap your arms and legs around me," he told her. "Can you cast a ward around us?"

"I don't know. There are too many of us, Paap, but I will try," she said. She concentrated and tried with all her might, but she could not hold the ward around everyone. "I'm sorry, Paap, I cannot hold it around all of us."

"Then hold it around as many as you can," said Tavat.

"It won't do any good. They have spotted us and they will soon be upon us," she said forlornly.

"It is all right, little one. I think it is time now to turn and fight," shouted Tavat.

Joran and Lynette turned to face the hoard, as did the warriors. "Mattern, take Lynette and Aerielle and go," said Joran.

"No," said Lynette, "I will not leave you." Joran knew it would do no good to argue with her.

"Father, go please! Take our daughter and get her to safety. Go to Cliffside." Lynette shoved her pack at her father. He took it and slung it over his shoulder with his own pack. "There is some Mother's Milk Root powder in my pack and everything you need for Aerielle," said Lynette to Mattern. "Please go now, Father! Hurry!"

"Take Ooloo with you," yelled Tavat.

"No, Paap! Morren is going to take me. I have seen it. I just couldn't tell you. It's all right. I will survive," said Ooloo, tears streaming down her face. "I love you, Paap." She let go of her grandfather and dropped a wingspan. Her wings opened with a snap and she flew toward Morren and the hoard pursuing them. Maybe her grandfather and the others would be spared if Morren got what he wanted and captured her.She turned to the Malakand and said, "Gormon, you must take Bicken and Fessa and run and hide. You are important to the future of your kind."

"But I want not to leave you," cried Gormon.

"You must go, now!" Ooloo insisted. Fessa and Bicken grabbed Gormon's arms and pulled him away. They began to run as fast as they could away from the approaching hoard while tears streamed down Gormon's face.

Mattern was torn whether to stay or go, but he decided to do as she asked.He looked at his daughter one last time before turning and flying away with Aeri clutched to his chest.

Morren saw Ooloo coming toward him and ordered the hoard not to harm her. She threw fireballs at him but they merely bounced off the shield of protection he created around himself. Saarnak had given him a powerful spell he could use to capture her. He threw a net of power at her knocking her from the air before she could make a shield of her own. She plummeted to the ground and almost lost consciousness. The net tightened around her. The more she struggled, the tighter the net became.

The warriors and Tavat flew after her but they were soon overcome by the undead. They were outnumbered five to one. Lynette, Joran, Kevar, and Hanoera fought as bravely as the warriors, but they were soon surrounded by the undead. They fought and continued to slash with their swords and knives even though each was soon wounded. They were forced to the ground and fought back to back, while the rest of the warriors circled around Ooloo trying to protect her and keep the undead from her. They stabbed the undead in the heart, which they soon discovered was the only way to kill them and many of them fell, but more just kept coming.

Morren landed his dragon and approached the fighters. Tavat was surrounded by a group of undead and had taken two serious wounds. He fell to the ground, but not before taking several of the undead with him. Three of the undead fell on top of him as he lay there bleeding from a wound in his side and left arm. The last thing Tavat saw before he passed out was Ooloo on the ground, captured in the energy net.

Kevar was down and Hanoera was seriously wounded. She wouldn't last much longer, but she stood protectively over Kevar slashing at the undead. She was able to stab several in the heart, but then she was overcome and fell.

"Do not kill them," shouted Morren. One by one the warriors, who were all bloodied and injured, succumbed to the overwhelming numbers of undead fighters flurrying around them and were forced to the ground. Morren didn't waste time and enthralled the warriors, taking control of them.

Lynette and Joran, who were fighting back to back a few wingspans away from the others, were horrified to see Morren enthrall the warriors. Conoc, Ingni, and Batab turned on Lynette and tried to capture her while Kivik, Ramar and Samas attacked Joran. They tried to disarm him. He and Lynette were now fighting against those they had come to consider friends.

Lynette looked around for Mattern and Aerielle, but when she saw no sign of them she was relieved and believed they had gotten away safely. Both Hanoera and Kevar were down and injured. Morren enthralled them to his will and they turned to attack Joran and Lynette.

"Joran, I will not become one of those things," Lynette screamed, knowing she was not going to last much longer. She looked into Joran's eyes and said, "I love you." She turned her knife upon herself, prepared to plunge it into her own heart. Joran looked at her and turned his knife upon himself, preparing to end his life.

A few wingspans away, Ooloo, who was fighting against the energy net surrounding her, saw Lynette and Joran and cast a spell at them. Light flared around them and they suddenly disappeared. Ooloo was barely conscious, but she had saved the young couple from Cliffside. She hadn't known she could do such a thing until that very moment, but she knew it was important that Lynette and Joran survive. 'If only she could have saved everyone,' was the last thought she had before she passed out.

Morren walked to where Ooloo lay unconscious on the ground. He waved his hand over her and the energy net disappeared. He bent down and placed a special bracelet, that Saarnak had him instructed to make, on each of her wrists. The bracelets were etched with runes and symbols that would prevent her from accessing and using her magic. He picked her up and climbed onto the back of his dragon. He flew away toward his fortress in the Wastelands, his army of undead and enthralled warriors followed.

# ~
## CHAPTER 3
# LARE

Gormon, Fessa, and Bicken, slowly came out from behind the bushes and rocks where they were hiding and made their way back to the battle site. Gormon pulled several bodies off of Tavat to discover he was surprisingly still alive.

Fessa and Bicken thought maybe they could save Tavat. The wound on his side was severe and his left arm had a bad cut along his bicep. They bound his wounds with strips cut from the clothing of the undead which had succumbed and gathered spears. They set to work making a stretcher they could drag. He needed help if he was going to survive.

None of them had ever been further south than the Borderlands north of the Wastelands where they lived after fleeing the desert. They had traveled under the Wastelands by going through the long tunnel Joran and Lynette and their group used to get to the cavern where they found Halalouma. Now that they were in the Southern Borderlands, they could only follow the road south in hope of finding help for Tavat. The sun was setting when they felt Tavat was stable enough to move. Fessa gathered her cooking pot and put it in her backpack as Gorman and Bicken broke camp.

They moved Tavat gently onto the stretcher they made with the clothing and spears. Bicken and Gormon each picked up the front end of the stretcher and dragged it between them. As they began their journey down the road, the three Malakand hardly spoke. They were so full of grief over the loss of their friends that they all turned into a dark indigo blue, which blended well with the night. But since they could see in the dark they traveled as quickly as possible. Wug rode on one of the poles of the stretcher and whined plaintively.

By the next turn, they still had not arrived at a village and decided to rest and eat. They moved to the side of the road and stopped in a small glade. They laid the stretcher down gently and Fessa checked on Tavat. She laid her hand gently on his brow. He was feverish and delirious and mumbled something about Ooloo. Fessa looked at Bicken and Gormon worriedly.

"We must find help soon," she said in Malakand. She took her canteen from her pack and put it to Tavat's lips, coaxing him to drink while Bicken and Gormon gathered more berries.

Tavat took a few sips of water and coughed. The wound on his side and arm were still bleeding and Fessa was afraid he was losing too much blood. She tightened the bandages and hoped they soon find a village.

They quietly ate some berries and drank from their canteen. After resting for a few moments, they picked up the stretcher and started back down the road. Before they had gone far they saw someone coming toward them. He was a wingless man sitting on a saddle on a garing. They didn't know what to do, whether to flee or ask the stranger for help. Fessa decided for them. As the stranger slowed down and approached them, she stepped into his path and placed her hands on her hips so that he had to stop.

She looked pointedly at Gormon. "Ask him to help us," she ordered.

Gormon and Bicken laid the stretcher down as the stranger dismounted the garing. He walked over and squatted down to look at Tavat. Wug curiously plucked at his shirt.

"Our friend, Tavat, needs help," said Gormon in the language Ooloo had taught him. "This Fessa and this Bicken. I is Gormon," he said patting himself on the chest.

The stranger seemed to understand because he turned to Gormon and asked, "What happened?" His accent was different, but Gormon understood him well enough.

"Big bads dragon man and army..." Gormon tried to explain but was at a loss for words.

"Nevermind," said the stranger as he took his pack off and laid it on the ground. "My name is Lare. This is Nart," he indicated the garing. "Your friend is in a bad way. There is a village about half a turn back the way I came. I can help you get him there. I don't know if they have a doctor, but we have to try to get your friend some help."

Lare had never seen a Malakand before, although he had read about them. He had never seen a creature like Wug, a bacanu, either. Malakand rarely came out of the Wastelands, at least not this far south. He wasn't sure the wingman they called 'Tavat' was going to survive, but he was willing to help them. He didn't have anything better to do and he was curious as to how they had come to be in this predicament.

He took some rope from his pack and rigged the stretcher to his garing. The Malakand had never seen a garing and they chattered away in their language and stared and pointed at Nart. For that matter, they had never seen a wingless man before either.

"Where you's wings?" asked Gormon as he offered his canteen to Lare.

Lare laughed and accepted the canteen. He took a drink before answering, "I was born without wings. None of my people have wings. Where I come from the wingless serve the

Wings. They call us Grubs, but we prefer to be called 'ground-dwellers.'" He handed the canteen back to Gormon.

Gormon nodded his head as if he understood what Lare was saying. He translated for Bicken and Fessa who also nodded politely.

"We better get going," said Lare. He mounted the garing and took off at a better speed than the Malakand had been making carrying the stretcher between them. They ran beside the garing, easily keeping up. Wug rode on Lare's shoulder with his tail wrapped around one of the wingless man's arms. Lare didn't seem to mind.

Just as Lare had said, it took about half a turn to get to the village. The sun was high in the sky when they arrived. There were five giant trees with various buildings in the limbs. Lare pulled to a stop in what was apparently the town square. Some of the townsfolk saw them and flew down from the various limbs to find out what was going on. A few ground dwellers strolled over to get a look at the strange-looking group. Few people this far south of the Wastelands had seen a Malakand, much less three.

"We need a doctor or a healer," said Lare to the group gathered around the stretcher. Wug hopped from his shoulder to Gormon's. He wound his tail around Gormon's arm and rubbed his head against the Malakand's face.

One of the wingmen said to another, "Gullip, go fetch the doctor." The wingman turned to Lare and said, "What happened?"

"I'm not sure. I came upon these three Malakand dragging this injured wingman about half a turn up the road. They said something about a dragon..."

"Dragon," laughed one of the townsfolk. "There haven't been any dragons for thousands of cycles," said one of the others.

"I'm just telling you what they told me," said Lare defensively.

Just then the doctor swooped down from a building in one of the trees. He looked at Tavat's wounds and said, "Get him to my surgery. I don't know if I can save him. He's lost a lot of blood and he has a fever. Someone go get the priest. It's going to take both of our skills if he is to survive."

Several of the townsfolk helped Lare unfasten the stretcher from Nart. Two of the winged townsfolk flew the stretcher holding Tavat up to the doctor's office in the middle of the five giant trees.

Lare and the Malakand weren't sure what to do now. Lare looked at one of the ground-dwellers standing around and said, "Is there somewhere we can wait, an inn or a tavern where we would be welcome?"

"Well," said the ground-dweller, "our kind aren't welcome in the inn, but the tavern is in that tree over there," he turned and pointed to the tree farthest to the west. "You'll have to take the lift up, of course. It's almost time for the last meal and my Wing Master won't mind if I break off work a little early. My name is Wellim, and I work for Tree Erboer." He held out his hand and Lare took it in his and gave it a firm shake. Gormon, Fessa, and Bicken looked at Lare for guidance.

"I'm Lare," he said. He deliberately did not say more and Wellim looked at him curiously.

"What brings you to these parts?" asked Wellim.

"Just business," said Lare. "This is Gormon, Bicken, and Fessa," he said changing the subject. "I don't know the little critter's name."

"Wug," said Gormon.

But Wellim was not willing to let it go. "What kind of business?" he asked.

"The wood business," said Lare impatiently.

"Well there's plenty of that around here," laughed Wellim. "You can tie up your garing over there. Plenty of grass to eat." He indicated an area under the tree where the tavern was located. A hitching post and a water trough were off to the side of the grassy area. Lare put a long lead on Nart so he could graze and drink with ease.

Lare and Wellim looked at the Malakand who were huddled together chattering away and appeared to be having an argument. Quite a few townsfolk had come to get a look at them and they were rather uncomfortable with all the attention.

"Are you going to bring them with you to the tavern?" asked Wellim. "There has never been any Malakand around here before. I don't know if they are welcome in the tavern or not.

"I suppose so," said Lare. By now the crowd around the Malakand had become quite large. Lare could tell it was making the Malakand nervous so he said to Gormon, "I think you three should come with me to the tavern." He pointed to the tavern to indicate where he wanted them to go.

Gormon was relieved. He translated for Fessa and Bicken who were relieved as well. They all three nodded to Lare. He ushered them toward the lift, pushing through the crowd. A ground-dweller tried to get on the lift with them, but Lare glared at him and put his hand on his blade. The ground-dweller got the hint and stepped away from the lift.

The lift was operated by the two ground-dwellers with a system of pulleys. Once it stopped at the limb on which the tavern was located, they got off and walked to the entrance. Wellim pushed open the door and said to Lare, "After all of you." Lare and the Malakand entered the tavern closely followed by Wellim.

The winged barkeeper looked up from drying glasses in surprise as he saw the group and came from behind the bar to greet them. "Welcome, welcome, take a seat anywhere." He didn't seem to object to the Malakand entering his establishment, although he stared at them warily. He snapped his fingers at a wingless serving girl who scurried to show the group to a table near the fireplace. Some of the patrons whispered to one another about the strange sight.

"They are tamed, aren't they," said the barkeep indicating the Malakand and Wug.

"Of course they are," said Wellim. "Ain't you ever seen Malakand before?"

"No, and neither have you," huffed the barkeep. "And I don't want any trouble in my establishment." He went back behind the bar and continued to dry glassware, all the while keeping a wary eye on the group.

"What can I get you?" asked the serving girl looking at the three Malakand curiously. "Um, what do they eat?"

"I have no idea. What do you have?" asked Lare.

"We have a nice tioldoer roast with tarog roots and a green salad," said the serving girl. Gormon was listening carefully and seemed to understand what she had said. He translated for Fessa and Bicken. They both nodded their heads.

"I'll have the roast and roots and the salad," said Lare. He looked at Gormon who nodded his head.

"We eat roasts and roots and salads too. We drink water, please," said Gormon politely.

"I'll have an ale," said Lare.

"I'll have the same," said Wellim, taking notice of Wug who was playfully sniffing at his shirt. "What does this little guy eat? What'd you call him?" he asked Gormon.

"Wug," said Gormon. "is bacanu." Wug hopped back over to Gormon and plopped down next to him to take a nap.

Shortly the food arrived and they all started eating. Wug woke up and picked at Gormon's food, stuffing pieces of salad in his mouth.

"Well, I guess that answers that question," laughed Wellim. "He eats what we eat."

As they were finishing up their meal, the wingman named Gullip came into the tavern and walked over to their table.

"Doc says your friend is stable right now. He stitched him up good and the Wind Dancer priest said a healing spell. Doc thinks he is going to be okay. You can go see him whenever you want," said Gullip.

"Thank you," said Lare. Gormon translated what Gullip said to Lare for Fessa and Bicken and they seemed relieved.

"We go see Tavat now?" Gormon asked Lare.

"Yes, we go see Tavat now," agreed Lare.

Lare paid the barkeep and they left the tavern with Wellim. They took the lift down and walked over to the tree where the doctor's office was located, but Wellim stayed behind this time to speak with a few townsfolk. They took the lift up to the office and Lare knocked on the door. The doctor opened the door and ushered them in. He led the group to another room where Tavat was reclining in a bed. He was pale and weak but looked a lot better than the last time they had seen him.

He turned his head and said, "Ooloo? Where is Ooloo."

Gormon went to his side and took one of Tavat's hands in his. "Bads man on big dragon take her," he said sadly. He turned dark blue with sorrow.

Tavat groaned and tried to sit up. The doctor rushed to his side and gently pushed him back down. "Not so fast. You lost a lot of blood," he said. "I just got you all stitched up. Maybe you can sit up tomorrow. For now, just rest."

Gormon turned and signaled for Lare to come forward, "This is Lare. He help us get you here before you die," he said, "He is a friend."

Tavat looked at Lare and nodded weakly. "Thank you," he said and then shut his eyes.

"That's enough for now," said the doctor. "He needs his rest. You can come back tomorrow."

Lare and the Malakand left the doctor's office and found Wellim waiting for them outside. He had taken the lift up while they were visiting Tavat. "You can stay with me since you aren't welcome at the inn. We ground-dwellers look out for one another. Your little friends are welcome too," he said, indicating the Malakand and Wug. "My place is between the roots of Tree Erboer not far from here."

They all took the lift down to the ground and Lare went to get Nart where he had left him grazing at the hitching post. He didn't mount though, deciding to walk instead of ride since the others were walking.

"You ready to go?" asked Wellim.

"Yep," said Lare as he signaled Gormon and the others to follow him. They set off down the road and soon arrived at Tree Erboer.

"My master is Mayor of this village. That's why it is called Erboer. I work in his office since I can read and I'm good with numbers," said Wellim proudly. "What'd you say you do for a living?"

"I didn't," said Lare pointedly.

"Sorry, just curious," said Wellim. "Don't mind me. I was just wondering why you were looking for wood here."

"Because my master told me to," said Lare. He'd had enough of Wellim's unwelcome questions.

"Yeah, yeah. Who is your master anyway?" persisted Wellim.

"Look," said Lare angrily. "Maybe we'd better find somewhere else to stay."

"No, no. Never mind," said Wellim. "Like I said. I'm just the curious sort. I meant no offense. Just ignore me." He held up his hands in surrender.

They arrived at Wellim's house between the roots of Tree Erboer. It was a modest-looking home. "You can put your garing in the stall around the side there," he said as he pointed the way to Lare, who walked off to tend to Nart. "There should be some straw too," Wellim shouted. He turned back toward the front door.

"It's just me. I'm not life-mated," he said as he opened the door and ushered the Malakand into his dwelling. "Here, let me get us some light and get the fire going." He lit a lamp and poked at the coals in the fireplace. He threw on a few small logs and soon had a nice blaze going. The Malakand sat close to the fireplace to get warm. The evening had become chilly as the sunset.

Lare finished unsaddling Nart and gave him a handful of straw. He checked to see that there was water in the trough and was relieved to see that there was. He walked to the front of the house and knocked on the door. Wellim opened it and welcomed him in.

"I'm afraid there's only one bed, but you're welcome to spread your bedrolls out around the fire here," said Wellim. "Let me know if you need any extra blankets or anything,"

"Thank you," said Lare. "This will be fine." He and the Malakand took their backpacks off and spread out their bedrolls as Wellim bid them goodnight after locking the front door.He went into the only bedroom and closed the door gently. Lare noticed that Wellim locked the bedroom door as well as if he didn't trust his guests.

Lare was not sure about Wellim. He asked a lot of questions. It took Lare a long time to get to sleep.

# CHAPTER 4
# CAPTIVE

Ooloo awoke with a terrible headache and she hurt all over. She was lying on a pallet that was lumpy and uncomfortable. She noticed the bracelets on her wrists and tried to pull them off to no avail. She sat up slowly and looked around. She was in a cell roughly two wingspans by three wingspans. There was a bucket in one corner, which she thought might be where she was supposed to relieve herself. A table and chair sat in the middle of the cell. There was a small barred window along one side of the cell.

Opposite the window was a wooden door. She didn't bother checking to see if it was locked. She knew it was. On the floor next to the pallet was a plate with some kind of gruel on it with a heel of bread. Next to the plate was a cup of water. It was exceedingly hot in the cell so she drank all of the water greedily. She picked up the plate and sniffed the gruel suspiciously. Foregoing the gruel, she ate the bread and wished she had saved some of the water. Then she relieved herself in the bucket.

She stood on tiptoe and looked out the window. She saw only sand and a tall dark wall. It wasn't quite nighttime yet. She walked to the door and tried to open it anyway. Pain shot up her arm. The door was locked so she banged on it with her fist ignoring the pain. She lowered herself to the floor and looked under the door but she couldn't make anything out other than sand.

"Hello, is anyone there?" she called as she got to her feet. She couldn't sense anyone outside the door. She decided to examine the bracelets on her wrists. She tried to take them off again, but there were no seams and they were tight like cuffs. There were bizarre symbols and runes engraved on them. She had a sinking feeling about the cuffs and tried to form a ball of fire in her hand. When she couldn't, her fears were confirmed. She could not access her gifts, at least not at the moment. She concentrated and thought she sensed...something, but she couldn't be sure.

Much time passed as she paced back and forth in the cell and it grew dark. Before long she thought she heard a key being inserted into the lock. She quickly got behind the door so that when it opened she would be hidden from the view.

Morren walked into the cell and conjured a ball of light that floated up to the ceiling. Ooloo came rushing around the door and tried to push past him and escape. But he grabbed her and lifted her off her feet and pulled her to his chest. She bit him on the arm and kicked and screamed, but he held on tightly.

"Stop it!" he said. "I'll let you go when you settle down." That only made her fight him all the more fiercely, and she continued to kick and contort in his arms. Finally losing patience, Morren walked over to the pallet, threw her down on it, and conjured a net to confine her. The more she struggled, the tighter the net grew. She felt she was going to pass out again.

Ooloo finally realized it was futile to keep struggling, so she became quiet and still. She glared at Morren defiantly.

"Fierce little thing, aren't you," he laughed.

"Let me out of this net!" she said. "I'll show you how fierce I really am!"

"No, I don't think so. Not until you agree not to fight me," Morren said as he pulled out the chair and sat down.

"I agree, I won't fight you," she said after thinking for a moment. He released the net of energy and she immediately ran for the door. She almost made it out, but just at the threshold, she slammed into an invisible wall, knocking her senseless. She sat down hard on the floor and shook her head to clear it.

"Devious and determined, and a liar," commented Morren.

"I did not lie. I said I would not fight you. I did not say I would not try to escape," she said.

Morren sighed and said, "It is useless for you to continue trying to escape. The sooner you realize that the sooner you can get out of this cell."

"Why would you let me out of this cell?" she asked, suspicious of his intent.

"Because I need your help," he said and smiled benignly.

"I will never help you," she said defiantly.

"We will see about that," said Morren. He raised his hand and Ooloo convulsed with pain. She shrieked in agony. The pain seemed to go on forever, but it was only a few moments. He lowered his hand and unclenched his fist. The pain stopped and Ooloo panted with relief.

"I do not enjoy torturing little winglets," he said, "but I will do what I must in order to get your cooperation. I will have your cooperation one way or another," he assured her.

"You are an evil creature besides being ugly," said Ooloo glaring at Morren with hatred. "What happened to your wings?"

"You have no idea what I have been through," he said angrily as he remembered his suffering in the void, the pain he had experienced. He shuddered just thinking about it. "I lost my wings in a terrible accident. But you don't need to concern yourself with that."

"I...I would like some more water, please," said Ooloo. "I can't help you if I die of thirst." It was so hot in the cell and Ooloo was very thirsty.

"Come with me," he said and stood up. He offered his hand to Ooloo to help her get up. She just looked at it disdainfully and got up on her own. Morren waved his hand before the door and walked through. He turned to look at Ooloo. "It's all right. The energy barrier is gone. Remember I can bring back the pain if you try to escape again."

Ooloo grimaced and followed him out with as much dignity as she could muster. "Where are we going?" she asked.

"You wanted some water, so I'm taking you to get some," he said.

Ooloo looked around curiously and saw she was within some kind of very large compound or fort, surrounded by tall black walls. At each corner were guard towers and she could see they were manned. There was one entrance into the fort and a large wooden door barred the opening.

There were hundreds of undead soldiers lined up in the courtyard, their eyes glowing red. She thought she saw Hanoera and Kevar, but she wasn't sure. She wondered if her grandfather was alive or dead...or undead. Without her magic, she could not sense him or anyone else. The last she had seen of him he was surrounded by undead warriors and fighting for his life. She hadn't seen him fall because she had been busy throwing fireballs at Morren. And then she had been caught in the energy net and lost consciousness when she fell from the sky.

She had to walk fast to keep up with Morren, but it was difficult because the ground was sand. She considered leaping into the air and flying away but remembered the energy net and the pain Morren had inflicted upon her.

Heat radiated off the sand and it was still stifling hot even though the sun had set. The two moons shone down brightly so she could easily see where they were going. Ahead was a large building with two spires or towers rising into the sky. It was made of the same black material as the wall and guard towers, dark and foreboding, and she didn't want to go there, but her thirst kept her feet moving.

They walked up a set of seven steps to the front double door. Morren raised his hand and the doors swung inward. He ushered Ooloo through the doors into a great hall. Along one side was a large dining table where several wingmen sat. They were a rough-looking and rowdy bunch, but at least they were alive and not undead. She wondered where they had come from.

"Who are those men," she asked.

"They are brigands and thieves," said Morren. "They won't help you. They have come into my service willingly. I did not even have to enthrall them," he bragged.

Morren went to a sideboard and poured a cup of water for Ooloo from a large, glass pitcher. She drank it down quickly and held the cup out for more. Morren refilled the cup and she drank that also.

"If you have had enough, there is someone I would like you to meet," he said.

He guided her over to a staircase the led up to one of the towers. She followed him up dozens of steps as they wound their way to the top. They came to a room in the center of which was an immense pedestal. Upon the pedestal sat a large black sphere or orb. Swirls of fire coalesced within its depths and across its surface. Morren waved his hand over the orb and a window opened upon a terrifying scene. In the window stood a large, three-horned demon-like creature, with long fangs. He was all red and his eyes glowed malevolently. Ooloo took a step back, but Morren pushed her forward.

"I have brought her," said Morren. "Here is the winglet Ooloo and she is everything we hoped she would be."

Saarnak stared at Ooloo as if he could see all the way into her soul. It made her very uncomfortable. She raised her chin in defiance and clenched her fists.

"Hello, Ooloo," said Saarnak. "Finally, we meet. I have been watching you for a long time."

"How?" she asked. "I have never seen you before. How have you been watching me?"

Saarnak laughed. "It is too complicated for you to understand, but suffice it to say I created a sort of window into Eruna, long before you were born. I have been waiting a long time for one such as you."

"One such as me?" she said. "What do you mean?"

"You are Ans'Isna, are you not? But you are also innocent," he said.

"So," she said defiantly.

"So, you can help me open a bigger window, a sort of door or portal into Eruna," said Saarnak.

"Why would I ever do that? I will never help you," she said.

"Oh, but you will," he said and held out his hand and squeezed his fist. Ooloo gasped for air. Pain exploded in her mind and body and she felt she was choking to death. Just before she passed out, Saarnak released his hold on her and she dropped to the floor. Tears streamed down her face. Ooloo was ashamed she was crying, but she couldn't help herself. The pain had been unbearable and she had never been so afraid.

"Take her back to her cell," said Saarnak. "Let her think about what I have said. Bring her back in a few turns and we will talk again."

"As you wish," said Morren. He tried to help Ooloo to her feet, but she slapped his hand away and stood proudly while wiping away her tears. They left the room with the black orb while Saarnak watched and laughed. Ooloo shuddered inwardly with anxiety, wondering what the next turn might bring.

Then they returned to her cell, the door was wide open. She stopped stubbornly at the opening, but Morren shoved her in the back and she stumbled into the room.

"I will have more water brought to you," said Morren amiably. "As you said, we wouldn't want you to die of thirst. Do not try to pass through the door or you will experience severe pain." Then he turned and walked through the door before slamming it shut. He locked it, conjured an energy barrier in front of it, and made his way back to the fortress.

As soon as he was gone Ooloo walked up to the door and put her hand on it. She immediately snatched it back because a shock of pain went up her arm. She tried again and was able to withstand a few more seconds of pain. If she could withstand the pain long enough maybe she could somehow get the door unlocked and escape. It wasn't much to base her hope upon, but it was better than giving up.

After a long interval of trying to build up a tolerance to the pain of touching the door, she heard a key being inserted into the lock. The door swung open and Ooloo immediately ran toward the threshold. She slammed into a wall of energy and startled the old wing-woman who was standing just beyond the opening. She held a large pail of water in her gnarled hands.

Ooloo picked herself up from the floor where she lay and looked at her. Her face was wrinkled and she looked to be older than Paap. Her brown wings were a bit scraggly and she was dressed in a dirty grey shift. Her eyes were dark and she looked straight ahead as if she were in some kind of trance. Ooloo moved to the side so the old wing-woman could enter. To Ooloo's amazement, she walked through the door without slamming into the invisible wall. That was interesting. So, the wall only applied to Ooloo. Maybe it had something to do with the bracelets.

"I have brought you some more water," said the wing-woman as she set a large metal pail down on the table.

"What is your name and where did you come from?" asked Ooloo.

"I am Gretna, and I am from the desert tribes of the western Wastelands," she answered.

"How long have you been here?" Ooloo asked, wanting to keep the conversation going for as long as possible. The longer the old wing-woman talked, the clearer her mind seemed to become.

"I have been here for many cycles, ever since the great dragon attacked my village," said Gretna.

"What do you do here?" asked Ooloo.

"I work in the kitchens," said Gretna.

"How many others from your village are here?" asked Ooloo.

A pained expression crossed Gretna's face. "I do not know. Many were killed," she said. "And those who weren't are now...undead." She shuddered and turned toward the door to leave, but Ooloo grabbed her arm.

"Can you help me? I need to get away from here," Ooloo said plaintively.

"I cannot help you," said Gretna as she removed Ooloo's hand from her arm. "I must return to the kitchens. I will bring you your first-meal in the morning."

She walked back out the door and closed it. Ooloo's heart sank as she heard Gretna lock it. Even if the door had not been locked Ooloo would have to deal with the wall of energy.She went to the table and dipped her cup in the pail of water and drank the lukewarm water. She also splashed some of the water on her face. Then she turned back to the door and began to work on withstanding the pain of touching it again.But she was eventually so frustrated and exhausted that she flopped down on the pallet.

She couldn't sleep. All she could think about was Paap and wonder where he was. Eventually, she fell into a troubled sleep. She was so tired that she didn't even dream.

She awoke as Gretna unlocked the cell door at the next turn. Gretna entered and laid a plate of food on the table. Ooloo got up and came to the table. She was disappointed to see more bread and gruel.

"I am so glad to see you, Gretna," she said. Gretna wouldn't look at her.

"I cannot talk to you," she said. "The master will punish me again."

Ooloo walked around the table and threw her arms around Gretna. "I'm so sorry, Gretna. Did he hurt you much?"

Gretna didn't answer. She pulled Ooloo's arms from around her waist and pushed her away. She hurried out the door and locked it. Ooloo sighed and sat at the table to eat apathetically.

Meanwhile, Morren was back in the tower talking with Saarnak. Rather, he was listening to Saarnak talk.

"She is not strong enough yet to open a doorway into Eruna," said Saarnak. "I did not expect her to be captured so soon. You have done well. But she must be trained before she is strong enough to help me."

"She defeated me the first time I attacked her group, so I know she is powerful. But the spell you gave me for the energy net enabled me to take her captive. Even if she were strong enough to open a doorway," said Morren, "her will is extremely strong. She will not willingly help us."

"We must find a way to break her will," said Saarnak. "I have seen she cares deeply for her grandfather, Tavat. Why didn't you enthrall him and bring him here as you did the other warriors?"

"I...I am sorry, Master, I lost sight of him as I was capturing the winglet," stammered Morren. "We should have him for our plan to proceed. Perhaps there is another way. In the meantime, we will work on breaking the will of this innocent known as Ooloo."

"As you wish, Master," said Morren as he scurried from the tower room.

Morren went to Ooloo's cell and unlocked the door. Ooloo was lying forlornly on the pallet. "

"Come with me," he said.

When she saw it was Morren, she leapt off the pallet and threw herself at him in a rage. She pummeled him with her fists and kicked his shins. He pushed her away from him, waved his hand and said, "Stop it!" She instantly dropped to the floor gasping in agony.

"I told you, it is useless to resist me. You will do as you are told or you will suffer the consequences. Now, do I have your cooperation?" he said.

"Yes," she uttered bitterly between clenched teeth. Morren released her from the pain and she stood up. She glared at him in fury.

"I have a surprise for you," said Morren. "Come outside with me." He led her out the door and through the plaza where the undead army was standing at attention. There was another group standing apart from the others. Ooloo realized it was the warriors who had traveled south with her and Tavat. They looked straight ahead and their eyes seemed unfocused. "They are enthralled and unless you do as I say I will begin killing them, one at a time and make them part of my undead army."

"What do you want from me?" Ooloo asked.

"I want to train you," said Morren. "You are not yet strong enough to open the portal for Saarnak, so I am going to teach you and help you gain the strength you need."

"What makes you think I won't turn my powers on you?" she asked, frowning.

"You doubt my determination to control you?" he asked, grinning vilely. He turned toward the group of warriors and focused his attention on Batab. He raised his hand and channeled a stream of red light at her. She threw her head back and opened her mouth wide to scream. The red light streaked down her throat and her eyes began to glow red. "She is now completely under my will."

"Is she dead?" asked Ooloo, horrified at what Morren had done.

"Oh, she is no longer alive, but she is much more than dead. Actually, she is undead, and unless you cooperate I will do the same to every one of these warriors. Now, when we return to your cell I am going to remove your bracelets. Do as I say or I will make every one of your friends undead," said Morren.

"What is it you want me to do?" asked Ooloo resignedly.

"What do you know about the four aspects of magic?" he asked as he led her back to her cell.

"I know nothing," said Ooloo.

"Well, at least you are now being honest," said Morren. "Sit down and I will tell you." He pulled out the lone chair for her and she sat down. He waved his hand over the bracelets on her wrists and they popped open.

Ooloo immediately threw a fireball at him. But it bounced off of him. He had already in anticipation put up a shield.

Morren laughed and said, "You are so stubborn and willful." He clenched his fist and Ooloo was struck with unbearable pain. It seemed to go on forever. Finally, Morren released her and she slumped to the ground. "Must I go back outside and make more undead of your warrior friends? Or maybe I should give you more pain." He clenched his fist again and the pain gripped her more strongly than before.This time she almost passed out before the pain stopped. "I will have your cooperation one way or another."

"Kill me," she said through clenched teeth. "I won't cooperate with you."

"Yes you will," he said, and the pain that hit her this time did make her pass out. When she regained consciousness,

Morren was gone. Ooloo got up from the dirty floor and went to lie down on her pallet. The bracelets were back on her wrists. She rolled over onto her side, curled into a ball and cried bitterly until she went to sleep.

When she awoke, she remembered she had carefully watched when Morren had removed the bracelets. Maybe she could duplicate his action, but for now, she was exhausted and her body still hurt as if she had been beaten. She began trying to access her magic, but she was weak from pain and gave up after only a few moments. She rolled over onto her side and began to cry again. Before long she was asleep once again. In her dreams, she was able to use her magic. She dreamed she was back in the Northern Plains. Tavat and her mother were there, but they acted like they couldn't see or hear her.

When she awoke the next turn, Morren was sitting at the table watching her.

"What do you want?" she asked. "Are you here to torture me some more?"

"I want you to try to move some of this water into your cup," he said, indicating the bucket of water and cup sitting on the table.

"I'm hungry," she said.

"You will eat when you do as you are told. Now, come here and let me remove your bracelets," he said.

She rose from the pallet and stood before the table. She held out her hands and Morren waved his hand over the bracelets. They once again popped open. She let them drop to the table and glared at him angrily.

"Don't you want to learn magic?" asked Morren. "Isn't that the reason you left your home, to go to Cliffside and become a Wind Dancer so you could study magic?"

"Yes," Ooloo said reluctantly. "What of it?"

"Then this is better. You don't have to wait until you become a Wind Dancer," he reasoned. "I will teach you everything you need to know about magic."

"What if I don't want to learn from you," she said stubbornly. "There are still many things I can learn at Cliffside."

"What does it matter?" asked Morren. "Besides, we are preparing to attack Cliffside and the Eight Realms. There will be no Cliffside when I am done. You may as well learn what you can from me...while you can."

Ooloo thought about it for a moment. "Alright. I will let you teach me," she said. "But one turn, I am going to kill you. This I swear!"

Morren laughed. "I'm sure you will try. Don't forget about your warrior friends. Their lives depend upon your cooperation."

"Leave them out of this. I will cooperate for now," she said. "You said you wanted me to move water from the pail to the cup." She picked up the cup and dipped it in the pail. She drank the water and put the cup down. "Now what?"

Morren frowned. "Funny," he said. "Now do it without picking up the cup. Reach out to the water from your center and move some water from the pail into the cup."

"My center?" she asked.

"Perhaps we need to start at the beginning. You have already discovered how to access your magic without knowing the first thing about it," he said.

"I am Ans'Isna," she proclaimed proudly. "I have been accessing my magic, as you call it, since I was a little winglet. I beat you the first time I met you. What do you think you can teach me?"

"I can teach you how you did it," said Morren. "Now close your eyes and focus inward."

Ooloo sighed and did as she was bid. She focused inward. Suddenly her eyes popped open and she gasped. "I see what you mean now," she said. "I saw my magic, rather I felt it, oh, I don't know what I mean. It's there like a glowing light and I can reach out and touch it."

"Yes," said Morren. "That is exactly right. Now take hold of it and use it to move the water."

Ooloo held her hand up over the pail and moved a small globe of water to the cup. Not a drop spilled. Morren picked up the cup and drank the water. "Very good, Ooloo," he said.

Ooloo beamed with pride in spite of her anger at Morren. "That was easy. Tell me more about the four aspects of magic," she said.

"You already seem to have a grasp on fire. The other three aspects are water, of course, and air and earth. We will spend the next few octurns working on your control of each of the aspects. But that is enough for this turn."

"I'm still hungry," she said. "You said I could eat afterward."

"I will send someone with your meal," said Morren.

"Can I have something besides gruel?" she asked hopefully.

"Alright," he said. "You have done well, so I suppose you deserve a reward." He picked up the bracelets and looked at Ooloo. "I can leave these off if you are going to continue to cooperate. But you need to know this cell is runed and warded. You cannot as much as touch the door or window."

Ooloo looked surprised. She hated the bracelets and besides she would be able to practice what she learned if they were removed.

"Well?" Morren asked. "What will it be?"

Ooloo had a choice. She could try to attack Morren again, in which case he would give her more pain or turn another one of the warriors into undead, or she could cooperate and learn as much as possible and grow in strength. She could then attack Morren once she was stronger and have more of a chance of defeating him. She decided on the second course, for now anyway.

"I will cooperate," she said. She would cooperate, for now, even though it grated against her. Morren put the bracelets in his pocket and left the cell.

Ooloo decided to practice finding her center and accessing her magic. She was determined to grow stronger in her magic. And when she was strong enough, she would kill Morren. She would free the undead or she would kill them all, free her friends, and she would find Paap. Or she would die trying.

# ~
# CHAPTER 5
# LIBRAENAIRE

A s Kerinelle and Libraen flew back to Cliffside they discussed the second message delivered by Swen. While they were elated over the birth of Joran and Lynette's winglet, they were horrified to learn about Morren and his plan to attack Cliffside School. For cycles, they thought he was dead, but now he was back and plotting revenge against them and everything they held dear.

"We must contact the Wind Council about the impending attack. We also need to let the High Matriarch know so she will send troops and reinforcements," said Kerinelle.

"Do you really think she will, Kerin?" asked Libraen, using her diminutive. "We would be better served to contact the Patriarchs and Matriarchs of the major Trees of the Eight Realms themselves. It is their sons and daughters who are students at Cliffside. Perhaps we should send all of the students home. If only we knew when the attack will take place."

"I don't think Morren will stop attacking the School," said Kerin. "If he really wants revenge why would he stop there?"

"You may be right, my dear," said Libraen. "The entire Eight Realms may be in danger. All of Eruna may be in danger."

They needed the Wind Dancers' help, as well as their magic, to protect the School. Morren was strong in magic and his attack would primarily be in that area. According to the message from Hanoera, he had created, and would surely use, an army of undead.

Kerin and Libraen arrived at the upper end of the Caverns, but instead of flying through the Caverns to Cliffside, they flew straight to the Wind Dancer's Ledge far above the School. The Ledge held a massive building with eight spires rising into the air far above the mountain behind Cliffside School. Eight colossal columns engraved with countless runes held up the front roof of the building and led to an open porch. Eight enormous steps spread across the entire front of the building leading to the front door, which was also engraved with runes. On each side of the main building were two wings–the west wing held the Council Chambers and classrooms while the east wing held dormitories for the Wind Dancers and student apprentices who studied magic.

Kerin and Libraen landed on the Ledge and walked up the eight steps and between the two central columns to the front door. The two guards standing at attention on either side of the double doors immediately bowed to them in respect and opened the doors.

"Greetings, Mother and Father," said an attendant as he met them in the entrance hall. "How may I serve you?"

"We need the Wind Council to assemble at once," said Libraen. "We have dire news we need to share which will affect the School and may even impact the Eight Realms and all of Eruna.

"At once, Father," said the attendant, his face turning ashen. The fact that Mother and Father wanted the Wind Council to assemble startled him to the core. Never before had such a request been made on his watch. He forgot to excuse himself and ran immediately to ring the bell that would bring the council members to the Chamber.

"Thank you," shouted Libraen to the frightened attendant's back as he ran to do their bidding.

"We should go immediately to the Council Chamber," said Kerin. She and Libraen turned left and made their way to the Chamber. It was empty but soon the eight council members made their way into the Chamber and to their seats at a large table in the middle of a raised platform. They looked askance at Libraen and Kerin as they stepped up to a podium below the stage.

"You have called the Council to assembly," said Wind Master T' Kernoeryl Haddon. "What has compelled you to summon the Council in this fashion. What is this dire news you have to report?"

"We have reason to believe T'Ardis Morrenaire is alive and planning to attack Cliffside School," said Libraen.

"What? That is absurd. He was killed in that awful experiment, as you two well know," said the Wind Master reproachfully.

"I thought he was dead," said Council Member Campule of Tree Drusca. Several other council members muttered and whispered among themselves.

"As did we. But as you know his body was never recovered. We don't know for certain what really happened to him," said Mother Kerinelle. "The message we received was clear. Morren is alive and he is out for revenge."

"Are you sure," asked Wind Mistress Grenbole of Tree Verdan. "How can this be?

"Apparently, he has been seen by one of my agents, T'Redbole Hanoeraelle. We just received the report less than three turns ago when we were in Esteryia. We flew back here immediately to warn you and elicit your aid."

"But how can you be sure it is Morren?" asked Wind Mistress Grenbole.

"That is the second part of what we need to tell you. There is a young winglet from the Northern Plateaus who is very gifted beyond anything we have ever seen or heard. Hanoera said she and her grandfather and a group of six warriors have been traveling for over a cycle to get to Cliffside," said Kerinelle. "They call her the Ans'Isna, and she is supposed to be some kind of savior of her people according to the legends of the High Plateau Clans."

"Do you know her name?" asked the Wind Mistress.

"She is called Ooloo Noo'Loon and her grandfather is called Tavat Noo'Loon," said Kerinelle. "As you notice their names are unusual. It has something to do with their belief system and the "circle of life" as they call it. Hanoera indicated they were on their way here and should be arriving by the next Turn of Winds."

"Apparently this winglet has the sight," said Father Libraen. That pronouncement elicited exclamations of surprise and delight from the eight council members.

"She saw Cliffside and described it perfectly without ever having been there."

"She sounds remarkable. We have not had anyone with the gift of seeing for over seven hundred cycles, since my ancestor T'Kernoeryl Benonaire had the gift."

"Not only does she have the gift of sight, but she also has the gift of knowing," announced Libraen. "That is how we know for certain that T'Ardis Morrenaire is alive. She knew his mind, what he was thinking during a recent attack on the group she is traveling with in Halalouma."

"Great Winds, there has been no one with the gift of knowing for over two thousand cycles," blurted Council Member Paelmin of Tree Lembe.

"Did you say Halalouma?" asked Wind Master Haddon incredulously. "Are you serious? You just forgot to tell us Halalouma has been found. When were you going to tell us that fact?"

"I apologize, Wind Master. There is much we need to tell you, but our main concern is the impending attack on Cliffside School," said Libraen.

"Of course, we understand. But perhaps you should start at the beginning," suggested Wind Mistress Grenbole.

Mother Kerinelle sighed and said, "Very well. As you may not be aware the High Matriarch's daughter Lynette and T'Ardis Joranaire underwent the Desideratum together."

"Oh, Great Wind," exclaimed Wind Mistress Grernbole. The other members of the Council all began to speak at once.

"Silence," shouted Wind Master Haddon. "This news is...disconcerting, to say the least."

"Yes, exactly. However, we thought it best not to interfere and let matters proceed along their natural course," explained Father Libraen.

"Their natural course?" exploded Wind Master Haddon. "What did you think was going to happen?" "Ahem," Father Libraen cleared his throat. "I found an ancient prophecy which I believe has relevance to the situation. It reads, "*When the roots of the lowest entwine the highest, a seed of destruction will float in the wind. Not only of destruction but also of creation, this seed will bring forth a Tree of great power. But with the power comes great suffering and much sacrifice."* This is a prophecy by Canawerelle, The Prophetess, and I found it in her journal entitled, "Sightings."

"She also had the gift of sight," said Mother Kerinelle, blithely.

"And what, you think this prophecy has to do with Tree Algren and Tree Ardis?" asked Wind Master Haddon.

"Yes, I most certainly do," said Father Libraen. "That is why we did not interfere with Lynette and Joran when they went through the Desideratum."

"We suspect they went through the life-mating ceremony as well," said Kerinelle.

"Oh, Great Wind," exclaimed Wind Mistress Grenbole again. She put a hand to her throat in shock. "Does the High Matriarch know?"

"I am sure she has agents and spies at Cliffside. So, yes, she probably knows," said Mother Kerinelle. "She also probably knows they have run away from Cliffside with two other students, my agent, T'Redbole Hanoeraelle and Joran's roommate, T'Drusca Kevaraire."

"The High Matriarch has surely sent a squad of soldiers after them and no doubt plans to arrest both of them, especially Joran," interjected Father Libraen. "Knowing her, she will execute him for daring to life-mate with her daughter without the High Matriarch's permission."

"The Royal Consort, Mattern, also knows," Mother Kerinelle continued. "He came to see us shortly after the runaways left Cliffside to inform us he has left the High Matriarch for good. He immediately went after them. He apparently used a blood spell to find his daughter and caught up with her in Halalouma."

The Wind Master sighed heavily and massaged his brow with one hand. "So how does Halalouma figure in this tale?" he asked. "How did they find it? No one has been able to find it in four thousand cycles. What makes you think these runaways found it?"

"The description given by Mother Kerinelle's agent, Hanoera, was as close to the ancient records as possible," said Father Libraen. "I won't go into detail here. But suffice it to say, I am convinced they have found a cavern containing the ancient city."

"Please continue," said Wind Master Haddon when there was an uncomfortable lull in their dissertation.

"The runaways made their way to the cavern containing Halalouma through a long tunnel under the desert. They came upon the winglet, Ooloo, and her grandfather, along with six warriors, as they were under attack by Morren and a squad of undead soldiers. He was riding a giant black dragon."

"Undead soldiers, giant dragons," huffed Council Member Pineal. "This story just gets better and better."

"Please, let them continue," said Wind Master Haddon. He glared at the other Council Members. "Please stop interrupting."

"They were able to repel the attack, but not before Ooloo sensed what Morren was thinking," said Mother Kerinelle.

"And what was he thinking," asked Wind Mistress Grenbole.

"First, he was going to return with an army of undead to capture her..."

"Capture whom?" asked Wind Master Haddon.

"Ooloo, he wants to capture the winglet Ooloo for some nefarious reason, I'm sure," said Father Libraen, frustrated with the interruptions. "And secondly, Ooloo sensed that he is planning to attack Cliffside in the near future."

Mother Kerinelle picked up the story at this point, "The group with Ooloo and the runaways decided to travel together back to Cliffside. They were able to make their escape from Halalouma as Morren returned with his undead army. As they were leaving they ran into Mattern in the tunnel. When they exited the tunnel and set up camp Hanoera met up with one of the Wing Guard we sent after them. She sent him back to us with the message about Morren, Ooloo, and all the other events that occurred. They are all on their way to Cliffside as far as we know," she concluded.

They purposefully said nothing about the birth of Lynette and Joran's daughter and hoped it would not be brought up. But they were not so lucky.

Council Member Pineal said, "And what of the life-mating ceremony. You have said nothing about it. Has there been a conception?"

Mother Kerinelle turned to Father Libraen. A knowing look passed between them. They decided to tell the truth, all of it. They felt the birth of the winglet was significant and the Wind Council had a right to know.

"What I have to tell you must never leave this chamber," said Father Libraen seriously. "I need everyone to swear an unbreakable oath before I proceed."

Wind Master Haddon stood to his feet immediately, and slowly each member of the council stood to his or her feet. They made their way down to the podium where Father Libraen and Mother Kerinelle stood holding hands and formed a circle around them. Each of them placed a hand on Father Libraen's shoulder.

Haddon led them in a chant, and a glow surrounded the group, binding them to the oath to never reveal what Libraen was about to tell them. When he was finished, the glow dissipated and the council members returned to the table on the stage and sat down.

"Now, please proceed," said Wind Master Haddon.

"Very well," said Father Libraen. "T'Algren Lynettelle and T'Ardis Joranaire have a daughter. They have named her T'Ardis Aerielle. She is also Ans'Isna according to Ooloo. You must never reveal knowledge of her existence to anyone. Her life may depend on your silence."

"You are probably right about that," said Wind Master Haddon. "If the High Matriarch finds out she might order the death of the winglet. But you said they are on their way back to Cliffside. Surely the High Matriarch will find out about the winglet then."

"We are sending back instructions for them with several flights of our Wind Guard as an escort, so they can return from the Borderlands without being apprehended by the High Matriarch's soldiers," said Kerinelle. "If not for the impending attack by Morren we would meet them in Esteryia and decide the best course of action. But I'm afraid we need to concentrate on protecting the School."

"We are at your disposal," said Wind Master Haddon. "Do you have any idea when the attack is coming?"

"No, unfortunately not," said Father Libraen. "When the attack comes we will alert you with the signal fire set up for such events. It will be the first time the signal fire has been lit in over a thousand cycles. We have yet to notify the Matriarchs and

Patriarchs of the Eight Realms, but we will arrange messengers as soon as we return to Cliffside."

"I suggest you allow us to send Wind Dancers, instead," said Wind Master Haddon. "They will be much more effective than messengers."

"Thank you," said Mother Kerinelle. "You are correct that Wind Dancers bringing the alert will bear more weight. We need for the Matriarchs and Patriarchs to take us seriously. I am particularly concerned that the High Matriarch will ignore the warning. She is no doubt preoccupied with the disappearance of her daughter."

"Then I will carry the message to her myself," said Wind Master Haddon. "You need to concentrate on fortifying the School. We will send every Wind Dancer we can spare when the attack comes."

"Thank you, Wind Master. Surely the High Matriarch will heed the warning coming from you," said Father Libraen.

"I suggest a test of the signal fires once all the messages have been received," said Mother Kerinelle.

"That is an excellent idea," said Wind Master Haddon. "I suggest we conduct the test three octurns from now. That will be sufficient time for all the messages to be delivered and for the Wind Dancers to return to the Ledge with the responses."

"Please let us know what the responses are," requested Father Libraen. "We need to know who will come to our aid and who will not. I sincerely hope all of the Eight Realms will be behind us."

"Certainly," said Wind Master Haddon. He turned to Wind Mistress Grenbole and said, "Will you please compose the messages and arrange for our fastest flyers to take them to the Eight Realms. I will compose the message for the High Matriarch."

"Yes, I will get started as soon as we adjourn," she said.

"Then if there is no further business, we are adjourned," said Wind Master Haddon. "Thank you, Mother Kerinelle and Father Libraenaire for bringing this matter to our attention. He pushed back from the table and went to where Kerinelle and Libraen stood at the podium.

"May the Great Wind protect you," he said as he clasped Libraen's forearm. Then he clasped Kerinelle's. "You are welcome to take last-meal with us, but I imagine you are eager to return to Cliffside."

"There is one other thing we would like to ask," said Libraen. "We'd like permission to teach the older students to access their magic."

Every member of the Wind Council began to protest immediately. Finally, Wind Master Haddon intervened.

"Silence, everyone, please," he said. "Father Libraenaire, you are asking too much. Only Wind Dancers are allowed to study magic! It has always been that way for as long as there have been Wind Dancers...many thousands of cycles. Your request is denied."

"But, Master Haddon, we must protect Cliffside," said Mother Kerinelle.

"You have my answer," he said. "We will send as many Wind Dancers as possible when the time comes. A call will go out to them as we warn the Eight Realms of the coming attack."

"Will you at least consider it?" asked Father Libraen.

Master Haddon sighed. "We will discuss it..." The other Council members started shouting again. "I said we will discuss it! Now if there is nothing further..."

"No, nothing further, thank you. We must return to Cliffside immediately," said Libraen.

"Thank you," said Mother Kerinelle. "We have much to attend to. We appreciate all you are doing to help us." She put her hand on Libraen's arm, signaling that it was time for them to go.

"You are welcome," said Wind Master Haddon. "T'Airiat bless and keep you."

"And you," Libraen and Kerinelle both said.

They turned and immediately left the Council Chamber and returned to the front door. Testing the wind strength Libraen said, "Do you want to go down through the Caverns or are you willing to take the risk and fly directly down to Cliffside?"

"I think we can risk the wind currents this time," said Kerinelle. The winds blowing down the cliff from the top of the Ledge were treacherous most of the time. But it was almost as if the wind was holding its breath, waiting for the coming attack.

Together they leapt off the Ledge from where so many Cliffside students had leapt during the Wind Trials for over eight thousand cycles. They fought the currents successfully and landed on the flight platform outside their offices in the limbs of Central Tree. Whatever the future held they knew they would at least have the help of the Wind Dancers to protect the School.

# CHAPTER 6
# ESCAPE

**M**attern reluctantly flew away from the battle with his granddaughter. He followed the river and flew as close to the water as possible. He stayed beneath the trees in an effort not to be seen. He hated leaving Lynette and the others behind to fight Morren and the undead. He had only been reunited with his daughter for a few short turns. But he knew he must keep his granddaughter safe, as Lynette requested.

He flew for an entire turn to get as far away from the battle as possible. He only stopped long enough to feed Aerielle and see to her needs. For the most part, she slept in his arms and only stirred when she was hungry. Mattern kept the river in sight as he flew south. He knew that soon he would need to stop at a farm or a village where he could restock supplies for himself and the baby.

Aerielle stirred against his chest and began to cry. It was time to feed her again and he could smell that he needed to change her diaper. He flew down to the side of the river and gently laid the little winglet on his cloak. He changed her diaper while she made it known that she was hungry by wailing loudly. Mattern quickly mixed the Mother's Milk Root powder with water from the river in one of the bottles Lynette had purchased in the Caverns.

He didn't know what he would have done if Lynette had not had the foresight to be so prepared for the needs of the baby in case she was unable to breastfeed her. Now it was the difference between life and death for the infant. Mattern knew he had only enough of the root powder left for three more turns, and he was almost out of food himself. All he had left was some stale travel bread and a few strips of tioldoer jerky.

Mattern planned to stop in Esteryia to restock and to see the old priest, T'Brandle Gannaire. He would surely know where Mattern could purchase more Mother's Milk Root powder. Fortunately, Esteryia was only about three turns away if he didn't stop for more than a few hours at night to rest.

Aerielle finished the bottle and dropped back to sleep in his arms. He gently laid her back on his cloak and went to the river to refill his canteen. Then he washed the dirty diaper in the river and spread it out on a rock, hot from the sun, to dry. In this heat, it wouldn't take long. He took out the travel bread and ate a few bites–just enough to assuage his gnawing hunger. Then he lay down next to the baby to rest.

When he awoke, the moons had risen. He picked up the sleeping baby and gathered his cloak and packs and flew south again, following the river. He followed this pattern until he finally arrived at the outskirts of Esteryia.

He flew directly to the tree where the temple was located to see Gannaire. Mattern knocked on the door to the temple and the priest's assistant, Jamen, opened it. It was mid-turn and Mattern didn't know if the old priest was there.

"How may we serve you?" asked Jamen.

"I need to see the priest," said Mattern. Aerielle began to cry loudly.

Just then Gannaire came out of his office and said, "What is all this racket?"

"Um, this gentleman needs to see you..." said Jamen.

"It's good to see you again, Milord. Who is this?" asked Gannaire, indicating the crying infant.

"I must speak with you in private," said Mattern.

"Jamen, please go fetch some more wood," ordered Gannaire. The attendant immediately turned and left the Temple to do as he was bid.

"This is my granddaughter, Aerielle," said Mattern. "I need your help. I'm almost out of Mother's Milk Root powder. Do you have any idea where I can get some more?"

"What about her mother? Is she not able to breastfeed the baby?" asked Gannaire.

A pained expression passed across Mattern's face and he slumped down onto one of the pews. "I do not know if she is alive or dead," he said.

"Maybe you should start at the beginning and tell me what has happened," said Gannaire as he sat down next to Mattern on the pew. Mattern told him everything that had happened since they had last seen each other. He told him about Ooloo, Tavat, and the warriors from the Northern Plateaus as well as the Malakand. He also told him about leaving the scene of the battle to save Aerielle.

"I had no choice but to take the winglet and leave if Aerielle was going to survive," said Mattern as he hung his head in shame. "Lynette wouldn't leave Joran..."

"I remember the young couple well," said Gannaire. "And you don't know if they survived the attack?"

"I feel in my heart that my daughter is alive, but I just don't know for sure," said Mattern. "I'm afraid I am all Aerielle has left. I know I cannot allow the High Matriarch to get her hands on her. You must tell not one about her!"

"Yes, you are certainly right about that. What do you plan to do?" asked Gannaire.

"Well, first I need more root powder to feed Aerielle," said Mattern.

"Of course, of course. I'm sure Selene and Merium keep a supply of just about every root and herb there is," said Gannaire.

Mattern groaned. "You mean the two witches I got the blood spell from, don't you?"

"Yes, I'm afraid so," said Gannaire. "They aren't so bad..."

"That's a matter of opinion," said Mattern holding up his hand where Selene had stabbed him to get blood for the blood spell."She could have just pricked my finger. Do you think they would be any danger to my granddaughter?"

"Oh! No, they would never harm an innocent. Of that I am certain," assured Gannaire. "I've known them for as long as I have been here at the Temple, and although they are peculiar, they have never killed anyone or done permanent damage. They've meted out justice in a few instances. One such instance was when..."

"As long as you are sure they won't hurt Aerielle," interrupted Mattern. "I think I will be on my way there."

"Wait, we were about to take mid-meal. Won't you stay and join us?" urged Gannaire.

"Well, Aerielle is hungry and she probably needs changing. I suppose I should go ahead and feed her," said Mattern. "I am out of food and I am hungry, so I will take you up on your offer."

"Excellent," beamed Gannaire. He opened the door to his office to find the attendant struggling through the front door with an armload of wood. "Jamen, take the wood to the fireplace in the kitchen and set an extra place at the table please."

Jamen scurried through a side door that lead to the small kitchen where he dropped the wood near the fireplace. He threw a couple of logs on the fire and quickly set another place at the table for their guest.

"I need to change Aerielle," said Mattern. He spread his cloak on the pew, laid her down and changed her diaper. Fortunately, she was only wet. "Is there somewhere I can wash this out?" he asked.

"Jamen," hollered Gannaire. The assistant came running from the kitchen to see what the priest wanted now. "Here, take this to the stream and wash it out," instructed Gannaire.

"Sir?" asked Jamen as he stared incredulously at the diaper Mattern held out. "You want me to wash this diaper?" He did not think his duties included the washing of dirty diapers.

"You heard me. That's what I said, and when you are done, bring it inside to hang by the fire to dry," said Gannaire glaring at his assistant. Jamen reluctantly took the diaper from Mattern, and left the temple holding a corner delicately between a finger and thumb to do as the old priest bid.

"Right this way." Gannaire directed Mattern to the side door that led to the small kitchen where a pot of stew was hanging in the fireplace bubbling. The aroma made Mattern's mouth water. "Would you mind?" he asked, holding the fussy infant out to Gannaire.

"Of course not," he said, taking Aerielle and placing her on his shoulder. He bounced up and down and she immediately grew quiet. Mattern mixed the last of the root powder with water from his canteen in a bottle and held his arms out to retrieve the baby.

"Why don't you let me feed Aeri while you eat," said Gannaire. "The ladle is on the mantle and the bowls are on the table."

"'Aeri,' I like that. Thank you," said Mattern as he ladled stew into the three bowls and set them back on the table. Jamen returned from washing out the diaper and hung it from a hook on the mantle to dry over the fire. Then he sat down at the table and quietly began eating his stew. There was a large loaf of bread on the table. Jamen broke it into three pieces and handed one to Mattern, who took it gratefully.

"We need to talk a little more about this Morren and the undead army you say he has at his disposal. Just how dangerous is he?" asked Gannaire. He sat down at the table with Aeri in his arms and fed her the bottle. Before long she had emptied it and Gannaire put her on his shoulder and burped her.

"I'm afraid I don't know much," said Mattern. "The young winglet, Ooloo, is convinced he is going to attack Cliffside. She seems to be extremely gifted and sometimes knows what people are thinking. She is called the Ans'Isna by her people and she thinks Aerielle, um, Aeri, is also Ans'Isna,"

"What does that mean?" asked Gannaire. "What is an Ans'Isna? I vaguely remember reading something about that when I was a student at Cliffside." He picked up his piece of bread and dipped it in his stew. He ate as Mattern continued his tale.

"I think it means 'one who saves,'" said Mattern around a mouthful of stew. "According to the Northern High Plateau Clans there is a legend that in a time of great need an Ans'Isna will be born and she will save her people. But I'm sorry I don't know any more than that, and I don't know what it means for my granddaughter. For all I know this Ooloo is dead along with everyone else who fought against Morren. I escaped with Aeri before the battle was finished." He sighed and again hung his head in shame for having deserted the others during the battle. If not for the need to take his granddaughter to safety he would never have left them to fight Morren alone.

"Did she say when the attack on Cliffside would come? Morren and his hoard of undead will have to pass by Esteryia to get to Cliffside. We need to prepare our defenses," said Gannaire. "I need to warn the townspeople."

"I don't know what defenses you can prepare against the undead," said Mattern. "It seems the only way to kill them is by stabbing them in the heart. Besides, do you really think the townspeople will believe you?"

"You have a point there," said Gannaire. "Can you stay around long enough to talk to the Mayor with me?"

"I suppose so," said Mattern. "But first let me go get more Mother's Milk Root powder from Selene."

They finished their bowls of stew. Mattern took Aerielle back from Gannaire and returned to where he had laid his cloak and packs on one of the pews. He refastened his cloak and threw the packs over one shoulder. Gannaire followed him to the door.

"You can sleep here tonight," said Gannaire. "I'm sure Jamen won't mind you using his cot. He can sleep on one of the pews." He looked pointedly at Jamen who knew better than to object.

"Thank you, Jamen. I am most grateful to you for your kindness," said Mattern. "I'll be back before dark."

"Don't you want to leave the winglet with us while you go see the witches?" asked Gannaire.

"No, thank you. I promised my daughter I would not let her out of my sight. And you said she would be in no danger from the witches anyway. He leapt into the air with Aeri clutched tightly to his chest. She was asleep and oblivious to the goings on around her.

Mattern flew to the tree where Selene and Merium lived. He was glad it was still light. It was just as creepy as the first time he had been there. He landed on the platform in front of the door and knocked. Merium opened the door.

"Well, well. I knew you would return," she said. "And you are not alone, just as I also knew."

Mattern entered the dwelling and held on protectively to Aerielle. Merium ushered him into the main room where various herbs, roots, and flowers hung from the ceiling to dry.

"Let me guess," said Selene as she came out of the back bedroom. "You need some Mother's Milk Root Powder."

"How did you..." Mattern started to say. Selene waved away the question.

"Her mother is not in the land of the living," said Merium. "And neither is the father also."

Mattern was at a loss for words. He moaned sorrowfully and sat down on the floor.

"You wouldn't be here with their infant otherwise," said Selene.

"But they are...they are dead?" asked Mattern.

"They might not be dead, but they are missing," said Merium. "I can assure you of that. They are no longer of this world."

"My sister is never wrong about these things," said Selene sympathetically. "Now let's get you what you came for." She walked over to a large shelf that held many jars of varying sizes. She took a large jar down and walked over to where Mattern sat on the floor. She held out the jar to him. "This is all we have. It should last you until you get to the Caverns on your way to Cliffside. There is an apothecary shop there where you can get more."

"How do you know I'm going to Cliffside?" asked Mattern.

"Merium is not the only one who can see things," said Selene. "Besides, where else would you go?"

"May I hold your granddaughter?" asked Merium.

"I'm not sure about that..." said Mattern, not really wanting to let the witch hold Aerielle.

"She is perfectly safe with us," interrupted Selene. "Merium just wants to see her."

Mattern relented and held the baby out to Merium. She took her and lightly ran her fingers over the child's face.

"You're blind!" he said. It finally dawned on Mattern that Merium was totally blind and she was "seeing" Aerielle with the sense of touch.

Merium cackled with mirth. "Yes, I am blind. But I see far more than you do. For example, I see there was a battle and your daughter asked you to take this baby to safety."

"Yes, she did," admitted Mattern. We were attacked by an army of undead..."

"Yes, but there was someone leading them, wasn't there," she said. It was more of a statement than a question. "Someone who was thought to be dead."

"T'Ardis Morrenaire was leading the undead," said Mattern. "May I have her back please?" He stood and held out his arms to take the baby back from Merium. She gently kissed Aerielle on top of her downy head and handed her back to Mattern.

"This one will have great power and there will be one with her who also has great power," said Merium. "Her life will be hard. You have a decision to make concerning her. You must not hesitate to make the hard decision to let her go. Her life depends on it. The High Matriarch will never let her live, and you know it."

Mattern gasped and a cold chill crept up his spine. He did have a decision to make and it was not going to be an easy one. He knew he could not keep Aerielle with him, in spite of his promise to Lynette. It would put her in too much danger from the High Matriarch. But he first needed to talk to Mother Kerinelle and Father Libraen before he decided anything.

"You must tell no one about my granddaughter," he said. "Her birth must be kept a secret, especially from the High Matriarch."

"You don't need to tell us that," said Selene. "We know as well as you do how ruthless the High Matriarch is. This winglet is special. She must live."

"What do you mean?" asked Mattern.

"I do not know why, but her survival is vital to the future of Eruna," said Merium. "When I held her I felt her power and I saw...many things."

The more Selene and Merium spoke, the more afraid for his granddaughter Mattern became. He just wanted to get away from the two witches and return to the Temple.

"Thank you for the root powder. What do I owe you?" he said as he put the jar in one of the packs."

Selene put her hand on his arm and said, "You owe us nothing. Just take good care of this winglet. Keep her safe."

"Don't forget what I said, you must make a hard choice for her safety," said Merium. "Do not fail to do what is best for her, no matter how hard it is for you."

Mattern left the witches' tree and flew back to the Temple. He didn't bother to knock, but went right in. Jamen met him at the door and led him back to Gannaire's office.

"Were the witches helpful?" asked Gannaire.

"Yes, they had what I needed," said Mattern. "They gave me some advice and I have yet to decide if it was good advice or bad advice."

"Speaking of advice, I advise you not to go into the town proper after all. I think I will have to speak to the Mayor without you and tell him about the impending attack from Morren. I sent Jamen to buy supplies for you and he says there are soldiers of the High Matriarch at the inn. I'm sure you don't want to run into them," said Gannaire.

"No, I do not. Maybe I should be on my way as soon as the sun sets," said Mattern. "You will have to speak to the mayor on your own now. What kind of supplies did you pick up for me, Jamen? How much do I owe you?"

"I bought you several loaves of travel bread and some tioldoer jerky," replied Jamen. "You can make a donation to the Temple of five Beck or eight Gren, whichever you have."

"Here is ten Gren. Keep the change for your trouble," said Mattern. He held out the ten Gren. Jamen accepted it and bobbed his head in gratitude.

"Thank you, Milord," he said. He turned and gave the money to Gannaire who put it in the temple's offering box.

"I think it is a good idea to travel at night. I recommend you follow the river south and stay away from the normal routes. There have been more and more of the High Matriarch's soldiers passing through Esteryia lately," said Gannaire.

"They are probably searching for Lynette, but they could also be looking for me. I didn't exactly leave the High Matriarch on good terms," said Mattern. He and the old priest talked at length while Jamen worked in the kitchen preparing last-meal. Pleasant smells wafted into the Temple from the kitchen.

Aerielle began to stir and finally woke up. She began to cry hungrily.

"I need to feed this hungry little winglet again," said Mattern. He prepared the bottle and fed her. He also changed her. Just as he finished someone began banging on the temple door.

"Open up in the name of the High Matriarch," shouted whoever was banging on the door.

"Quickly, this way," said Gannaire. "Jamen, do what you can to stall them."

Mattern scooped up the baby and Gannaire grabbed his two packs. He led Mattern to his office and around his desk. He moved a rug out of the way and pulled open a trap door. A ladder led down to a small room under the office.

"In here, and pray the baby doesn't start crying," said Gannaire. "Hurry!"

Mattern quickly descended the ladder and Gannaire tossed down the two packs. He slammed the trap door shut and put the rug back in place. He put the extra bowl in the sink and checked the room for any other signs of Mattern's presence. Then he sat down at his desk just as Jamen knocked on the door to the office.

A soldier shoved past Jamen and barged into the office. Two other wingmen came into the office after him.

"How may we serve you, my son," said Gannaire sedately.

"We are looking for some runaways. We need to search this temple," said the winged soldier. "It has been reported they were seen in this area. We are also looking for the Royal Consort. Have you seen any of them?"

"You will find no runaways here," said Gannaire. "Who are you and who is it exactly that you are looking for?"

"I'm Captain T'Cotyla in service of the High Matriarch. The High Matriarch's daughter, T'Algren Lynettelle, has run away from Cliffside," said the soldier as he directed his wingmen to look in the kitchen and side rooms. "She would be traveling with a young wingman by the name of T'Ardis Joranaire. And the Royal Consort is also missing."

The wingmen returned a short while later. They reported that they had found no one.

"You see, it is just I and my assistant, Jamen," said Gannaire.

"If you should see them you must get word to one of my wingmen immediately," said the Captain. "I am leaving two of them at the inn."

"Of course," said Gannaire. "Is there anything else? We were just about to sit down to last-meal."

"Yes, we are also searching for the Royal Consort. You haven't seen him, have you?"

"The Royal Consort, you say?" said Gannaire. "No, we haven't seen him either, have we Jamen? Why would the Royal Consort be so far from Algren?"

"Just let my men know if either of you sees him," said the Captain.

"Of course, of course," assured Gannaire.

The Captain and his wingmen left temple. Gannaire waited to make sure they had flown back to the inn before removing the rug once more. He opened the trap door and Mattern tossed up the two packs and then climbed up the ladder with Aeri who was thankfully sound asleep in one of his arms.

Gannaire shut the trap door and rearranged the rug. "Jamen has prepared a nice meat pie for last-meal," said Gannaire. "The sun still hasn't set so you have plenty of time.

"Thank you, I am hungry," said Mattern. "And thank you for not giving me away."

"I never have cared much for the current High Matriarch," said Gannaire. "Oh, beg your pardon," he said realizing he was speaking to her mate.

Mattern laughed ruefully. "I haven't much cared for her either for a very long time. I will never go back to her," he said.

"Now tell me what Selene and Merium had to say," said Gannaire as he served Mattern a healthy slice of meat pie. They talked over the meal and before long the moons rose. Mattern decided not to stay the night and felt it was time to go.

"Let Jamen check before you leave," said Gannaire. Jamen hopped up from the table and went outside the Temple. He flew around the flight platform looking in all directions.

He went back into the temple and said to Mattern, "All clear, Milord," as if he were a co-conspirator.

"Thank you, Jamen. I appreciate all you have done for me," said Mattern. "And thank you, Gannaire. I won't forget your kindness."

"Just take care of this winglet," Gannaire said as he placed his hand on Aerielle's head. He chanted for a few moments, speaking a spell of protection over her. When he was done, Mattern shook his hand, went out the door and flew off into the night.

# CHAPTER 7
# BETRAYAL

Lare dreamed he was surrounded by soldiers and awoke with a start. He realized there was a knife at his throat and it wasn't a dream. Wellim stood over him and said, "Sit up slowly and don't try anything." There were three other winged men in the room in addition to the three Malakand who were cowering in the corner. One of the winged men stood over them with an arrow nocked to his bow.

Lare did as he was told. "What is this about?" he asked as he turned to look at Wellim who had stepped back but was still brandishing the knife threateningly.

"You fit the description of a wingless man wanted for robbery and for questioning concerning his missing master down in Algren," said Wellim. "I told you I work for the Mayor and I see everything that comes across his desk. There was a bulletin from Tree Ferndoren that came in a while ago about it."

"I haven't murdered anyone," said Lare. This was true as it had been an unfortunate accident that had caused the death of Master Ferndoren. Lare had taken the money from the strong box, but he considered that back wages as he was convinced Master Ferndoren had been cheating him out of his fair pay for many cycles. Still, he felt badly about it and he figured his crime was bound to catch up with him sooner or later.

"Stand up and put your arms behind your back. And don't try anything," said the winged man in charge, Captain T'Oseria. Lare complied and the Captain bound his hands together.

"What about them?" asked the winged man guarding the Malakand. "What do we do with them?"

"I only met them a few turns ago," said Lare. "They needed my help getting an injured winged man here for treatment with the doctor. Leave them out of this."

"We don't need them. Go on get out of here," said Captain T'Oseria to the Malakand. They scurried past the man with the bow and arrow and went to the door after picking up their packs.

Gormon looked at Lare and said, "Don't worries. Tavat know what to do. We not leave this village yet." Then he turned and followed Bicken and Fessa out the door.

"You're coming with us," said Captain T'Oseria. "You will be held until Tree Ferndoren can be notified of your capture." He roughly poked Lare in the back with his sword to get him moving.

"Take care of Nart, please," shouted Lare to the fleeing Malakand. They went to the stall was and where the garing untied him. They led the garing away toward the town of Erboer.

"What about my reward?" protested Wellim. "The bulletin said there was a reward."

"You'll have to contact Tree Ferndoren about that," said the Captain.

"But, but..." stuttered Wellim.

"Now move out of the way so we can get this prisoner to a holding cell," said the Captain.

"But I work for the Mayor himself," said Wellim indignantly.

"Then take it up with him," said Captain T'Oseria. He shoved Lare out the door and the other two winged men followed. Wellim was left standing with fists clenched and an angry glare on his face.

Since Lare was wingless, the winged soldiers escorted him to the village on foot as the sun rose. They walked all the way to the tree where the holding cells were located. They had to take a lift up to the landing and entrance to the building. The wingless men operating the lift looked with sympathy at Lare and quietly speculated about the reason for his arrest. They, like almost everyone else in town, had seen him bringing an injured Tavat to the doctor with the three Malakand the turn before.

Captain T'Oseria unlocked one of the cells and untied Lare's hands. Then he shoved him through the door.

"You've just missed first-meal," he said and laughed obnoxiously as he relocked the cell door. "I'm sure you can last until mid-meal."

Lare looked around the small cell. Along one wall was a cot and in the corner was a bucket. There were no other furnishings and the cell contained one small barred window on the back wall and a smaller one in the door.

Lare sat down on the cot. It was hard and lumpy. After a while he stretched out on it to wait, for what he did not know. He supposed some guardsmen from Tree Ferndoren would come for him eventually.

Gormon, Fessa, and Bicken came into the town and tied Nart to a post. They went to check on Tavat at the doctor's tree. They rode the lift up and knocked on his door. The doctor answered it and looked surprised to see them so early in the turn.

"I suppose you are here to see my patient," he said.

"Yes, please," said Gormon politely. "We is here to sees Tavat."

The doctor laughed at Gormon's grammar. "Right this way," he said and led them to a side room where Tavat was sitting up in bed.

"I'll let you visit with your friend, but don't tire him out. I'll be in my office if you need me," the doctor said.

Tavat looked much better than the last time they had seen him. He had his color back and his wounds were bandaged properly. He smiled when he saw the three Malakand.

"I understand you saved my life," said Tavat to Gormon, Fessa, and Bicken. "The healer says there was a wingless man with you who brought me here. Where is he? Who is he? I would like to thank him."

Gormon proceeded to tell Tavat everything that had happened since the Malakand found him after the battle with Morren. He learned that the wingless man's name was Lare and that he was being held for questioning. Tavat asked if they had seen what happened to Ooloo, but they said they had not. They had been hiding when the wizard and his hoard attacked.

Tavat sighed and said, "We have to find her. But first, we need to figure out how to free Lare. I owe him a debt for helping to save my life. The healer says I should be able to get out of bed in another turn or two. In the meantime, you three need to stay out of trouble. Gormon, do you still have any of that drink you gave us when we were at your chooch?"

"Yes, I has a full flask of it. Why? Is you thirsty?" asked Gormon.

"I have an idea," said Tavat. He worked out his plan with Gormon who then translated it for Fessa and Bicken. They all seemed to like the idea.

That night and the next, Gormon and Bicken watched to see what time the guard was changed. At a certain time each night only two guards were on duty. Gormon told Tavat what they had observed and they finalized their plans to rescue Lare.

On the third night and after Tavat was sufficiently recovered from his wounds, the three Malakand and Tavat went to the tree where the holding cells were located.

"We is here to sees the wingless man Lare, please," said Gormon to the winged officer in charge, Wing Guard T'Elmin. He was on duty with Wing Guard T'Cotyla. He sat behind a desk, which held several stacks of bulletins and other paperwork. Wing Guard T'Cotyla sat across the room on a stool sharpening his sword. He looked at Tavat suspiciously.

"I'm afraid that will not be possible," said T'Elmin as he got up and walked around to the front of the desk. "No one can see the prisoner without permission from Captain T'Oseria."

"We sees the Captain then," said Gormon.

"Yes, can we see the Captain, please?" asked Tavat.

"He's not here and won't be back until morning," said T'Elmin.

"We waits here then," said Gormon. He plopped down on the floor and reached into his pack. He pulled out a flask and took a long drink. When he was done he passed the flask to Bicken who also took a drink.

"Here now, what do you think you are doing?" asked the Wing Guard, who seemed confused at the strange behavior of the Malakand.

Bicken passed the flask back to Gormon. Gormon held the flask out to T'Elmin who looked even more confused.

"Please take, drink," said Gormon.

"It is a great insult to refuse," said Tavat. "Malakand are sensitive about such things."

T'Elmin looked at T'Cotyla who shrugged.

"What could it hurt?" said T'Cotyla.

"Is it safe?" T'Elmin asked Tavat

"Of course. I'll take a drink first if that will make you feel better," said Tavat who took the flask from Gormon and pretended to take a big swig. "It's actually quite tasty and just a little intoxicating." He held the flask out to T'Elmin who readily accepted it.

"Well, I wouldn't want to insult the little fellows," said T'Elmin. He accepted the flask from Tavat and took a drink tentatively.

"Uh, that one is female," said Tavat indicating Fessa.

"Oh sorry," said T'Elmin. "Hey, you weren't kidding. This stuff tastes great."

"Have another drink," said Tavat, tipping the bottle and encouraging T'Elmin to take another drink. He did and then passed the flask to T'Cotyla who also took a drink.

"This is good," said T'Cotyla. "What did you say it is called?"

"It is called carasum and is made from nectar of cara plant found only in Wasteland desert," said Gorman.

"Do you have any more of it?" asked T'Cotyla. "This flask won't last long if we all take a drink."

"Yes, we's got plenty, plenty" said Gormon. "Is important to finish whole flask once it is opened." He took it back from T'Cotyla and took a drink. Then he passed it to Bicken, who took a drink and then passed it to Fessa. She drank from the flask and then passed it to Tavat. He didn't take a drink but handed the flask to T'Elmin who greedily took a long swig.

They kept drinking until the flask was empty and Bicken brought out another flask. By then T'Elmin was quite drunk and had passed out behind his desk. T'Cotyla drank the last bit from the second flask and dropped it on the floor. He fell over and passed out also.

Tavat went through the desk drawers until he found the keys to the cells. He found Lare's cell by calling out his name and banging on the cell doors. Once he unlocked the correct door Lare looked up from the cot where he was reclining. He stood and squinted at Tavat.

"You look a lot better than the last time I saw you," he said to Tavat.

"Yes, I am much better thanks to you," said Tavat. "Help me move these drunken fools into your cell." The two of them carried the guards into the cell although Lare did the majority of the work since Tavat was still recovering from his wounds. They locked the cell door and took the keys with them.

By this time, it was very late and everyone in the village was long asleep. Even so, Tavat went outside and looked around to be sure it was safe to make their escape.

No one was around, not even the lift workers. The Malakand and Lare were forced to climb down the lift ropes while Tavat flew to the ground.

They retrieved Nart from where the Malakand had tied him and the group left the village quickly. Tavat wanted to go back to where they had last seen Ooloo flying toward her captor, but Gormon and Lare argued against it finally convincing Tavat that there would be no way to rescue Ooloo from Morren without help. So, they decided to go south, to Cliffside, which was Ooloo's original destination. They had nowhere else to go.

Lare knew the quickest way to Cliffside would not necessarily be the safest. They decided not to travel the roads but would instead travel through the countryside as much as possible. Tavat flew ahead to scout the way and make sure there were none of the High Matriarch's soldiers in their path.

They traveled as far as they could before sunrise. They stopped to rest and discussed what they would do when they got to Esteryia, which was the next village they would come to on their journey south. They decided only Tavat would go into the village since the Malakand would bring too much attention.

They needed a disguise for Lare since wanted bulletins were probably sent to Esteryia as well as Erboer. Fessa knew of a common plant that would darken Lare's skin several shades. While Fessa went to find the plant Lare decided to cut his hair and thin his eyebrows. He would let his beard grow as they traveled. He was unwilling to part with his garing, Nart, though.

Lare suggested that perhaps he should go his own way so as not to endanger the others. But Tavat convinced him to stay with the group since he was the only one who knew the territory and the way to Cliffside School. Lare decided to take the risk, especially since he felt he owed an explanation to a certain girl he had left behind when he ran from the Wing Guards of Tree Ferndoren. Even if they believed the death of Master Ferndoren had been an accident, Lare was a ground-dweller and his master was winged. If caught, Lare would be summarily executed.

Fessa returned with the succulent plant and proceeded to slather Lare's face and neck with the juice from the leaves. She showed Lare how to squeeze the leaves to get the most juice and he finished covering his arms and the rest of his body with it. Before long he was swarthy looking and with his short hair and thinned eyebrows he looked like a different person. He also practiced walking with a slump so that he looked shorter than he actually was. Hopefully, he could pass for someone else at the border checkpoints.

They also came up with a story that Tavat was Lare's master and they were transporting the Malakand to Algren to sell. Malakand had never been seen in the Eight Realms so it was a feasible story. Gormon, Bicken, and Fessa were reluctant but finally agreed to allow themselves to be tied up once they got to the border checkpoint to facilitate their cover story.

According to Lare, they would not arrive at the border for at least two octurns. They knew the Wing Guard from Erboer was probably not far behind them so they would have to be careful as they traveled. Wing Guards from Tree Ferndoren were probably on their way to Erboer by now to take Lare back to Algren. They would not be happy to discover that Lare had escaped and the group would have to avoid being apprehended by them.

"We should be on our way," said Tavat. "I'll fly ahead to see if the way is clear."

"Follow the river south since that is the route we are going to take," said Lare.

"If I spot any trouble I'll come back to warn you," said Tavat as he leapt into the air and flew quickly away.

Lare mounted Nart and nodded at the Malakand. They set off toward the river. They had not gone very far when Tavat returned.

"There are some soldiers flying this way," he said. "There are at least eight of them. We must find somewhere to hide." Gormon translated for Bicken and Fessa.

"They could be either from the High Matriarch or from Tree Ferndoren. Either way, I don't think we stand a chance against them," said Lare.

"I spotted a gulch to the west of the river. Follow me," said Tavat. "I will run with you instead of flying so the soldiers won't spot me. But we must hurry."

He quickly ran west toward the gulch with the Malakand following. Lare brought up the rear-riding Nart. Before long they spotted the gulch and all hunkered down in it. Lare made Nart lay down and he and Tavat pulled limbs and brush over the group. They hoped it was enough to hide them from sight as the soldiers flew by over the road and not far from where they were hiding.

As it turned out, the soldiers were from Tree Ferndoren and Captain T'Oseria was with them. Lare recognized him as the one who had locked him up a few turns ago in the village where the doctor helped Tavat.

After the soldiers had passed, Tavat and Lare pulled the branches away and the group set off traveling south again. Tavat hoped the people at Cliffside would be willing to help him get Ooloo back, but he feared they would be too busy when the wizard Morren attacked. Tavat would help them fight the wizard and he sincerely hoped they would help him get his granddaughter back. He didn't know what else he could do but hope she and the warriors who traveled from the High Plateaus with them were still alive.

~
## CHAPTER 8
# DREAMS

One moment Lynette and Joran were fighting for their lives against Morren and the undead army and the next they found themselves standing alone, surrounded by a thick fog. They were somehow transported away from the fight just as they each were about to take their own lives to prevent themselves from being turned into the undead.

Lynette lowered her knife and looked around. "What happened?" she asked Joran. He looked just as surprised as she felt. "Where are we?"

"I don't know," said Joran as the fog began to slowly dissipate. The fog, which hung on the ground, gave everything an eerie appearance. They were in the camp by the river, but there were no undead warriors attacking them and their friends were nowhere to be seen.

"You are in the world of dreams," said Ooloo. She was sitting on a log a wingspan away whittling on a stick. "I didn't know what else to do." She looked up from her whittling. "I knew you were about to kill yourselves and I couldn't let that happen. I was about to pass out so I sent you here."

"But how can we get back?" asked Joran. "We need to go to Cliffside."

"And find my father and daughter," added Lynette.

"I do not know," said Ooloo as she continued to whittle on the stick. "I am only here now because I passed out. I'm not really here. I'm dreaming. This is the world of dreams, and you must be careful." She finished whittling and got up to hand the stick to Joran. "What is this?" asked Joran. The stick was covered in strange, faintly glowing runes and symbols.

"I do not know for certain," said Ooloo. "I saw these runes in Halalouma somewhere. I feel they are important. Perhaps they will help you here."

"But what do these runes mean?" asked Lynette. "We learned about runes at Cliffside, but these do not look familiar."

"Protection, healing, power, I suspect," said Ooloo. But I really do not know for sure what they mean."

"Protection from what?" asked Joran.

"I do not know," said Ooloo. She squirmed uncomfortably. "I wish I did."

"Well, what do you know?" shouted Joran, who was losing patience.

"I am sorry, but I am waking up now. Be careful," said Ooloo as she began to fade away. "Go back to Halalouma. You will find what you seek there. Use the runes on the stick as your guide...find the runes on this stick..." And then she was gone.

"Blast it all!" yelled Joran. He looked around and noticed he and Lynette were suddenly standing in Halalouma again, just outside the inn where she had given birth. But they were no longer in a cavern. They were under the open sky. There were phantoms wandering the streets.

"What in the Eight Realms is going on?" asked Lynette. "How did we get here? And who are all these people?" She reached out to touch a wingless woman dressed in elaborate robes, but her hand passed right through her. It seemed that none of the people were anything more than wisps of smoke or perhaps ghosts. Lynette tried to get the attention of the woman, but she didn't even stop or look at her. She just continued walking down the street. There were other winged people flying between the buildings and flitting from place to place, as well as ground-dwellers walking and milling around.

"The last thing Ooloo said was for us to go back to Halalouma, and we would find what we seek there," said Joran. "I just thought about it and then here we are, back in Halalouma. But I don't think this is the Halalouma of our time. She said go back…I wonder if this is the Halalouma of the past? And these people must have lived here once."

"Yes, according to the legends, Halalouma was originally under the open sky. And then the whole city vanished one turn, never to be seen again and only heard of in legend," said Lynette. "The Ancients must have somehow hidden the city in the cavern, the same cavern where we originally found the city."

"I think you are right," said Joran. "We sure aren't in the same Halalouma as before. I wonder what else is different? Besides these people, that is."

"She said this is the world of dreams," suggested Lynette. "We are supposed to find something or learn something that will help us."

"But I don't understand what it is we are here to find," said Joran.

"I would think it is something to help us defeat Morren," said Lynette. She looked down at herself and noticed something unusual. "Have you noticed we are no longer wounded?" she asked Joran. "Ooloo must have healed us when she sent us here."

"You're right," he said. "I'm not hungry yet, either."

Lynette laughed and said, "That is unusual. You are always hungry. Why don't we start by looking in the buildings here and see what we find?"

"Okay, but we stay together," said Joran. "Ooloo said something about the runes on this stick. Maybe it will help us locate whatever it is we are supposed to find. See how the runes are glowing weakly? Maybe we can use it like a divining rod."

They first went into a building across the street from the inn. It looked like some kind of government building. They went inside and looked around. There were ghostly winged men and women inside scurrying around as well, and ground-dwellers conducting some sort of business. Joran and Lynette looked in all the rooms, but most of them contained some kind of filing cabinets. The runes on the stick continued to glow weakly.

"This is ridiculous," exclaimed Lynette when they had exited the building. "Why don't we just walk through the city until the runes on the stick glow more brightly?" Ooloo said she saw these runes and symbols somewhere in the city. I think we should just start with that. Maybe the runes will glow brighter the closer we come to whatever it is we are supposed to find."

"Well, I certainly don't have a better idea. Let's go to the next building and unless the runes glow brighter we won't bother going in," suggested Joran.

They continued through the city, watching the symbols on the stick. It seemed turns had passed before the runes began to glow more brightly. They were well into the center of the city, near where the lift was located. There was a magnificent building with eight wide steps leading up to eight columns across the front, similar to the building on Wind Dancers' Ledge. On the top of the building stood an elaborately decorated spire. The spire was at least a hundred wingspans tall and went all the way up and through what would have been the top of the cavern if they were still in the cavern.

There were fantastic sculptures and other artistic structures in the park area in front of the building. The fog swirled and curled around the objects as if stirred by the wind, and ghostly winged and un-winged men, women, and children walked through the park as if they were enjoying themselves, conversing and laughing.

The closer Joran and Lynette came to the building, the brighter the runes glowed. Similar runes were carved into the columns of the building. The big double doors also contained runes, which glowed brighter the closer they came. The runes on the stick glowed so brightly they were almost blinding.

"This has to be the runes Ooloo spoke of," said Lynette.

As they pushed through the door they realized they were not alone with ghosts any longer. A tall, ethereal wingless man holding a long staff stepped in front of them. He was glaring menacingly at them. Both Joran and Lynette pulled their swords from their sheaths.

"Who are you and what are you doing here?" he demanded imperiously. "You do not belong here! How did you get here?"

"I...I'm sorry, sir," stammered Joran brandishing his sword at the man. "We don't know what is going on. We were sent here by a young winged girl, the Ans'Isna." It was the only thing Joran could think of to say. He held up the stick Ooloo had given him. "She gave us this stick and told us to find these runes."

"Come with me," said the tall man upon seeing the stick. He ignored the sword. He turned on his heel and led Joran and Lynette to an elaborate inner door decorated with brightly glowing runes and symbols, the same as the ones on the stick.

He pushed through the door and stood back for Joran and Lynette to pass.

They didn't know what to expect, but they came upon a scene where eight individuals, four-winged men and four-winged women, were standing around a pool of what appeared to be water. They were all dressed in elaborate robes and were more solid looking than the wisps and ghosts outside the building. Each one of them had a timeless look, neither old nor young. They were holding hands and chanting. The surface of the pool was silver and shimmering with swirls and whorls. When the eight beings noticed Joran and Lynette standing in the room, they stopped what they were doing and turned to stare at them.

One of the men stepped forward and said, "You do not belong here. How did you get here?"

Joran sighed impatiently and said, "As I told this man, we were sent here by a young winglet named Ooloo. We were in the middle of a battle with a wizard named Morren and his army of undead..."

Several of the winged beings gasped and others murmured. "So it has begun," said one of the women. She walked up to stand beside the man. "They are the ones," she said to the winged man.

"The battle for this world, it has begun," said the man. "We have been watching and waiting."

"Who are you?" asked Lynette. "What do you mean you have been watching and waiting?"

"What battle?" demanded Joran.

"We are the guardians of the dream world," said the woman gently. "We watch the worlds from here. But there are some things we cannot see."

"Worlds?" asked Joran.

"Yes, well, there are many realities, you see..." she began.

"They do not yet understand," said the man as he gently laid a hand on the woman's arm. "Maybe we should start by introducing ourselves. I am Wind Master Dainenaire of Tree Queric, and this is Wind Mistress T'Feulla Joanelle. You may call me Master Dainen. Everyone here is a Wind Master or Wind Mistress."

"Wait a minute," said Joran. "I've heard of you. We read about you in our studies at Cliffside. But you were Wind Master over a thousand cycles ago, if I remember my history correctly. And Mistress T'Feulla was Wind Mistress over seven hundred cycles ago. How can you be here now?" he asked.

"Ah, but we are not really here. Only our spirits are here although we are more corporeal here than those you saw throughout the city. Each of us was selected by our various Wind Councils in our time to become a guardian. We have watched and waited for just such a time as this," Master Dainen said.

"But what do you mean we are the ones?" asked Lynette.

"You are fully here, as was predicted..." began Mistress Joanelle.

"We have known for countless thousands of cycles that one turn Eruna would be faced with destruction from another realm and the battle would begin with the use of undead warriors," interjected Master Dainen. "But we have been unable to see exactly when it would occur. Something has been blocking our sight of the event."

"We knew that two young Wind Dancers would come to the world of dreams, fully, not just in spirit," said Mistress Joanelle.

"But we are not Wind Dancers," said Joran.

"Ah, but you are in another realm and therefore you are, or will be Wind Dancers," explained one of the other Wind Masters. "You would have been chosen in this realm..."

"Don't confuse them," said Master Dainen. "It is not important that they understand. What is important is that they learn what is needed."

"What is it we need to learn?" asked Joran.

"Why magic, of course," said one of the other Wind Mistresses.

"But that takes many cycles," said Lynette. "How can we learn magic in time to do any good? We need to go to Cliffside to help defend it against the attack of the undead and a wizard named Morren."

"You have all the time in the universe," said Master Dainen. "We know about Morren, but there is something about him we cannot see. Until you arrived we were not sure which way events would unfold."

"I don't understand," said Joran as he and Lynette sheathed their swords.

"You do not need to understand," said Wind Mistress Joanelle dismissively. "Allow me to introduce the rest of the guardians."

After the introductions, Master Dainen and Mistress Joanelle led Joran and Lynette into another room. It appeared to be a large dining room. It was late in the turn and they realized they were hungry—hungry and tired.

"Since you are fully here, your bodies have needs. You need sustenance and rest," said Master Dainen. "Please sit and refresh yourselves. It is time for last-meal." He led Joran and Lynette to a large dining table covered with food and pitchers of water, ale, or wine. "I know you have many questions, but all will be answered in due time. For now, just eat. When you are done, it will be time to rest. You will need your rest."

Joran and Lynette did as they bid. Master Dainen and Mistress Joanelle sat across from them and watched them eat. When they were finished, Master Dainen waved his hand over the table and the food, plates, and pitchers vanished.

Joran was startled and jumped to his feet. "What the..." he exclaimed.

"Oh, I'm sorry. I didn't mean to startle you," said Master Dainen. "I see you have a lot to learn. But now, it is time for you to rest. You must be exhausted." He got to his feet and pulled the chair out for Mistress Joanelle.

"I will show you to your rooms," she said. "Follow me."

They left the dining room and walked down a long hall. She led them up an exquisite staircase to another hall and finally to a group of rooms. She opened a door on the left and led them into an elaborately decorated room. Lynette and Joran took off their backpacks and laid their swords on a round cushion in front of a large sofa.

"This is the salon and the bedroom is through that door. If you would like to take a bath, this is the door to the bathroom and privy," said Mistress Joanelle indicating another door.

"Yes please, a bath would be heavenly," sighed Lynette. She followed Mistress Joanelle into the bathroom. There was a large tub against one wall with pipes leading to it.

"You just turn this knob here for hot water and this one for cold," said Mistress Joanelle as she showed Lynette how to work the elaborate tub. "And here are some towels on this rack over here."

"I've never seen anything like this," said Lynette. "But if we are in the world of dreams, how can any of this be real."

"It is as real as it needs to be. I imagine there is a lot you have never seen in the city," said Mistress Joanelle. "In the morning, return to the dining room for first-meal. Sleep well." She smiled, turned on her heel and left their rooms.

Lynette sighed again. The explanation left her with more questions than answers. She filled the tub with steaming hot water as Joran went to check out the bedroom.

"Why don't you join me," Lynette shouted to him. He came into the bathroom just as she lowered herself into the steaming water.

"Wow, that is a large tub," he said.

"Yes, large enough for the both of us," she said as Joran began eagerly stripping off his clothes.

"Everything is happening too fast," said Joran as he sank into the tub. "I don't know what to think." "Me either," said Lynette. "But for now, let's just enjoy this bath and then see what happens tomorrow."

When they were finished bathing, they climbed into the large bed and were asleep almost as soon as their heads hit the pillows. Since they were in the world of dreams, their dreams were of Halalouma.

The next morning Joran and Lynette put on fresh clothes and made their way back to the dining room, where the table once again was covered with dishes of food. Master Dainen joined them and sat across the table from them. When they were finished, he once again waved his hand over the table and the plates and scraps vanished.

"We may as well begin now," he said. "Follow me." He led them to another room down the long hallway. He waved his hand over several lamps. Bright flames sprang up in the lamps, bringing light to the room. It was full of scrolls and manuscripts. A large, round table sat in the middle of the room. Above the table, the ceiling seemed to be open to the sky and Lynette and Joran could see the stars.

"How could this be?" asked Lynette. "We are in a building, aren't we? And it's morning, isn't it?"

"Yes, well, that is a projection of the sky far above the building in which we are located. It is nothing you need to worry about now. Please, have a seat," said Master Dainen.

Joran and Lynette sat on one side of the table with the Wind Master on the other. "I know you have many questions, and all will be answered in due time. But first, let us begin with me teaching you how to reach or access your magic. It's simple really. You must first find your center. Close your eyes and visualize your center."

"What does that mean?" asked Joran a bit impatiently. Lynette laid her hand gently on his arm.

"Just try it, Joran," she said. Joran closed his eyes and tried to imagine what his center looked like.

"Breathe deeply," said the Wind Master. "Turn your thoughts inward. And relax."

"That's easy for you to say," grumbled Joran. But he closed his eyes and did as he was bid. Before long, he felt something.

"Yes," said Master Dainen. "That's it. That is your center. Now expand your vision beyond yourself. Reach out of yourself."

Lynnette gasped and her eyes popped open. "I felt it, I felt some kind of power," she said. "It was as if I could almost reach out and take hold of it."

"That's exactly what you are going to do," said Master Dainen. "But for now, I want you to try centering yourself with your eyes open."

Joran and Lynette had much more difficulty reaching their center with their eyes open. But eventually, they were successful.

"That is enough for now," said Master Dainen. "Just listen. There are four aspects of magic you will need to learn to use. They are earth, fire, water, and air. The easiest aspect to work with is air. One of the uses is to make a shield of energy with air. You can use air to protect yourselves during battle."

"But how can air be a shield?" asked Joran. "We learned about the four aspects of magic at Cliffside, but we were not allowed to practice magic, although we were taught certain runes that we could use on our weapons."

"In your world or realm," said Master Dainen. "But in others, you were able to practice magic as students at Cliffside."

"That would have been nice," said Lynette.

"Yes, well, until you arrived we didn't know which realm you would come from. Anyway, back to using air. You shape the air and compact it into any shape you like," said Master Dainen. "Like this."

All of a sudden Joran huffed and was pushed back from the table, the legs of his chair scraping the floor. "Wow, it felt like a fist punched me in the chest."

"Now try to hit me," said Master Dainen." He came around the table as Joran rose from the chair and walked stood before him. Joran threw a punch at him, but his hand slammed into something solid.

"Oww," said Joran, shaking his hand. "That felt like a rock."

"That is what an energy shield of air is supposed to feel like," said Master Dainen. "You must be hungry by now. It's time for last-meal."

"It can't be," said Lynette. "We haven't had mid-meal yet."

"I must apologize for that," said Master Dainen. "You were doing so well I kept you working throughout the entire turn. I assure you it is time for last-meal now. More time passed for you than you realize when you had your eyes closed and were trying to reach your center. Let's go back to the dining room now."

Joran and Lynette followed him to the dining room. Again the table was laden with plenty of food and drink. They realized they were ravenous. After they had eaten their fill, Mistress Joanelle and another Wind Mistress came into the room.

"Mistress T'Oleeva Mianelle will continue your lessons this evening," said Master Dainen. He waved his hand a cleared away the plates.

"Please call me Mian," she said amicably. "Come with me." She led them back to the room with the round table and after they were seated she began to speak.

"I know you were wondering what happened to the cavern in which you found Halalouma the first time. You no doubt have heard of the Cycle of Dragons," she said.

"Yes, that was more than five thousand cycles ago," said Lynette.

"Correct, as reckoned by your time," said Mistress Mianelle. "The winged people of that time, my time, actually, were almost wiped out by the dragons. The dragons ruled the skies and were more plentiful and powerful than you can imagine. We knew we had to do something in order to survive. So we gathered our most powerful Wind Dancers from all over Eruna and developed a spell to change the dragons."

"Change them how?" asked Joran.

"We wanted to make them peaceful, to change their natures and remove their lust for blood and death, to enable them to live among us on Eruna," said Mistress Mianelle.

"So, what happened?" asked Lynette. "Where are the dragons now?"

"I will get to that," said Mistress Mianelle. "We built a device that would magnify the power of the Wind Dancers. You no doubt saw the central spire in the middle of the city?"

"I thought that was a work of art or something," said Joran.

"No, it was to intensify the Wind Dancer's magic and focus it," said Mistress Mianelle. "When we were ready, the Wind Dancers gathered and began channeling their energy through the device. The power shot into the sky. Some of the dragons were indeed changed."

"Changed to what," asked Joran. "There are no dragons on Eruna now, except for the one belonging to Morren, the one he calls 'Death.'"

"You have met them. You have met what they became, the Malakand," said Mistress Mianelle. "They fell from the sky and were changed into what they are now."

"The Malakand were once dragons?" asked Lynette incredulously.

"But you said some of the dragons were changed," said Joran. "What happened to the rest of them?"

"The device's beam of power ripped a hole, or portal, in the fabric of reality and some of the dragons were thrown into a void, for the lack of a better word," said Mistress Mianelle. "And they have changed also. But not into Malakand."

"How were they changed then?" asked Lynette. "What did they become?"

"They were changed into all manner of demons," said Mistress Mianelle. "And the leader of the dragons was the worst of all. His name is Saarnak, and he has been trying to get back into this realm ever since, for thousands of cycles."

"But what happened to the Wind Dancers and all the people of Halalouma? In our time or realm, or whatever, there are no people living there," said Lynette. "Where did they all go?"

"What we didn't expect was that the use of that much power would have an effect on the people living here. We began to get sick with a wasting disease. You see, power was pulled from every living being in Halalouma...too much power. Once we realized what was happening it was too late. The damage had been done."

"Yes, but how did Halalouma come to be in a cavern?" asked Joran.

"Ah, yes, in order to prevent the sickness from spreading we moved earth and rock and enclosed the city entirely. We excavated the tunnels for the Malakand to come and go. They were immune to the disease and they took care of us as the sickness slowly wiped us out," said Mistress Mianelle.

"But didn't they know what you had done in changing them? Didn't they know they were once dragons? Why would they help you?" asked Lynette.

"No, they never knew. They became a simple, mostly peaceful species. They completely forget who they really were," said Mistress Mianelle. "It took several cycles but the Malakand began to leave the underground city and move into what is now the deserts of the Wastelands. You see, the power of the device also changed the land and devastated it. The Wind Dancers decided to form the guardians to watch over Eruna from the world of dreams, for the time when Saarnak would make his move."

"But the guardians all come from different times in the past. I don't understand..." said Joran.

"You see, the world of dreams is timeless," explained Mistress Mianelle. "Once we decided to form the guardians, the Wind Councils elected a representative throughout time and reality. Each Wind Dancer chosen made the sacrifice to become a guardian. Our spirits exist here, but our bodies have long since deteriorated and turned to dust. Do not worry if you do not understand. As I said, the world of dreams is timeless. Except for you, as you are fully here, time will seem to pass for you. It is now time for you to rest again. You must keep up your strength. In the morning you will continue your lessons. I bid you good night," said Mistress Mianelle. She left them sitting in the room looking amazed.

"That is a lot to take in," said Joran.

"Yes, it is," agreed Lynette. "The Malakand, Bicken, knew how to get to Halalouma and brought Ooloo and the warriors there...or here, as the case may be. Oh, it's so confusing!"

"I know," said Joran. "Forget about it for now. I wonder how your father and Aerielle are."

"Perhaps one of the guardians could tell us?" said Lynette. "I miss her so. I hope she is safe."

Joran put his arm around her shoulders and squeezed her gently. "We may as well go to bed," he said. "I'm really tired. Looking for my center was hard work." They returned to their rooms. Both fell asleep almost immediately.

The eight Guardians were back in the room with the silver pool. They held hands and chanted as the pool swirled.

"They are concerned about their daughter," said Master Dainen. "Let's look in on her."

The silver pool coalesced and the guardians could see Mattern flying with the baby, Aerielle, in his arms. It was nighttime and he stopped and made camp. In another octurn Mattern would be back at Cliffside.

"They seem to be fine," said Mistress Joanelle. "Mattern has to make his decision soon. The High Matriarch must not get her hands on the baby. She is too important."

"What about the Ans'Isna, Ooloo?" asked Master Robellaire of Tree Whalnu. The silver pool coalesced again and the scene changed. Ooloo was sitting on her pallet in the dark fortress tugging at the bracelets that encircled her wrists.

She sat up straighter and appeared to look straight at Master Dainen. "Who's there?" she asked. The guardians looked at one another in surprise.

"She is more gifted than we thought if she can sense our presence. When she goes to sleep let's see if we can contact her," said Mistress T'Oleeva.

Ooloo shrugged her shoulders and went back to working on the bracelets. She was concentrating on breaking one of them. Morren had been displeased with her for continuing to try to get through the door and wall of energy and had put the bracelets back on her wrists. But after a while, she laid down in frustration and slowly went to sleep.

She immediately found herself in the world of dreams. She was in the city of Halalouma outside the building with the runes. Master Dainen and the other guardians came out the door and stood in a line staring at Ooloo. Fog swirled around her feet.

"Hello, Ooloo," said Master Dainen, speaking for the group. "We have been expecting you."

"Expecting me?" she asked. "Who are you?" She thought about drawing her knife but decided against it. She could sense the power emanating from the group.

"We are the guardians of the dream world," he said. "We know what you have done. We know that you agreed to let Morren teach you."

Ooloo stuck out her chin defiantly. "What of it?" she asked.

"Morren seeks to use you. You must be very careful," said Mistress Joanelle.

"I will learn everything I can from him and then I will kill him," declared Ooloo vehemently. "He is almost as evil as Saarnak. I will kill him also," she said with a certainty borne of her loathing for them.

"Come inside and we will speak of many things before you awake," said Master Dainen. "We have many questions."

# CHAPTER 9

# CHAINS

Morren stood before the pedestal holding a black orb and opened a window into the void. Saarnak immediately appeared in the window.

"What do you want," he asked Morren.

"When can I proceed with the attack on Cliffside?" he asked.

"You must create more undead warriors first," replied Saarnak. "The Wind Dancers will not be easy to defeat. Go into the western Wastelands and round up more of the desert tribes. You will need at least five hundred more warriors."

"Yes, Master," said Morren. "And I will be able to make more undead as we travel south and attack the villages in the Northern Provinces along the way."

"Yes, of course, you could also do that," agreed Saarnak. "The more undead warriors we have the better. How is the training of the innocent going? Is she a willing and cooperative student?"

"Once I showed her the futility of her resistance, she yielded completely. Although, she does keep trying to break through out of the cell, but, I put the bracelets back on her as punishment. She already knows quite a lot, and she is a fast learner. I will have to be careful and keep my guard up, though. She has sworn to kill me," said Morren.

Saarnak burst out laughing. "Yes, I imagine she has," he said. "She is quite stubborn and willful."

"She is that," agreed Morren.

"When do you think she will be powerful enough to open the portal for me?" asked Saarnak.

"Probably not until I have taught her how to use all of the aspects of magic," said Morren. "Until then she will not have the power required to safely accomplish our goals."

"Yes, we wouldn't want her to end up as you," said Saarnak. He was referring to the ill-fated experiment when Morren had tried to use a powerful spell to open a portal to another world. He had not been strong enough, even with the help of his friends, Kerin and Libraen, to avoid the backlash of power that had landed him in the void where Saarnak and his demons lived. He had been horribly disfigured and his wings had been burned away.

Morren shuddered as he remembered the event. "You promised to heal me and give me back my wings," reminded Morren.

"Yes, I remember. I will keep my promise once I have entered Eruna," said Saarnak. "I suggest you concentrate now on acquiring more undead and on training Ooloo. The sooner she is trained the sooner we will both achieve our goals.

"Yes, lord," said Morren. He closed the window and turned on his heel. He left the tower and went outside. He climbed on the back of Death, his great dragon. They flew off toward the Western Wastelands. He took along some of his undead army.

He flew over several of the villages from which he had already captured tribesmen and women. The villages were burned to the ground. Death had been efficient. After half a turn he arrived at another village, this one full of winged people. They rose up in the air to attack him and protect the village. Morren conjured a shield and their arrows and spears bounced off it harmlessly. They were attacked by the undead and began to succumb.

Morren cast the spell to enthrall the tribesmen and those attacking him immediately succumbed. He landed his dragon and walked through the village enthralling men right and left, even those injured. He killed the rest, the women and children, and Death began to feed. Many of them tried to flee, but Morren burned them down with fire, and Death killed the rest. He gathered those he had enthralled and led them back to his dark fortress.

He made them stand at attention as he cast the spell to make them undead. He raised his hand and a red light flashed out and encompassed them. As they opened their mouths to scream, the red light shot down their throats and their eyes began to glow red.

Ooloo watched from her cell through the little window. She was horrified by what she saw. She became even more determined to learn what she could from Morren so that she might kill him. But she would make it as unpleasant for Morren as possible.

The next turn, Morren went into the Wastelands again and returned with more enthralled tribesmen. He again turned them into undead warriors also. He did this for several turns until he had over five hundred additional warriors. He was finally ready to begin his attack. But first, he knew he must consult Saarnak.

He went up into the tower where the black orb sat on the pedestal in the center of the room. He opened a window into the void and Saarnak appeared once again.

"I am ready to begin my attack soon," said Morren.

Saarnak frowned at him and asked, "What of the innocent? What about her training?"

"That's what I wanted to ask you about. I thought I would take her with me and continue her training," he said.

"You may take her, but be warned, if she escapes I will not give you back your wings," said Saarnak. "I suggest you keep her bracelets on her and keep her chained except for whenever you are training her."

"I will have a special wagon built for her where she will stay when I'm busy. I won't be able to keep my eye on her all the time," said Morren.

"That is a good idea," said Saarnak. "But I want her to see the destruction you and your warriors wreak. She must be fully convinced of your power. This will dissuade her from any foolish notions of escape. Don't forget, she bested you during your first attack on Halalouma. Be very careful she does not have the opportunity to do so again."

"Yes, lord," said Morren, anticipating the reign of terror he would bring upon the unsuspecting inhabitants of the Eight Realms. But for now, it was time for Ooloo's training.

He made his way to her cell and opened the door. Ooloo was sitting on her pallet forlornly. She jumped to her feet and glared at Morren angrily.

"Have you been practicing finding your center?" he asked. "I left your bracelets off last night so you could practice. But if you displease me I will put them back on you and you will not be able to practice tonight. Come here and show me what you have accomplished." He set the lamp he was carrying onto the table and lit it by conjuring a ball of fire. He sat in the lone chair behind the table as she stood before him.

"I can do more than that," she said. She threw a ball of fire at him. But he had come into the cell with a shield of energy already around him, and the ball of fire was deflected. He had to be constantly on guard with her.

"Why do you persist in your useless attempts against me?" he asked. He squeezed his hand and she was suddenly stricken with pain. She writhed on the floor of the cell as he rose from the chair to go stand over her. "Perhaps you need another lesson in pain to convince you that I am in no danger from you."

"For now," she said under her breath. "I beat you once. I will beat you again."

"What was that?" he asked. "Speak your mind."

"Nothing," she said between clenched teeth. Pain was still coursing through her body. It was all she could do not to cry out and scream for mercy.

"Now are you ready for your training, or do you need more pain?" Morren asked.

"I'm ready," she screeched. "I'm ready, blast you."

Morren released her from the pain, and she lay there for a few moments regaining her composure. "How many more lessons like this are you going to have to experience?" he asked, shaking his head. He didn't really expect an answer as he went back to the chair and sat down.

"Now come here and show me how well you can control yourself," he said. "Show me how you can reach your center and the power there. Until you can control it better you will not proceed in your training."

Ooloo stood in front of the table and focused inward. She immediately found her center and gained control of the power.

"I have it. Now what?" she asked.

"That is very good, Ooloo. I want you to try to move all the water from the bucket and form it into a globe," said Morren. "This should be easy for you."

Ooloo grabbed the water in the bucket with her power and formed a globe over Morren's head. Then she released it all at once and the globe of water splashed all over him as she laughed uproariously. He jumped up in a rage and slapped her across the face.

"So, you think that is funny?" he asked as he used his magic to dry himself off. "We'll see how funny you think it is when I do this."

He grabbed her by the arm and dragged her out of the cell. He led her to the cell where her friends were being held. He practically ripped the door from its hinges as he used his magic to open the door. He waved his hand at the warriors within the cell and they all fell to the ground writhing in pain and screaming.

"I'll stop, I'll stop. I promise! Just stop hurting them!" she pleaded.

"Are you going to take your training seriously, or must I make them all undead?" he asked in a rage.

"I promise, I'll take it seriously, blast you," she screamed. "Please don't hurt them anymore." He released the warriors and reattached the door to their cell. He slammed it closed.

"One more display of your defiance and I swear I will turn them all into undead," Morren said. He jerked Ooloo by the arm and dragged her back to her cell. He threw her into the cell and then sat back down in the chair. "Now, I want you to take the water, form it into a globe and hold it above your head."

Ooloo did as she was told. "Now I want you to move the globe around the room, but don't let any of the water spill from it," Morren said."Once you have done that, I want you to put the water back in the bucket."

Ooloo moved the globe from corner to corner around the cell and then dumped it back in the bucket. Once the water was back in the bucket, Morren picked it up and poured all of it out on the dirt floor.

"Why did you do that?" she asked. It was her drinking water he had just poured out. She wondered what she was going to drink.

"I want you to gather the water together and put it back in the bucket. You have all night to try," said Morren.

"But it's all dirty now," she protested.

"You will have to separate the water from the dirt, unless you want to drink dirty water," he said, grinning with spite. "I'll be back tomorrow to see how well you did." He rose from the chair and went to the door. "If you haven't done it by the time I return, I will punish you. All you have to do is separate earth from water."

He opened the door and turned to look at her. "Remember, you are not to touch the door or you will experience pain." With that, he left and closed the door behind him. Ooloo was just stubborn enough to go to the door and touch it anyway no matter how much pain it brought her. And it did bring her pain.

When she stopped hurting from touching the door, she stood over the spilled water and tried to get the water to rise from the dirt. It was harder than she thought. Water was hard to control, but she was determined to do it.

She decided to try finding her center again and she was able to get a small amount of water to rise from the dirt, about a handful. She carefully guided the water to the bucket that she had moved from the table to the floor. She repeated the process until all the water was off of the dirt floor. It looked cloudy to her, as if some of the dirt had remained in the water.

She sighed and dumped it all back out on the floor. She would keep trying until she got it right. It was hot in the cell, even though the sun had finally set. If she was going to have something to drink she had better try again.

Finally, after several attempts, the water was clear. She moved some from the bucket to her cup with her magic and took a sip. It tasted delicious. She drank it all down and refilled her cup using her magic again and drank that down too.

Then she relieved herself in the other bucket and lay down to go to sleep. It was then she realized that Gretna had failed to bring her last-meal. Morren must have told her not to bring it as punishment for spilling the globe of water over him. It was worth it to go without a meal to see his ugly, wet face, but she was sorry her friends had to suffer for her rebellion. She would try to refrain from such actions from now on. She didn't want to see any more of them become undead, like Batab. Finally, she went to sleep.

She found herself in a horrible nightmare. She was standing in a square surrounded by strange-looking buildings. Shadows in the street rose from the ground and took the form of winged people. They flew around her head and began to attack her. She was knocked to the ground. Every time she got up she was knocked down again.

She tried fighting them off with her magic, throwing fireballs at them. But they merely dissipated, the fireballs just passing through them, and then reformed. More and more shadows began to surround her. And she was sinking into the ground as if it were quicksand.

Then the shadows coalesced into one large being. He looked like Saarnak. "You see?" he said. "You cannot escape me, even in your dreams."

Ooloo willed herself to wake up just before her head went beneath the sand. She was drenched in sweat and her clothes stuck to her. She got up from the pallet and went to the table for a drink of water. She didn't want to go back to sleep, but she knew she needed some rest. Maybe if she concentrated on something pleasant, like her Paap, she would dream about him. When she went to sleep this time, she found herself back in the Northern Plains and could see the High Plateaus in the distance.

Tavat was there. He was hunting and she was watching him. She tried to speak to him, but he couldn't hear her. She wanted to talk to him so badly, but it was as if he couldn't see her at all. She awoke again and rolled over on her pallet.

She decided to try thinking about Lynette and Joran. She pictured them in Halaloluma, in the dream world where she sent them. She fell asleep again and found herself in a dining room.

Joran and Lynette were sitting at a table and were surprised to see her. They had just finished eating last-meal.

"You're here," said Lynette. "I'm glad to see you. What happened to you? You said you had passed out, and the last we saw of you before you were here and gave us the stick you carved the runes into, Morren had thrown some kind of net over you."

"Yes, he captured me," said Ooloo. "I had hoped he would let the others go if he caught me, but he didn't. He enthralled my friends, the warriors from the North. Have you seen Paap? I looked for him before I passed out but I didn't see him. I dreamed about him earlier, but he couldn't see or hear me. Do you know what happened to him?"

"No, we didn't see him either," said Joran. "We were too busy fighting the undead. We were about to kill ourselves when you transported us here to the dream world. Thank you, by the way. You faded away last time before we could thank you for saving us."

"You are welcome," said Ooloo. "Have you found anything to help you against Morren?"

"Well, we are learning a lot about magic from Wind Master T'Queric and the others," said Lynette.

"I'm being trained by Morren," Ooloo said as if she was ashamed of the fact.

"What?" asked Lynette. "Isn't that dangerous? He is clearly evil, Ooloo. Please be careful."

Just then Master T'Queric and Mistress T'Feulla entered the dining room. They were not surprised to see Ooloo again. She had been to the world of dreams before, but she had awakened before she had a chance to talk to Lynette and Joran. The guardians had kept her busy with their myriad of questions.

"Hello, Ooloo," said Mistress T'Feulla. "How are you coming in your lessons with Morren?"

Ooloo grimaced. "He punishes me a lot," she said. She told them about how she had dumped water on him and they all laughed. "I just can't help myself. It is almost worth the pain. But I don't like when he hurts my friends."

"How are they," asked Lynette. "Have the warriors been changed into undead?"

"They are not undead yet, except for Batab. Morren made her undead to get me to cooperate with him. Sometimes he gives the rest of them pain too," she said sadly. "I don't like it when he does that."

"Maybe you shouldn't aggravate him then," said Lynette gently. "Maybe you should just cooperate with him."

"I know," said Ooloo sullenly. "I just wish I could escape from him. But he put a powerful spell on the door to my cell and it brings me pain when I touch it. And sometimes he makes me wear bracelets that make it impossible for me to use my magic."

"Don't lose hope," said Joran. "We are learning as fast as we can and we will help you when we return to our realm."

"But Morren is going to attack Cliffside soon," said Ooloo.

"Do you know when?" asked Master T'Queric. "We haven't been able to see anything concerning him. It's almost as if something is blocking our sight."

"No, I just know it is soon," said Ooloo. "I think Morren is using dark magic more and more. And he is under the control of the demon Saarnak."

"Ah, Saarnak," said Mistress Feulla. "We should have known he would be somehow involved. The signs are all there. The dragons have waited for thousands of cycles. We must consult the others." She rose from the table and went to find the other Wind Masters and Wind Mistresses. When she had found them they all gathered in the dining room.

"Tell us what you know of Saarnak, Ooloo," said Master T'Queric. "Tell us everything. Don't leave anything out."

"I only see him through a window in a black orb. The orb is on a large pedestal in one of the towers above Morren's fortress. He is in some kind of void. Morren says they want my help to open a portal so Saarnak can come through into Eruna," said Ooloo. "He said only an innocent can open the portal for Saarnak. That's why they want my help."

Master T'Queric gasped and everyone started talking at once. "Everyone, please! So that is his plan. Listen to me, Ooloo. You must not open the portal. Saarnak must not come into Eruna. He is far more powerful and dangerous than you could ever imagine," he said.

"But Morren will hurt my friends," said Ooloo. "I have to go now. I am starting to wake up." And with that she was gone.

"Is there some way we can help her?" asked Joran. "There must be something we can do."

"You must learn as much as you can about magic while you are here," said Master T'Queric. "That is the only way you can help Ooloo."

Ooloo awakened when Gretna unlocked the door to her cell. She held a plate of food in her hands.

"Hello, Gretna," said Ooloo. She ran from her pallet and put her arms around Gretna's waist. Gretna pulled away from her and set the plate down on the table.

"I brought you some fresh berries. I know you are getting tired of gruel," said Gretna.

"Are you still under Morren's control?" asked Ooloo hopefully. "You seem different."

"If you mean am I enthralled, then no, I am not," answered Gretna. "There is nothing I can do to escape and besides, I have no where to go. My village was completely destroyed and those I love have been made into the undead."

"Oh, I'm so sorry, Gretna," said Ooloo. "If I find a way, I promise I will set you free."

Gretna laughed ruefully. "Just eat now, and don't do anything foolish," she said. Then she left the cell and relocked the door.

Ooloo ate her first-meal, savoring the berries, and then sat back down on her pallet to wait. She didn't have long to wait before Morren came to the cell.

He sat at the table and looked at Ooloo speculatively. "I have a surprise for you," he finally said. "We are leaving the fortress and heading south."

"We?" asked Ooloo.

"Yes, I am taking you with me. We will continue your training as we travel. But I'm going to have to put your bracelets back on," said Morren. "Come here."

Ooloo rose from her pallet and went to the table where Morren was sitting. She reluctantly held her arms out and Morren put the bracelets on. "Don't try anything to make me regret taking you with me." He got up from the chair and walked to the door.

"Follow me," he said as he waved his hand before the door. "You can leave the cell now." She followed him out the door and up to a wooden wagon. There was a door in the back with a tiny barred window in it. "I've constructed a special wagon for you to ride in, but for now you can ride on Death with me. But you will have to wear this chain."

The chain was attached to a large collar around the dragon's neck and ended in another collar that Morren fastened around

Ooloo's neck. The collar was constructed of the same metal as the bracelets and had runes carved in it. She was connected to the dragon as she sat in front of Morren on the dragon's back.

"You will wear the chain as long as you are riding with me. Otherwise, you will spend the rest of the time in the wagon," said Morren.

"I'd rather ride in the wagon than with you," said Ooloo.

"Oh but I want you to see what is happening," said Morren. She had to sit there as Morren gave instructions to his legions of undead warriors. She didn't like what she heard. Morren instructed them to capture or kill everyone in their path as they swooped through the Northern Provinces.

They all took to the air and flew away from the black fortress heading south. Several wagons pulled out of the compound, pulled by several garings each, and followed them across the sand. Ooloo could see Gretna sitting next to the driver of one of the wagons. The drivers were the rough, wingless ground-dwellers she had seen in the fortress. She wondered why they were helping Morren. What had they been promised for their service?

When they stopped for the night, Morren unhooked the chain from the dragon's collar but did not immediately remove the collar from around Ooloo's neck. He hopped down from the dragon's back and waited for Ooloo to slide down. He tried to catch her, but she pushed him away and landed in a heap on the sand.

Morren sighed, "I would have helped you off the dragon," he said.

"I don't want your help," said Ooloo as she stood up. "When are you going to take this blasted collar off?"

Morren shook the chain, making her stagger as he led her to a table set up in the middle of the camp. "You have a choice, Ooloo. You can either go straight to your wagon and eat by yourself, or you can dine with me," he said. "But you will wear this chained collar until I take it off for your training."

She thought about it for a moment and decided to eat with Morren. It was still stifling hot and she didn't look forward to being confined in a hot wagon until the night cooled down. Besides, she was sort of looking forward to learning more magic.

Morren politely pulled out her chair for her and she plopped down in it. Then he went around the table and sat down across from her. He poured each of them a cup of water, which Ooloo drank down greedily. Before long, Gretna brought two plates and set them down in front of them. They ate last-meal in silence until Morren said, "I will take your collar and bracelets off now for your lesson. But do not try anything to escape."

Ooloo just looked at him. "Well, what is it going to be?" he asked.

"Alright," she agreed. "I won't try anything."

"Good," he said as he removed her collar. She rubbed her neck where the collar had irritated it. Then he removed the bracelets and set them on the table.

"I thought I would teach you about the aspect known as earth tonight. First, find your center and then I want you to use the sand to form a pyramid," he said, "Like this." He raised his hand and the sand began to form itself into a small pyramid shape about as tall as a man.

"But couldn't I use air to do that?" she asked.

"You could, but try it by taking hold of the sand and moving it, like you did when you separated the dirt from the water," he said.

She took hold of the sand with her power and it went flying into Morren's face. "I'm sorry, I'm sorry," she said. "I lost control of it."

Morren sighed angrily, wiped the sand from his face and glared at her. "I'm not sure you didn't do that on purpose," he said. "But I will give you this one chance. Try again, and unless you form a pyramid you will spend the entire night in agony."

Ooloo took hold of the sand again and formed a pyramid. "Good," said Morren. "Now form the sand into the shape of a cube."

Ooloo did as she was told and formed a cube. "Is that all?" she asked. "Am I just going to make geometric shapes?"

"No, you can take the sand and do this," Morren said and demonstrated for her. He propelled the sand against an undead warrior and stripped the skin from his bones as he screamed. As he began to fall, a man-shaped figure of red light came streaming out of his mouth and then dissipated. The bones clacked together as they toppled down to the ground.

Ooloo shuddered in horror and pulled away from Morren. "I want to go to my wagon now," she said.

"Fine," said Morren. "But first I'm going to put your bracelets, collar, and chain back on. After he was done he led Ooloo to the wagon he had specially prepared for her and pulled open the door. He pushed her up the steps and through the door and followed her into the wagon. He connected the chain to a ring in the floor of the wagon. "Remember, do not touch the door unless you want pain. And don't fool with the chain either." Then he left and slammed the door shut. She heard the key turn in the lock. She went to the door and touched it out of spite. It definitely caused her pain.

She pulled her hand back, sat down on the pallet that had been provided for her and looked around the wagon. It was smaller than her cell had been, but there were two buckets and a cup for her use. One bucket held water for her to drink and one was for her to relieve herself. It was stifling hot in the wagon, so she picked up the cup, dipped it in the water bucket and drank. It was lukewarm. She splashed some of the water on her face and then lay down to sleep. The collar was uncomfortable around her neck and sleep never came. She lay there thinking of ways she could kill Morren. When she finally went to sleep she dreamed of killing both Morren and Saarnak.

~

## CHAPTER 10

# MESSAGE

The High Matriarch of the Eight Realms had just dismissed her courtiers and left the throne room when the head of the Wind Council himself barged into the throne room demanding to see her immediately. One of her wing guards was sent to fetch her as she was on her way to her dining room to have last-meal. With irritation, she returned to the throne room and ordered her courtiers to return also. A lesser person would not have dared to send someone to "fetch" her. She swept into the throne room indignantly and sat down on her throne. She glared at Master Haddon as she sat there with her chin in one hand, her other hand tapping impatiently on the arm of the throne with her long fingernails. Her long black hair hung in a braid over her left shoulder. She impatiently grabbed the braid and threw it over her shoulder to hang down her back. There was a lot on her mind, not the least of which was the situation with her missing daughter and the upstart T'Ardis with whom she had life-mated. The High Matriarch wondered if that was the reason Haddon was here.

"Master Haddon, what do you want that you felt was necessary to interrupt my last-meal?" she asked as her courtiers scurried back into the throne room.

"Your Majesty, Mother Kerinelle and Father Libraenaire sent me here to warn you that there is going to be an attack on Cliffside by T'Ardis Morrenaire and an army of undead."

This caused a commotion among the courtiers who began to murmur and whisper. The High Matriarch frowned and shouted, "Silence! Continue, Master Haddon."

"You must send re-enforcements to Cliffside immediately," said Master Haddon. "We do not know for certain how soon the attack is going to come, but we must be prepared."

"Really? T'Ardis Morrenaire? You want me to believe someone who has been dead for over forty cycles has come back to life and is going to attack Cliffside? And that he is bringing an army of undead?" she asked mockingly.

"Yes, Your Majesty," said Master Haddon. "Mother and Father called the Wind Council to assembly over an octurn ago to report the impending attack. They assure us that Morren is quite alive and is set on revenge for what happened to him."

"Mother Kerinelle and Father Libraen," she said sarcastically. "Well, why didn't you say so?"

"Your Majesty?" asked Master Hadden not understanding her attitude.

"Mother Kerinelle and Father Libraen have never been supportive of my reign, and now they want my help," she said. "Why should I help them?"

"Because, Your Majesty, winglets from all over the Eight Realms are students there and because Mother Kerinelle and Father Libracn believe Morren will not stop at Cliffside," said Master Haddon. "They believe he will bring his undead army into the Eight Realms when he is done with Cliffside."

"When will this attack take place, did you say? "she asked, continuing to tap her nails on the arm of the throne.

"The Ans'Isna did not say. She only knows that Morren is going to attack soon," said Master Haddon. "She has the gift of sight."

"Who is this Ans'Isna?" asked the High Matriarch.

Master Haddon proceeded to tell her about the winglet Ooloo and the warriors from the north. He purposely left out the fact that her daughter and her life-mate were on their way back to Cliffside. He also did not mention the birth of their daughter.

"So this Ooloo has the gifts of both sight and knowing," she said. "And they are on the way to Cliffside as we speak." Her interest was piqued now. She could use someone with the gifts of sight and knowing. She felt there was something Haddon was not telling her though. "What are you not telling me?" she asked.

"I am telling you exactly what Mother Kerinelle and Father Libraen told the Wind Council," said Master Haddon. "I decided to come to see you myself so that you would take this threat seriously and send help to Cliffside.

"And that is the problem with your story," said the High Matriarch. "How can I believe anything Mother Kerinelle and Father Libraen say? I have never trusted those two. They allowed my daughter not only to life-mate with this T'Ardis character of whom I never approved, but also to run away from Cliffside with him. I will not commit any of my soldiers to protect Cliffside from an attack that may or may not even happen."

"But...but, Your Majesty. They were adamant about Morren..." said Master Haddon.

"Besides," she interrupted. "I am concentrating all my efforts on finding my daughter and her so-called life-mate. You wouldn't happen to know anything about their whereabouts would you?"

"No, Your Majesty," said Master Haddon. "I have no idea where they might be." He was telling the truth as far as he knew it at that moment. Kerin and Libraen had not told him much about Lynette and Joran, other than they were on their way back to Cliffside. He had no intention of telling her that or about their winglet.

The High Matriarch looked at Master Haddon suspiciously. "I do not believe you. There is still something you have not told me," she said. "Take him." She snapped her fingers at her Wing Guards.

Two Wing Guards stepped up and grabbed each of his arms. He tried to pull away but they held on tightly.

"This is outrageous and unprecedented," said Master Haddon. "I came to warn you about an attack and ask for your help. Am I under arrest, now?"

"Call it what you like. I am going to hold you for questioning until you tell me everything you know. You will tell me everything and hold nothing back," said the High Matriarch with conviction. "Take him to a cell below."

Master Haddon tried to use his magic against the Wing Guard holding him, but he could not access it for some reason. Something was preventing him from using his magic. He should have noticed it when he first entered the hall, but he had been too intent on trying to convince the High Matriarch of the danger of Morren's attack.

Seeing the shock and confusion on Haddon's face as he failed to use his magic the High Matriarch laughed. "Tree Algren is warded against your magic, and everyone else's magic," she said. "I am the only one who may use magic here."

"You mean dark magic," said Master Haddon as they dragged him from the court. "You will not get away with this."

One of the High Matriarch's ladies-in-waiting quietly slipped from the throne room without being seen. She made her way to her own room and quickly wrote a message to Mother Kerinelle. She was secretly one of Mother's agents, placed in the court to spy on the High Matriarch. She sealed the message concerning what had happened to Master Haddon with wax and put her special mark in it. The she flew to the messenger's station.

"Hello Mistress Gwendelle," said the winged man behind the desk at the station. "Another letter to your mother?"

"Yes, Framen," said Gwendelle. "I thought I might go for a visit at mid-cycle, with the High Matriarch's permission, of course."

"Humph, like you'll ever get her permission," said Framen.

"Well, maybe this time she will allow it. I'll wait until she's in a good mood to ask her," Gwendelle said.

"Ha, then you'll never ask her," said Framen.

"Now, now, don't be that way," said Gwendelle. "I'd better be getting back to court." She handed Framen five Gren coins for the message to be delivered.

"You take care, Mistress Gwendelle," said Framen as he put the Gren in his money pouch.

"You too, Framen," she said. She flew back to Tree Algren and slipped back into the large throne room unseen.

Meanwhile, the High Matriarch was just dismissing court for the second time and all the courtiers were beginning to disperse. Gwendelle made her way to her room to await the High Matriarch's beck and call. She hoped Mother Kerinelle would know what to do about Wind Master Haddon. He was, after all, the head of the Wind Council. Gwendelle was appalled that he had been taken to the cells below Tree Algren. She uttered a quick prayer for him. There were terrible rumors about what transpired beneath the roots of Tree Algren.

The High Matriarch made her way down to the special chamber beneath Tree Algren where Master Haddon was being held in a cell. Each of his hands was chained to the wall of the cell. He was furious at the treatment he received.

"Your Majesty, this is outrageous and is not at all necessary. I will gladly answer any questions you have to the best of my ability," he assured her.

"Of course you will," said the High Matriarch. "Now, how did this Ans'Isna get a message to Mother Kerinelle and Father Libraen."

"As I said earlier, she, her grandfather, and the warriors from the Northern Plateaus have been making their way to Cliffside for over a cycle. They apparently found the ancient city of Halalouma," said Haddon. He thought she might be distracted if she knew about Halalouma.

"Halalouma?" asked the High Matriarch. "She began pacing back and forth in front of Haddon. "You are sure of this?"

"Yes, and while there they were attacked by T'Ardis Morrenaire," said Haddon. "The winglet, Ooloo was able to discern from his mind that he plans to attack Cliffside."

"Yes, but how did she get word to Mother and Father?" she asked.

"According to Mother Kerinelle, when they exited Halalouma they ran into a commander of a Wing Guard from Cliffside School, who was searching for your daughter. He sent his squad into the Wastelands to continue the search while he circled back to look for them."

"And has this squad from Cliffside found any sign of my daughter?" she asked.

"I do not know, Your Majesty. All I know is that Swen carried a message to Mother and Father telling them about Morren and his planned attack," he said.

"Swen? Is that the commander of the Wing Guard at Cliffside?" she asked.

"Yes, Your Majesty," said Haddon.

"What else did this Swen have to say?" she asked.

"I do not know, Your Majesty. I have told you what Mother and Father told me," said Haddon. He was leaving out the part about Lynette, Joran, and their winglet, but he hoped the High Matriarch would accept the rest of what he said as truth. But he was not so fortunate.

"You are not telling me everything," she said, "And I am losing patience with you." She turned away from him and called to Jathen, a wingless man of special skills she had saved from execution when she first became High Matriarch. Jathen had no qualms about doing her bidding, even when it required the use of those skills. He came scurrying into the chamber from a room not far from Haddon's cell.

"Yes, Your Majesty?" he asked as he rubbed his hands together.

"I need information from Wind Master Haddon here," she said as she indicated the unfortunate winged man chained to her chamber wall. "He is holding something back, and I wish to know what it is.

"Yes, Your Majesty," said Jathen. He went to his room to retrieve his bundle of instruments. He returned to Haddon's cell and unrolled the bundle onto the table in the center of the room. Master Haddon realized then that he was about to be tortured and would probably never leave his cell alive.

"I will return after last-meal to question my guest," she said. "See that he is still alive when I return."

"Yes, Your Majesty," said Jathen. She left the chamber and flew back to her dining room.

Master Haddon glared at Jathan and said, "Is that all you can say? Just, 'Yes, Your Majesty?' Do you know who I am?"

"You are Wind Master Haddon," said Jathen as he nodded his head. "Like she said."

"Yes, I am head of the Wind Council and I am being held against my will and illegally. I demand that you release me. The Wind Council will reward you, but only if you let me go now," said Master Haddon.

"No, now I couldn't do that," Jathen assured him shaking his head back and forth. "She wouldn't like that. No, she wouldn't like that at all. No. Not going do it."

"Then you are as evil as she is," said Master Haddon. "You will pay for your crimes."

Jathen burst out laughing. "My crimes...that's enough talking now. Let's get started." He picked up one of his evil looking instruments and set to work.

Haddon screamed until he was hoarse. He decided that he would die before he betrayed his oath to Father Libraen. He would not divulge his knowledge of the baby, Lynette, or Joran, no matter what Jathen did to him. If only he could have accessed his magic. He would have burned Tree Algren to the ground and the High Matriarch and Jathen with it.

After last-meal, the High Matriarch returned to the cell to find Wind Master Haddon beaten, bloody and subdued. Jathen stood to the side wiping his hands on a dirty rag.

"What of the other arrangements?" she asked. "Did you find someone who fits my needs?"

"Yes, Your Majesty," said Jathen. "She is in the other chamber."

"You haven't defiled her, have you?" she asked sternly.

"No, Your Majesty," said Jathen. "She is still pure, and she is ready for the ceremony whenever you are."

"I will question our guest to see what else he knows first," she said. She sauntered over to Haddon and lifted his chin. He was barely conscious. "Now, what do you know of my daughter?"

"You are going to kill me no matter what I say," said Master Haddon through clenched teeth. "There is nothing more I can say."

She slapped him across the face. His head jerked to the left and then hung down toward the floor. "There is nothing more you can say, or will say?" she asked. She grabbed his chin and yanked his head up to look him in the eyes. "Tell me what you know!"

"You will pay for this. This is what I know," he screamed at her. "I have nothing else to say."

"That is a shame," she said. "Jathen, I leave him to you. I have a business to attend to in my private chamber. When I return he had better talk."

She turned on her heel and left the cell as Haddon began to scream and curse at her. She slammed the door to the cell in disgust. She flew down a long hall to another chamber. Tendrils of roots hung from the ceiling. A stone altar was in the middle of the chamber, and on the altar was a young winged girl, drugged and dazed. Against one of the walls of the chamber was a shelf covered with bottles and packets of various powders and liquids, scrolls, and manuscripts. Across from this on the opposite wall was a fireplace with a cauldron hanging over a low flame.

The High Matriarch pulled her knife from her boot and made a small cut across the girl's arm. She put a bowl under her arm to collect some blood. Then she turned to the cauldron and poured the blood into it. She went to the shelf and selected a few jars and packets. Carefully measuring out specific amounts, she then dumped them into the cauldron also. As she slowly stirred the contents of the cauldron she began to chant in an ancient language, the language of blood magic...dark magic.

As she peered into the cauldron a scene began to appear. She could see Lynette and Joran, but the view was very foggy. They appeared to be practicing spells using air, but she could see little else.

So, was this what Haddon was hiding? Her daughter and life-mate were learning magic? But who was teaching them? Where were they? She could see nothing other than the two of them no matter how much she chanted. At least now she knew what she wanted to ask Haddon. But that could wait.

She looked into the full-length mirror leaning against one of the walls of the chamber. She did not like the small wrinkles at the corners of her eyes, which also had dark circles under them. And her figure was not what it once was and her beautiful black wings had lost some of their shine. This would not do at all. But she would take care of it now.

She returned to the slab and collected more blood from the young girl's arm. She picked up a piece of chalk from the shelf and drew a circle with an eight-pointed star in the center. She dipped her finger in the blood and touched it to each point of the star. She stood in the center of the circle and cast the dark blood spell that kept her looking young. She closed her eyes as the spell began to take effect. Walking back to the mirror she snapped her wings open and gazed at her image. There were no more wrinkles or dark circles under her eyes, her figure was once again firm, and her wings glistened as if they were covered in oil.

When she returned to the cell holding Haddon he had stopped screaming. But he was still alive. She again questioned him, but he would say nothing more than what Mother Kerinelle and Father Libraen had told him.

"I know that my daughter and her life-mate are learning magic, but I do not know who is teaching them or where they are," she said. "Do you know where they are?"

"I have told you everything I know," said Haddon. "Now let this be done, and release me or kill me."

"As you wish, I am finished with you anyway," she said angrily. "You may return to Mother Kerinelle and Father Libraen and tell them I will not send any soldiers to Cliffside. I will, though, call all the Matriarchs and Patriarchs of the Eight Realms to court and then we will decide on a course of action." She released his hands from the restraints chaining him to the wall.

"Jathen, please summon a squad of my Wing Guard to escort Master Haddon to the edge of Algren. Remember,

Haddon, your magic will not work in or anywhere near Tree Algren. You will again be able to use your magic when you are well away from Algren."

"Your treatment of me will not be forgotten T'Algren Devoerelle," said Master Haddon using her given name. "Mother Kerinelle and Father Libraen will hear of this. And so will the Wind Council."

"I really do not care what any of them think," she said. "And besides, they have the impending attack by Morren to worry about."

"Someone is going to attack them?" asked Jathen.

"According to Wind Master Haddon, this Morren, who is dead, by the way, has an army of undead and supposedly he is going to attack Cliffside," she said.

"Do not think he will stop there," said Master Haddon as Jathen scurried from the chamber. "You will regret not sending soldiers to stop him at Cliffside. Other members of the Wind Council are warning the other realms of the impending attack."

"If and when he attacks Cliffside, I will reconsider my position. But until then, I have given you my decision," she said.

Jathen returned with a squad of Wing Guards. "Now go, before I change my mind and kill you," she said. "You will be able to heal yourself once you leave Algren, but not before."

"Take him through the lower tunnels and escort him to the border," she said to the commander of the Wing Guard. Give him a clean robe first.

"Yes, Your Majesty," said the commander.

The Wing Guard left the chamber with Haddon after helping him into a fresh robe. They practically dragged him through a tunnel running under the roots of Tree Algren and exited through a hidden door between two of the roots. As soon as they reached the border, Haddon felt his magic return.

"Are you able to fly, sir?" asked the Commander. He noticed that blood had seeped through the clean robe from Master Haddon's wounds.

"I will be in a few moments. I need to heal myself now that I can use my magic again," said Master Haddon. He chanted for a few moments and the wounds inflicted by Jathen began to close and disappear, but there was still blood on his clothing. He could have used his magic to remove the blood, but he chose not to. He wanted evidence of his mistreatment.

"For what it's worth, sir, I am sorry that you were tortured and so badly treated," said the Commander quietly so the rest of the Wing Guard could not overhear. "What will you do now?"

"I will return to report this to the Wind Council, as well as Mother Kerinelle and Father Libraen. Then we will prepare for the coming attack on Cliffside I told the High Matriarch about," said Master Haddon. "I suggest you prepare also. It will only be a matter of time before Algren is also under attack." Then he leapt into the air and flew north toward Cliffside. The Wing Guard flew back to Tree Algren.

"Do you think what he says is true?" one of the Guards asked the Commander.

"I have no idea," said the Commander. "We all were in the throne room when he delivered the message about the coming attack to the High Matriarch. Apparently, Mother Kerinelle and Father Libraenaire believe an attack is coming, and that's good enough for me. It wouldn't hurt to be prepared."

"But what about all the young winglets at Cliffside?" asked another Guard. "What will happen to them if the school is attacked?"

"That is a good question," replied the Commander. "Many of them are the offspring of the leaders of the Eight Realms. Surely, they will insist their winglet leave if there is enough time. At the very least they will send their own Wing Guards to help protect their own winglets."

"I hope so," said the other Guard. My sister's two winglets are students at Cliffside."

# CHAPTER 11

# WARNING

It had been an octurn since soldiers had flown over the gulch where Tavat, Lare, and the Malakand had hidden. They had been lucky that they weren't caught. Tavat was again on the hunt for food. He had found it necessary to replace many of his arrows with what he considered to be inferior ones that he and Lare made. They were not as good as the ones Tavat made in the Northern Plateaus, but they would do for hunting the small game that seemed to thrive in this area. In another turn, they would be in Esteryia and could purchase more travel bread and other staples, and perhaps buy some better-made arrows.

Lare was not far away, also hunting, while the Malakand males, Gormon and Bicken, were foraging for edible plants and berries. The female, Fessa was sitting near a small campfire stirring something that looked suspiciously like gruel in her ever-present pot. Tavat was willing to use the last few of his own good arrows if he must, to catch something decent to eat. He was not fond of Fessa's gruel.

He spotted a small animal loping across the meadow under the trees and loosed the arrow he had nocked. His aim was true and the animal fell to the ground dead. When he went to retrieve it he thought he heard something and froze. He could see Lare about fifty wingspans away, standing perfectly still, as if he were listening.

Tavat slowly nocked another arrow and looked in the direction of the noise as whatever it was rustled the tall grass again. He slowly stood and took aim. He heard a high-pitched squealing, which he knew to be one of the Malakand in trouble. It sounded like Fessa. Lare took off running in the direction of their camp to deal with whatever had caused Fessa's distress.

Tavat saw two wingless men creeping through the grass toward him. "Stand up," Tavat ordered. He could hear them whispering and repeating his order.

Slowly, the two men stood up. One had a sword and another was holding a spear, both aimed straight at Tavat. They looked hungry and desperate.

"Put your weapons down," said Tavat. "I can put an arrow in one of your eyes before you can throw that spear."

They looked at each other and dropped their weapons. "Come over here, slowly," said Tavat. Just then Lare came to where Tavat stood, pushing ahead of him a third-winged man. He had his sword at the man's back. Fessa walked timidly behind Lare and peered around him to glare at the man. Wug was perched on her shoulder and chattered angrily at the man.

The other two men moved to where Tavat pointed. Lare checked them for more weapons with his other hand while he held his sword steady in the third man's back. He pulled out a knife from one of their boots and handed it to Fessa. She took the knife and shook it meaningfully at the three men. She was bright orange with anger.

"I found this one in the camp holding Fessa," said Lare. "He was also trying to steal Nart."

"Now, I didn't hurt the little thing, I just snuck up and grabbed her so she wouldn't run off," said the third man. "And I wasn't gonna steal your garing. I was just looking for supplies."

"Why were you sneaking into our camp and why did you grab her?" asked Lare. "You didn't have to sneak."

"I just wanted some of what she was cooking," said the man plaintively. "We haven't eaten in two turns. I'm sorry for sneaking around. It's just you have to be careful with all that is happening."

"What about you two?" asked Tavat. "Why were you sneaking around in the grass."

"We weren't sneaking," said one of the men. "We were hiding. We didn't know if you were one of them."

"One of them?" asked Tavat.

"Them, the undead," he said looking scared. "They are headed for Erboer, them and a big dragon, and we've been running for our lives and hiding ever since. They're coming this way."

"What is this you are talking about," said Tavat. "What dragon?" He thought he knew exactly what dragon, but he wanted to hear what the men had to say.

"They came out of the Wastelands and have been killing and destroying everything. The dragon burned down some of the trees near Erboer," said one of the other men. "Those living in the trees were burned up too. That's when we took off, before they could get to Erboer."

By now they were back at the camp. "Sit down and behave yourselves and we won't hurt you," said Lare. The three men did as they were told and sat down in front of the fire. "Now who are you and where did you come from exactly?"

"My name is Nalor, and this is Chrim and Diln," said the man who had been holding the sword. His clothes were dirty and torn and his brown hair was scraggly. Wug hopped down from Fessa's shoulder and went to sniff at the three men.

Chrim, who had long blond hair and was extremely thin, was the one who had come into the camp and grabbed Fessa. Diln had held the spear. Diln looked a lot like Nalor, but was shorter. He tried to reach out and pet Wug, but Wug jumped back and chattered angrily at him. Wug hopped back to Fessa and perched on her shoulder.

"Diln is my younger brother," said Nalor. "We met up with Chrim just south of Erboer, which may not be there anymore. He saw more than we did. We're originally from the western desert tribes. When we heard about the wizard and his army of undead, we decided to leave the desert to make our way south."

Gormon and Bicken strolled back into the camp warily. They stared at the three men in front of the fire as they laid down their armloads of leaves, berries and roots. They sidled around the fire to sit near Fessa who set about stirring her pot again. She picked up a few of the roots, cut them into small chunks, and added them to the pot. Tavat grimaced as he watched her toil over her pot of gruel.

"Lare, please go get the animal I killed. It is at the edge of the meadow under the trees," said Tavat. "I do not think these men will be any trouble now." He lifted his nocked bow pointedly.

"No...no...we mean no trouble," assured Nalor. Chrim and Diln nodded their heads in agreement.

"That sure smells good," said Chrim smiling at Fessa. He hoped he could make it up to her for scaring her.

She lifted one shoulder and sniffed disdainfully after Gormon translated what the man said. She was not ready to forgive him just yet, but she wasn't afraid of him anymore, not with Tavat keeping an arrow nocked and aimed at them. Her color had returned to green as her scales reflected the firelight.

Just as the sun set, Lare returned with the tioldoer Tavat had killed. He began to skin it and prepare it for cooking. He devised a spit to cook it over the fire. He kept a watchful eye on the three men as he slowly turned the spit to roast the meat.

Fessa selected a few of the larger leaves and spooned some of the gruel and roots onto them. Bicken passed one of the leaves to Nalor. Then he gave one to Chrim and Diln. Nalor blew on it to cool it down before scooping some up with his fingers. Chrim and Diln just tucked into their portions without waiting for it to cool.

Soon the roasted meat was ready and Tavat finally lowered his bow and set it on the ground close by in case he needed it. He pulled his knife from his belt, cut a piece of meat, and handed it to Lare. Then he cut more and passed the pieces to the three men, who gobbled it down and asked for more.

"Easy," said Tavat. "You want it to stay down. Since you haven't eaten in a few turns you might throw it up."

"Sure is good," said Nalor. "You got anything to drink?"

"Water," said Lare. "I don't think you should drink anything else right now." He retrieved a skin full of water that was tied to Nart's saddle. He passed the skin to Nalor who drank greedily. Nalor passed the skin to Chrim, who also drank his fill. Then he passed it to Diln. Diln took a drink and then offered the skin to Tavat who shook his head.

"No, thank you. You keep it. Now, tell us more about these undead warriors you say are coming this way," said Tavat. "How many are there?"

"I don't rightly know. It isn't just that they kill everyone, it's that the wizard makes more undead by casting a spell on them," said Nalor, who seemed to be the spokesman for the group.

"Wizard?" asked Tavat. "There is a wizard?" Tavat thought it surely must be Morren Nalor was talking about.

"Yeah, and he rides a big, black dragon," said Diln. "He's as evil as they come."

"Are all the undead winged?" asked Lare.

"Some are, some aren't," said Nalor. "The winged undead go after the winged, while the wingless ones go after the wingless. Those that aren't killed or made into undead are captured."

"For what purpose?" asked Tavat.

"I...I don't rightly know for sure," said Nalor.

"Don't forget that winged girl," said Diln.

Tavat suddenly stood up and loomed over Nalor. "What winged girl?" Could he be referring to Ooloo?

"Chrim knows about her. I never got close enough to see any girl," said Nalor.

"Tell me about the girl. What does she look like?" said Tavat glaring at Chrim.

"She must be about eight or nine cycles old, and she has her hair in braids," said Chrim. "Her skin is light brown, like yours..."

"What is she doing with the wizard?" asked Tavat, afraid he already knew the answer.

"Sometimes the girl rides on the dragon with the wizard. She wears a collar around her neck with a chain connected to the collar on the dragon. It seemed like the wizard was teaching her magic and things," said Chrim.

Tavat groaned. The girl must be Ooloo! And what was she doing learning things from the evil wizard? Tavat was sick at heart with worry for her.

"Did you see any other warriors with skin my color?" He was also worried about the six warriors who had begun the journey from the north with him and Ooloo.

"No, all I saw was the girl," said Chrim.

"I must go and rescue her," said Tavat as he stalked back and forth in front of the fire.

"You will be killed or turned into one of the undead," said Lare. "What use will you be to your granddaughter then? We need to continue south to Cliffside and get help, just as we planned."

"Yes, yes," agreed Gormon. "Do not go. Ooloo is alive. If the bad wizard teaching her, he needs her alive for some reason. Is good news."

"What you say makes sense," said Tavat. "But I do not like leaving her there."

He picked up his bow and walked away from the camp to be by himself. He sat on a rock and thought about Ooloo and remembered how her hair smelled to him when he held her on the high plateau after she startled him so long ago. After a while, he went back to where he first saw Nalor and Diln and picked up their weapons.

When he made his way back to camp, the three men were settling down to sleep while Fessa wiped out her pot with a large leaf. When she was done cleaning it, she stuffed it into her pack. Then she began cutting pieces of meat from the roasted tioldoer and wrapped them in leaves. She also packed up the leftover roots, leaves, and berries. At least they would have something to eat on their way to Esteryia.

"I will keep the first watch," Tavat said to Lare.

"You sure?" asked Lare. "Let me go take my saddle off Nart first."

"I do not think I can sleep anyway," said Tavat. "We will leave just before light, before first-meal and eat on the road."

Lare went to where the garing was tied to a small tree next to the river and removed the saddle. He checked the bindings to make sure Nart had enough free rope to eat the grass around the tree and drink from the river.

"I keeps watch with you," said Gormon to Tavat. "No sleeps for me either. Too worried abouts my friend, Ooloo."

"I welcome your company," said Tavat. "I am also worried about Ooloo."

Lare came back with his saddle and set it down on the ground. He used it for a pillow and settled down to sleep on his back. He lay with his arms crossed, his sword in one hand. He didn't really trust the three men in the camp so he kept one eye open for as long as he could. He eventually dropped off to sleep.

Fessa walked over to Tavat and patted him on the back to comfort him. Then she went and lay down next to Bicken who had curled up by the fire. Wug was already curled up next to Bicken. Nalor, Chrim, and Diln went to sleep almost immediately and began to snore loudly.

After a while, Fessa sat up and glared at them. "Humph," she said disgustedly and lay back down. Before long she was sound asleep.

Tavat and Gormon walked about twenty wingspans away from the camp to keep watch and talk. Gormon was worried about Ooloo, but he was also worried about Tavat.

"Ooloo takes cares of herself," said Gormon. "She Ans'Isna. Strong magic."

"I know," said Tavat. "I just don't like her being with that evil Morren. She is still so young and impressionable."

"Im...pressnable? What that mean?" asked Gormon.

"It means that Morren may have an influence on her," said Tavat. "She is so innocent. I don't want to see her lose that innocence."

They eventually walked over to where Nart was tied up. Tavat checked his rope, although it was not necessary. Then they walked back to the camp. Everyone was sleeping soundly, or so it seemed.

Nalor was merely pretending to be asleep. While Fessa had been busy with cleaning her pot, he had picked up the knife where she had laid it after cutting strips of the meat. He also had his eye on his sword and Diln's spear where Tavat had put them a short distance away. He waited until Tavat and Gormon moved away from the camp again. Then he gently woke Diln and Chrim and held his finger to his mouth to keep them quiet.

Chrim crept slowly across the camp, picked up the sword and handed the spear to Diln. Nalor went to where Lare lay sleeping and put the knife to his neck. Suddenly an arrow thwacked into his back and he fell forward, dead before he hit the ground.

Lare immediately woke up, realized what was happening, and jumped up brandishing his sword. As another arrow took out Diln before he could kill Bicken with the spear, Chrim attacked Lare with the sword. Tavat and Gormon ran back into the camp to find Lare and Chrim fighting. By that time, the three Malakand had awakened.

"Do you want me to take him out?" asked Tavat.

"No, I got this," said Lare. He thrust his sword at Chrim who tried to block it, but he was unsuccessful. Chrim received a nasty cut on his side. Soon Chrim realized he was not going to win the swordfight with Lare. He dropped his sword and raised one hand while the other grasped his bloody side.

"I give up. It was Nalor and Diln who started this," he said.

"Give me a good reason why we shouldn't kill you too," said Lare between clenched teeth.

"I swear, if you let me go, I won't bother you anymore," said Chris. As soon as he finished speaking an arrow hit him in the neck, the point sticking out of his throat. He fell toward Lare who pushed him away and the dead man fell to the ground. Tavat had decided they could not trust him no matter what he said. As far as Tavat was concerned they were better off with the three men dead.

"Well, that takes care of that problem," said Lare. "We won't have to worry about these three anymore."

Fessa got up and walked to where Chrim lay and kicked him. Then she spat on him. Gormon and Bicken both nodded their heads in approval. Wug hopped over and kicked Nalor and then Diln, all the while chattering angrily. Bicken picked up the sword Chrim had dropped and handed it to Lare.

"I see the Malakand are in agreement," said Tavat. "These three could not be trusted. That is why I never moved far beyond the camp. I had a feeling about them. They were too desperate. And desperation can make a good man do things he would not ordinarily do."

"What should we do with the bodies," asked Lare. "We can't just leave them here. If Morren is making undead warriors I don't want to think these three could come back to kill us in the future."

"We should burn them," said Tavat. He piled the bodies into a heap and began placing wood and brush around them. When he was satisfied that they would burn, he lit the fire. It took the rest of the night for the bodies and he had to keep adding more wood and brush to the fire. No one felt like sleeping after everything that had happened. In the morning there was nothing left but a pile of bones and ash.

"We better get moving," said Tavat. "Someone from Esteryia might come to investigate the fire and smoke. We shouldn't be here when they do. And besides, if Morren and his army are coming this way, the sooner we leave the better."

Lare saddled Nart and untied him from the tree. He led him to the camp. Fessa grabbed her pack and hung it from the saddle. Then Lare climbed into the saddle and held out his hand to lift Fessa onto the saddle with him. Wug positioned himself on Lare's shoulder. Lare trotted Nart at a fast pace through the trees near the river while Gormon and Bicken ran after him. Tavat leapt into the air and flew ahead to scout the path beside the river.

As the moons set and the sun rose, they made their way toward Esteryia quickly. At least they could let the people there know what was coming. It wouldn't be long before Morren and his army would be there.

They had decided to stay off the road and follow the river to Esteryia as Tavat scouted ahead. He circled back occasionally to check on the travelers and report what he had spotted up ahead.

By the time the turn was almost over, and the sun was about to set, they came to the tree on the outskirts of Esteryia where the temple was located. Lare had told Tavat about the Wind Dancers and the temples spread throughout the Eight Realms.

Jamen was busily sweeping off the landing platform of the tree in which the temple was located. Tavat flew up to the landing to talk to him. Lare and the Malakand stayed on the ground and began making camp by the river, which was only a few wingspans from the temple tree.

"Hello," said Jamen curiously. "May we help you? The priest is in his office." He propped his broom against the wall, opened the door to usher Tavat into the Temple.

"Stay there by the river while I go talk to the priest," shouted Tavat to Lare and the Malakand. He needn't have bothered to tell them anything as Fessa had already jumped down from Nart and had her cooking pot out to prepare last-meal near the river. Gormon helped Lare unsaddle Nart as Bicken tied the garing to a small tree next to the river. There was plenty of river grass for Nart to eat.

Tavat and Jamen went to the priest's office and knocked on the door. He was sitting behind his desk with his feet propped up on it. He jumped up and grabbed his robe and put it on as Jamen knocked on the door again.

"Come in," he said as he made his way to the door. Tavat walked into his office and Gannaire's eyes widened in surprise. Tavat was an imposing sight.

"What can I do for you, my son," he asked, even though he was probably the same age as Tavat.

"I have come to warn you," said Tavat. "An army of undead is making their way here. They were last seen near Erboer."

"You are the second person to bring me this news," said Gannaire. "Maybe the mayor will believe me now. What else can you tell me?"

"There is an evil wizard who rides a big black dragon. He controls the army," said Tavat. "And he has my granddaughter."

"You are obviously not from around here," said Gannaire. "Tell me everything or as much as you are comfortable with."

Tavat felt he could trust the old priest, so he told him about Ooloo and her desire to go to Cliffside. He told him about meeting the Malakand, and the young winged couple with their friends in Halalouma. He spoke of the attacks from Morren and how Ooloo was now his captive. And he told him about Mattern. Finally, he told him about Lare, and about Nalor and his two cronies.

When he finished his tale, Gannaire said, "You have had quite an adventure so far. We must speak with the mayor of Esteryia and warn him about what's coming. But now it's time for last-meal."

"My friend Lare and the three Malakand are below waiting for me. I will eat with them," said Tavat.

"Then I will join you, if that is alright," said Gannaire. "When we are done I want you to come with me to town to talk to the mayor, if you will. He did not believe me when I told him before about Morren and his army of undead." He called Jamen and told him of his plans.

Gannaire flew down to the river with Tavat to find Lare and the Malakand preparing to eat. Tavat made introductions and then they all sat down to eat the leftover tioldor meat, berries, and root stew Fessa had prepared.

"You said I am the second person to tell you about Morren," said Tavat. "Who was the first?"

"Oh, that was Mattern, the Royal Consort," said Gannaire.

"When was he here?" asked Tavat. "The last we saw of him he was flying away from the battle carrying Lynette and Joran's new winglet."

"He was here about two octurns ago. He was also on his way to Cliffside," said Gannaire. "I need to warn you, there are Wing Guards from the High Matriarch staying at the inn."

Lare was concerned when he heard this. "I better stay out of sight then," he said quietly. Even though his appearance was different than before, he was still not willing to take a chance on being arrested.

"You are welcome to stay in the temple," said Gannaire. "If there is any trouble I have a good hiding place for you. But there is not anything I can do about your garing."

"Thank you, but I will stay with my garing," said Lare.

"We stays by river too," said Gormon.

"As you wish," said Gannaire. "Tavat, are you ready to go to town with me? The sooner we talk to the mayor, the better."

"Yes, I am ready," said Tavat.

Gannaire and Tavat flew straight to the tree where the mayor lived. They landed on the flight platform and Gannaire knocked on the door. It was answered by the mayor's life-mate, Cyntha. She was a little taken aback by Tavat but she recovered quickly and welcomed him and the priest into her home.

"This is Tavat, from the Northern Plateaus," said Gannaire. "This is T'Esteryia Cyntha, the mayor's life-mate.

Cyntha curtsied politely. "We need to speak to the mayor immediately," said Gannaire. "Is he here?"

Yes, he just got home. I think he is in the library," said Cyntha. "Um...right this way." She led them to a door down a short hall. She knocked on the door and then opened it without waiting for a response. The mayor was sitting in a large armchair reading some documents.

"Yes, my dear? What is it?" the mayor said, not bothering to look up.

"Lund, the priest is here to see you. He says it's urgent," she said.

Gannaire impatiently pushed past her pulling Tavat with him. "Lund, this wingman has seen the wizard Morren firsthand and has news that he is on his way here from Erboer with his army of undead."

"Oh my," said Cyntha. "Undead? What is he talking about Lund?"

"And who is this wingman?" Lund asked, rising from his armchair. He rose from the armchair to comfort Cyntha. He put his arm protectively around her. "Cyntha, why don't you go get something for our guests to drink?" he suggested.

As she left the room, Gannaire said, "This is Tavat, from the Northern Plateaus and he has seen Morren and..."

"You're a long way from home," said the mayor suspiciously.

"Lund, you're not listening," said Gannaire, becoming exasperated. "I told you before and you didn't believe me. Now I have brought you an eyewitness..."

"Alright, calm down, Gannaire," said the mayor. "Let me hear what he has to say. Have a seat." They sat on the couch across from the mayor's easy chair. The mayor sat back down. "Now, tell me exactly what you have seen."

"It is just as the priest says, I have seen this Morren. He rides a big, black dragon and commands an army of undead soldiers," said Tavat. "And he has captured my granddaughter."

Cyntha returned with a tray containing a pitcher of wine and three cups. "Oh my," she said when she heard what Tavat said.

"Thank you, Cyntha," said the mayor. "That will be all." He left no doubt that he preferred that she remove herself while the men conferred.

"But, Lund," she said hoping to stay.

"My dear, please," said the mayor. With that, she turned on her heel and left the room in a huff. But she didn't go far. She positioned herself just outside the door so that she could hear what was said. If what the man from the North said was true, then Esteryia was in terrible danger.

# CHAPTER 12

# LESSONS

Ooloo sat in front of Morren as they flew over Erboer on the dragon, aptly named Death. She still wore the chain that attached her to the dragon. She also wore bracelets that prevented her from accessing her magic. She watched the scene of carnage and destruction in horror, but she was helpless to do anything.

She saw the undead attack the hapless citizens, winged and wingless. Morren spoke a few words to Death and the big dragon spewed forth flames that set one of the giant trees of the village on fire. The flames leapt high into the sky as people flew from the burning tree.

"Why did you do that?" Ooloo asked. She was appalled at the wanton destruction. "Why did you have Death set that tree on fire?"

"Because that is Tree Erboer," replied Morren. "That is the home of the mayor of this village. With its destruction my conquest of Erboer is complete."

"But I thought you wanted to attack Cliffside," said Ooloo. "Why do you have to destroy everything in your path? What have these people done to you?"

"I am doing this for you, as a lesson," said Morren as he made Death circle over the village. Ooloo could see people flying or running everywhere, trying to escape the undead warriors. Some were being rounded up and forced into the town square. Some of the people tried to fight back and discovered that the way to stop the undead was by stabbing them in the heart. But the villagers were outnumbered and ended up dead or were herded into the town square.

"See, at least the citizens have a chance. But in the end, I will win this battle," he said smugly.

"But why..." Ooloo started to say.

"Enough! Stop asking questions," said Morren. "I have work to do." He landed Death in the center of the town square where many of the citizens had been rounded up. "Stay here." It wasn't as if she could go anywhere with the chain that connected her to the dragon

Ooloo knew what was coming next. She watched as Morren approached the remaining people, winged as well as wingless in the town square. The undead stood in rows awaiting orders. The battle was over, the destruction almost complete. Only a few of the giant trees were left standing.

"Good people of Erboer, you have a choice," said Morren as he stalked back and forth in front of the captives. "You can serve me willingly or you can serve me as undead. But you will serve me regardless."

"We will never serve you," said the mayor of Erboer. Several citizens shouted out in agreement with him.

"Speak for yourself," said Wellim and stepped forward. A handful of other citizens sided with him and also stepped forward. Some were winged and some were ground-dwellers. All were less than model citizens.

"But what of the children?" asked one of the winged women.

"Yes," said the mayor. "What do you intend to do with the women and children?"

"Ah yes, the children," said Morren. "The children and their mothers will go free." He turned to Ooloo and smiled benignly at her. "You see, my dear, I am not completely heartless. You have been a good influence on me." He ordered that the women and the children be separated from the group in the square and held to the side. Then he turned to the rest.

"I give you one more chance to serve me willingly," he said. A few others stepped forward. In all, there were about twenty total that had stepped forward. "Go with the commander of my regular soldiers, Captain Virn."

Virn led the group, some of them thieves and cutthroats, away from the square to be equipped and to begin their training. Morren used these men sometimes to scout ahead, and others he enthralled to be spies or otherwise do his bidding. They also hunted for game and other provisions for the living army. The undead did not require sustenance.

"The women who have no children will serve in the camp. But I will not allow any rebellion or trouble. The other women and children are free to go," he said. But there was nowhere for them to go. Most of their homes in the trees and among the roots had been destroyed.

"Now for the rest of you," said Morren. Ooloo looked away. She hated this part. It always made her sick at heart to see the making of the undead.

Morren chanted as he held up his hands. A red light went from his hands to surround the people in the square. They began to contort and scream. As they opened their mouths wide, the red light flew down each of their throats. Their eyes began to glow red. They were now undead. It had taken only a few seconds.

"Join the others," ordered Morren. The newly undead got in line with the rest of the undead. "We will stay here in Erboer for a few turns. Next, we will make our way to Esteryia, which is a much larger village than we have so far encountered. There is even a Wind Dancer's temple there."

He returned to the dragon and removed the collar from around Ooloo's neck, but he left the bracelets on her wrists. She hopped down from the dragon and stood next to Morren.

"Come with me. Let's find a suitable tree where we can stay," he said congenially.

"I prefer to stay in my wagon than stay anywhere with you," she said.

"But we must continue your lessons, so you will stay with me for now," said Morren.

"Well, I am hungry," said Ooloo sullenly, although she really had no appetite after what she had just witnessed. She hoped she could distract him for a while. She didn't want to learn any more magic from him, but he never gave her a choice.

"Alright then," said Morren. "I purposely did not destroy the tree containing the inn. It should be suitable for us." He turned to the women who had no children and ordered them to go prepare a meal and get some rooms ready.

Ooloo followed Morren and flew to the flight platform of the inn. But instead of going in, he stood at the edge to survey his armies. "By the time we get to Cliffside, my armies will be invincible," he said. "Do you know what lesson I am trying to teach you here?"

"No, I do not, and I do not care," said Ooloo.

"I'm trying to teach you that I am more powerful than you and that it is futile to continue trying to defeat me. My power grows stronger with every conquest," said Morren.

"I beat you once, and I will do it again," Ooloo said quietly.

"What did you say?" he asked.

"I said I beat you once, and I can beat you again," she said defiantly.

Morren burst out laughing. "I was unprepared then, I admit," he said. "But I have learned what is required to overcome you."

"Yes, Saarnak taught you," she said defiantly. "If not for him, I would have killed you already. That is why I let myself be captured by you."

"What do you mean?" asked Morren.

"I saw that you captured me, so I figured there must be a reason," she said. "The only reason would be so that I could kill you."

"Your reasoning is flawed," said Morren. "I captured you with an energy net Saarnak showed me how to make. And I am still alive."

"Take these bracelets off and I will kill you," she said.

Morren laughed again. "Then I won't be taking them off except for your training, and then only under controlled circumstances. Do not forget, you agreed to let me train you so that you could grow stronger."

"I haven't forgotten," she said. "What is it you are training me for exactly?"

"You have no need to know that now. You will find out when the time comes," said Morren. A woman opened the door and came out of the inn. It was Gretna.

"Master, your last-meal is prepared," she said. Ooloo ran to her and threw her arms around her waist. Gretna pushed her away and scurried back into the inn.

"You know she is enthralled to serve me," said Morren. "She has no feelings for you or anyone. Her one desire is to serve me."

Ooloo wasn't so sure of that. She was working on breaking through the enthrallment. She felt she was getting somewhere. She just needed more time.

"Let's go eat now," said Morren as he grabbed Ooloo roughly by one of her arms and pulled her into the inn. They walked into the main room where there were several tables and chairs, as well as a bar. However, the proprietor had been made undead along with the mayor and other men who refused to serve Morren.

Morren and Ooloo sat at one of the tables. A winged woman immediately brought two plates heaped with food from the kitchen. She placed them on the table. There was meat, baked roots, other vegetables, and some kind of salad. She sat a plate down in front of each of them.

Morren began to eat ravenously, but Ooloo only picked at her food.

"I thought you said you were hungry," commented Morren.

"I seem to have lost my appetite," said Ooloo. She pushed her plate away. "Can I go to bed now?" She was hoping to find her way back to the world of dreams. She felt sure the answer to her freedom was there.

"When I am done," said Morren, "We are going to do some more training."

"I am not in the mood to train," Ooloo snapped. It was a mistake. She had pushed Morren too far. He lifted a hand and squeezed it. Ooloo was struck with unbearable pain. She fell out of her chair onto the floor where she curled into a ball and lay panting.

"I told you, I decide when you train. I said, as soon as I finish we are going to do some more training," he said, seething with anger. He released her from the pain. "Now get up, sit down, and be quiet while I try to enjoy the rest of my meal."

Ooloo got up and sat in her chair. She glared at Morren as he ate, thinking of all the ways she could kill him. Finally, he was done and rose from his seat.

"Come, I want to teach you how to move heavier objects. There is probably a room where the proprietor keeps kegs of ale and such," said Morren. "Let's have a look around. It is most likely located between the roots of this tree, maybe even under the roots. That would be perfect for our use."

They exited the inn and flew down to the base of the tree. Sure enough, there was a cellar door near the lift. Morren open it and shoved Ooloo in ahead of him. The storage room was indeed under part of the tree. Tendrils of root hung down everywhere and it was chilly. It was the perfect storage area for wine and ale.

He channeled a flame to light a lantern. There was a set of stairs that wound down to a room containing large flasks, kegs, and barrels of wine and ale. He channeled flame to all of the lanterns in the chamber.

"Excellent," he said. "Just what I was hoping for."

"What? Are you planning on getting drunk?" laughed Ooloo.

"No, nothing as mundane as that," said Morren. "You are going to move these barrels with your powers."

"Where do you want me to move them?" she asked.

"Oh, from one side of the chamber to the other. But before I take your bracelets off, let me prepare the room," he said. He began chanting and turning in all directions. "Now, the entire room is spelled. If you try to leave you will find only more pain."

"What else is new?" she asked sarcastically.

"Be still and let me remove your bracelets," he said. He waved a hand over the bracelets and they popped open. He removed them from Ooloo's wrists and put them in one of the big pockets of his robe.

"Now what?" asked Ooloo. "Are you sure you would not rather just get drunk?"

Morren sighed and said, "See that big barrel right there on the end? I want you to use one of the elements of magic to move it all the way over there." He pointed to a spot way across the big chamber.

Ooloo concentrated and used air to lift the barrel across the room, just as Morren had asked. "Now what?" she repeated.

"Now I want you to move the next two, both at once," said Morren. "Then you will move three at once, then four at once, and so forth until all the barrels have been moved and stacked nicely against the wall."

Ooloo again concentrated and moved the two barrels. By the time she got to eight barrels at once she was sweating, in spite of the chill in the room. But she was done. She had moved all the barrels.

"Now I want you to move the entire stack back across the room," said Morren. Ooloo knew she could move at least eight at a time, so it would not take as long to move the barrels this time.

Then Morren said, "All thirty-six at once." Ooloo looked at him as if he were crazy. "Go on, I think you can do it."

Ooloo lifted her hands and pulled as much magic from her center as she could. She lifted the whole stack of barrels and strained mightily. Sweat poured from her brow. She slowly moved the stack across the room and set them down with a clunk. Then she sat on the ground panting.

"See, I told you that you could do it," Morren said clapping his hands. Then he picked up a large flask and took a drink. He wiped his hand across his mouth and poured the rest out onto the floor. Some of it splashed and splattered onto Ooloo.

"Now, I want you to channel water from the air into this flask."

"I do not think I can," she said.

"Well if you can't, then you will have nothing to drink until morning," said Morren.

Ooloo started giggling. Then she started laughing uproariously. Morren handed her the flask and turned on his heel. He left her sitting on the floor of the room laughing. Before he left, he extinguished all the lanterns with a wave of his hand. Ooloo wasn't worried. She could easily relight the lanterns with her magic.

"You can be thirsty in the dark for all I care," Morren snapped. "You will spend the night here." With that, he ran up the stairs and slammed the cellar door.

Ooloo channeled a flame for the lanterns so she wouldn't be in the dark. Then she got up and went to touch the door. She was assailed with pain just as she expected. She jerked her hand back and went back down the stairs.

She retrieved another flask and opened it. She took a big gulp of wine and sat down on the bottom stair. She started laughing again. She was surrounded by wine and ale and who knew what kinds of beverages. She wouldn't go thirsty, but she did get a little drunk. She remembered the wine that had splashed onto her. She certainly smelled drunk.

After taking another drink from the flask she decided to try to channel some water into the flask Morren had emptied. Concentrating, she pulled some of the moisture from the air and tried to get it to go into the flask. She was only partially successful as some of the water splashed on her arms.

She concentrated again and pulled the wine from her clothing into a globule and moved it away from her. She sent it flying across the room and it splatted against the wall. Then she drank some more wine. She realized she actually liked the taste. She drank herself into a stupor and soon fell over. Lying on the ground she decided to go to sleep. She was incredibly tired from working all the magic. But she felt great except the room kept spinning whenever she opened her eyes.

She wanted to talk to Lynette and Joran. She felt there was something that could help her escape from Morren's clutches somewhere in Halalouma. When she went to sleep she found herself back in the Wasteland, in the fortress of Saarnak.

She was in the room with the large black orb. Saarnak was staring at her from a window in the orb.

"Hello, Ooloo," said Saarnak. "I hear your lessons are going well."

"Oh really?" she said. "Who told you that? And how come you are in my dreams?"

"Morren reports to me every turn. I know everything that is going on. I know that you are growing stronger with every turn. And I am not really in your dreams. You are tied to me. You wouldn't understand," Saarnak said patronizingly.

"How am I tied to you?" she asked.

"You are tied to me by blood. Don't you remember?" asked Saarnak.

"Remember what?" asked Ooloo.

"Before I allowed Morren to take you from my fortress we performed a blood spell that tied you to me," said Saarnak.

"I do not remember this," said Ooloo.

"You were enthralled at the time," replied Saarnak. "It was performed in this chamber during the full moons. You are bound to me now, and soon you will be strong enough for my purposes," said Saarnak.

"And what would that be?" asked Ooloo.

Saarnak laughed. "You will know when it is time," he said.

"And when will it be time?" she asked.

"When Morren returns from taking Cliffside," said Saarnak.

"That will never happen," insisted Ooloo. "The leaders there are too strong for Morren. And besides, they know he is coming and has surely prepared for his attack."

"You mean Mother Kerinelle and Father Libraenaire," said Saarnak. "Yes, they are strong and I'm sure they are doing everything they can think of to prepare. But it won't be enough...because of you."

"What do you mean because of me?" asked Ooloo. "I will never help Morren. I am going to kill him."

Saarnak laughed. "You are probably right about that, but not before Cliffside is captured." He began to fade away from the orb and Ooloo's surroundings began to dissipate. She awoke with a start. She sat up and discovered she had a terrible taste in her mouth, and her head throbbed.

She pulled some water from the air directly into the empty flask. She drank it down greedily. Then she lay back down to go back to sleep. She concentrated on Lynette and Joran, hoping this time to make a connection with them. It took a long time, but finally, she dropped off into a deep sleep.

She found herself in the world of dreams, in Halalouma. This time she found herself sitting in the starred chamber at the round table. But instead of Lynette and Joran, it was Master T'Queric sitting across from her.

"Hello, Ooloo," said Dainen. "How is your training coming along?"

"Okay, I guess," she said. "At least I know I can move thirty-six barrels of ale all at once, though I don't know what good it does me."

Dainen laughed, "You would be surprised. You could crush someone by crashing the barrels down on top of them."

"Even a wizard?" she asked hopefully.

"If you mean Morren, then I'm afraid not. He surely will have taken precautions," said Master Dainen. "He is not going to be easy to kill."

"Maybe so, but I will kill him...Saarnak too," she said with certainty.

"I hope you are right, Ooloo, they both deserve to die," said Dainen.

"Why can't I learn magic from you here, in the world of dreams, like Lynette and Joran?" she asked.

"Because you are not fully here," he replied.

"I am not wearing the bracelets now. At least I wasn't when I went to sleep," she said. "I can just send myself here like I did Lynette and Joran as soon as I wake up.

The solution seemed so simple. She felt she finally had a way out.

"You are forgetting," said Dainen. "Morren has probably taken precautions. Did he spell the room where you are sleeping?"

"Yes, he did, blast it," she said. Hope melted away from her like snow on a sunny day in the High Plateaus.

"Do not lose hope, Ooloo," said Dainen. "You will find a way to escape. Just be prepared when the opportunity arises."

"But how will I know when that is?" she asked.

"You will know," said Dainen with certainty.

"Can you and the other Wind Masters and Wind Mistresses help me?" she asked.

"We have done what we can, Ooloo. Saarnak's influence is far greater than any of us once thought. You must not help him in any way," said Dainen.

"But why does he need my help if he is so powerful?" she asked.

"You are innocent," he replied. "He needs your help to open a portal into your realm."

"I will never help him," she said. "I will kill him."

"I'm sure you will try," said Master Dainen. He looked troubled.

"Can I see Lynette and Joran now?" she asked.

"They are training, but I'm sure they would appreciate a break," he said. "Come with me."

He led Ooloo from the room and outside the building. Ooloo noticed he floated rather than walked. He took her to one of the parks in Halalouma where Lynette and Joran were sparring with magic. Mistress Joanelle was cheering them on.

Joran was using fire and trying to attack Lynette, while she was using water as a shield to prevent him. It seemed to Ooloo that they were equally matched.

"Isn't that dangerous?" she asked Dainen.

"We would not let them hurt each other. And besides if one is injured the other would heal them," said Dainen.

"They have learned healing?" she asked. "I learned to heal when I was still in the Northern Plateaus."

"Yes, we are aware of many of your talents," said Dainen.

Just then Lynette gave the water flowing from her hands a big push and drenched Joran. He yelped as the fire coming from his hands extinguished under the deluge.

Lynette laughed as Joran used air to dry himself off. Then he raised his hands and a deluge of water soaked Lynette. She squealed and got a mouthful of water as Joran laughed. After she had dried herself off she ended up in Joran's arm. They finally noticed Ooloo and Master T'Queric standing off to the side.

"Ooloo," said Lynette. She extricated herself from Joran's arms and ran to Ooloo. She bent and hugged her.

"How are you doing? What have you learned? Where are you now?" she asked.

Ooloo laughed. "I am fine, and I learned how to use air to move things. And right now, I am asleep under a giant tree in Erboer."

Joran walked over to stand next to Lynette. "Erboer?" he asked. "Morren and his armies are as far south as Erboer?"

"I'm afraid so," said Ooloo. "Next, we are going to attack Esteryia, but not for a few more turns. Morren wants to stay in Erboer for a while."

"And it should take at least five turns for you to get to Esteryia from Erboer. So, the people of Esteryia have an octurn to get ready," reasoned Joran. "Then another two octurns to get to Cliffside. Mother and Father must be warned that they only have three octurns left before Cliffside comes under attack."

Lynette and Joran turned to Master Dainen. "Isn't there something you can do to warn them?" asked Lynette. "Can Ooloo send us back to our realm to warn them?"

"No, I can't. Morren spelled the room I am in and I can't access my magic," said Ooloo.

Master Dainen looked thoughtful. We can send you back to your realm, to Cliffside even. But you haven't finished your training yet," he said.

"I don't care about that," said Lynette. "Just send us to Cliffside."

"Yes, if you can send us there, then do so, please," pleaded Joran. "We have to warn Mother and Father."

"I think it is time we took action," Mistress Joanelle said. "We have waited and watched long enough. I will summon the others. She turned on her heel and went back the way Ooloo and Dainen had come.

"I hope you know what you are asking," said Master Dainen. "You will leave the world of dreams before you are fully trained. I just hope you have learned enough."

He led them back to the building with the runes on the door. They went inside the room with the silver pool. Mistress Joanelle had gathered the other Wind Masters and Wind Mistresses. They stood around the pool holding hands and chanting. Master Dainen joined them but didn't hold hands to close the circle yet.

"Step into the pool," he ordered Lynette and Joran. They climbed over the edge and dropped down into the pool. As they stood in the middle of the pool up to their waists Dainen joined hands with the others. The octet was complete. "Take a deep breath and sit or lie down so you are completely submerged."

Lynette looked at Joran and took a deep breath. He did the same and they both sat down with the liquid over their heads. They noticed the liquid did not feel wet but felt as if it rolled off their skin. They could hear the octet chanting louder and louder.

The liquid began to swirl and swirl around them. It began to bubble and boil, but it wasn't hot. Just when they thought they were going to have to take a breath there was a loud pop. They suddenly found themselves sitting on the floor of the office of Mother Kerinelle and Father Libraen in Central Tree at Cliffside.

Mother and Father had been each sitting behind their respective desks. They both hopped to their feet and raised their hands, preparing to cast defensive spells.

"Lynette, Joran? Is that you?" asked Father Libraen incredulously as he stepped around the desk.

"What are you doing here? How did you get here?" asked Mother Kerinelle.

"Yes, it is us," said Joran as he stood up from the floor. "We have so much to tell you."

"You have three octurns before Morren attacks Cliffside," said Lynette breathlessly. "We have returned from Halalouma to help you prepare."

# CHAPTER 13
# HADDON

Wind Master Haddon flew back to Wind Dancers' Ledge from Algren as quickly as he could. Although he had healed and bound his physical wounds, the mental and emotional wounds haunted him. The High Matriarch's man had been brutal in his torture, but Haddon had not revealed the secret of the baby born to Lynette and Joran.

He was convinced something had to be done about the High Matriarch. Her behavior toward him had been heinous. She was obviously delving into dark magic.

Haddon landed on Wind Dancers Ledge and pushed through the doors without saying a word to the guards. They barely had time to open it before he barged through on his way to the Council Chamber.

"Call the Wind Council to assemble at once," said Master Haddon to the chamberlain.

"At once," said the surprised chamberlain. He ran to do as he was bid.

Haddon practically ran to the Council Chamber. He was furious with the High Matriarch and felt she should be removed from the throne.

He jerked his chair out from the table on the platform of the Council Chamber and sat down quickly. He tapped his fingernails on the table as he waited as the Council members slowly made their way into the room and to their seats.

Wind Mistress Brena took one look at Master Haddon and was shocked at his appearance. His wings were tattered and he had dark circles under his eyes.

"Great Wind, what happened to you?" she asked as she pulled her chair out and sat down next to him.

"Wait until the others arrive," he said.

Council member Paelmin was the last to arrive. "I'm so sorry," he said. "I was teaching a class..."

"Yes, we all were," said Mistress Brena. "Now, I want to know what happened to you, Haddon. What happened in Algren?"

"The High Matriarch is what happened to me," said Haddon hotly. "She had me tortured."

"Great Wind, why would she do that?" asked T'Desidy Tarrylaire.

"She didn't take my warning about Morren seriously," said Haddon. "And she suspected me of hiding something important, which we all know that I am."

"You didn't break your oath to Libraen and tell her about the baby..." asked Mistress Brena.

"Of course not, blast it!" said Haddon vehemently. "I would have died first. I thought she was going to kill me actually."

"Why did she let you go then?" asked Council member Paelmin. "Why didn't she kill you?"

"I believe it was because she does not want to have an uprising of the Wind Dancers," said Master Haddon. "She is no doubt concerned about the messages we have been sending to all the Wind Dancers, Matriarchs, and Patriarchs of the Eight Realms and Northern Provinces."

"She knows full well the Wind Dancers would never stand for the murder of the leader of the Wind Council," said Tarryl. "There would surely be a revolt."

"That is exactly what I am going to recommend," said Haddon. "She must be replaced. T'Algren Lynettelle would make a much better ruler…"

All the members of the Council started talking at once. "Are you seriously proposing a revolt against the High Matriarch?" asked Tarryl.

"I don't think that is a good idea," said Council Member Campur.

"Also, Lynette is missing. She's somewhere in the Northern Provinces, along with other students from Cliffside," said Mistress Brena. "Are you sure she is on the way back, or even that she would be willing to overthrow her mother?"

"I'm sure we can convince her," said Master Haddon. "Her father would surely be on our side. From what Libraen and Kerinelle said, the Royal Consort has split from the High Matriarch. Mattern is a good man. He knows, more than anyone, what the High Matriarch is like. I'm sure he can testify that the High Matriarch is using dark magic."

"What you are proposing is all-out war," said Paelmin. "You would have to have the approval of the Matriarchs and Patriarchs of each of the Eight Realms…"

"I realize that," snapped Haddon. "I will visit each one personally, if I must, to get their approval. For now, the High Matriarch has called them all to Algren to discuss whether or not to send re-enforcements to Cliffside."

"I was wondering when you would get to that," said Mistress Brena. "That should be our main concern right now."

"Never fear, that is foremost in my mind," said Haddon. "We will table the discussion of overthrowing the High Matriarch for now, at least until this attack on Cliffside has been resolved. Have the Wind Dancers we sent to warn the rulers of the Eight Realms about Morren returned yet?"

"Yes," said Tarryl. "Fortunately, all the Wind Dancers we sent have already returned. You were the last to return, Haddon," said Tarryl.

"And what do they each report?" asked Haddon. "Are any of the Realms willing to send reinforcements to Cliffside?"

"The rulers all want to wait and see what the High Matriarch is going to do. I am sorry to say, they want to wait until they meet with her to make any decisions," Mistress Brena. "It is just a waste of time, as far as I am concerned. By the time a decision is made, Cliffside could already be under attack."

"It seems no one is taking the report about Morren seriously," said Paelmin. "Everyone seems to think he is dead. Even I find it hard to believe he is alive."

"Why would Kerinelle and Libraenaire make up a story about something like that?" asked Haddon.

"They wouldn't," said Mistress Brena. "I, for one, believe them. They got a message from the captain of the Wing Guard they sent after Lynette and Joran. I believe his name is Swen."

"I believe them too," said Master Haddon. "Who here doesn't believe them?"

Paelmin, Campur, and another Council Member raised their hands. Haddon wasn't surprised Paelmin and Campur didn't believe it, but he was surprised that T'Folar Liselle didn't either.

"You know that Libran and Kerin were involved with Morren's death or disappearance," said Liselle. "He tricked them into performing a dangerous spell with him, a spell that ended with his death."

"Yes, we all know the story," said Haddon impatiently. "But he wasn't killed after all. He was apparently cast into some kind of void or other realm."

"Maybe we need to send someone to the Northern Provinces to see what is really going on," said Campur.

"Yes, that is a capitol idea," said Tarryl. "I volunteer to go."

"But we cannot afford to wait for you to go and return. We must put out a call to all Wind Dancers to come to Cliffside," said Haddon. "We need to be prepared when, or if, Morren attacks."

"Most of them have been called already when the envoys reported the coming attack to the rulers of the Eight Realms," said Haddon. "But since there are no reinforcements coming we will need all the Wind Dancers from the outlying regions as well."

"When is the soonest the attack could happen," asked Mistress Brena.

"Kerinelle and Libraen did not specify a timeframe. They just know that he is coming," said Haddon. "This Ans'Isna they talked about was certain that Morren was going to attack."

"What is her name again?" asked Paelmin.

"Her name is Ooloo Noo'Loon and she is from the Northern Plateaus," said Mistress Brena. "She is quite gifted apparently. She has both the gift of seeing as well as the gift of knowing."

"They were attacked by Morren in Halalouma," said Haddon. "The message brought by Swen was adamant about that. He caught up with the group after they exited a tunnel to the cavern holding Halalouma, and Kerinelle's agent reported that Morren came out of the Wastelands.

"Why the Wastelands?" asked Tarryl. "What could be in the Wastelands but sand and more sand?"

"Morren has probably set up some kind of camp or fortification there," said Mistress Brena.

"If there is something there, the people in the Borderlands will surely know," said Tarryl. "I will go as far as Esteryia or Erboer. There are always traders coming from the desert tribes to sell their wares in the cities."

"So, we have decided to contact as many Wind Dancers as we can to come to Cliffside, and we have decided to send Tarryl on a fact-finding mission to the Northern Plateaus," said Master Haddon.

"I'll prepare another message to go out immediately to the out-lying Wind Dancers stressing the importance of their presence at Cliffside," said Mistress Brena. "I just hope the others took the call seriously and are already on their way here."

"If there is no further business?" Master Haddon said as he looked around. No one said anything. "I hold you all to your oath not to discuss anything said in this Chamber with anyone outside of the Wind Council. Meeting is adjourned."

Everyone except Master Haddon and Mistress Brena left the Council Chamber. She turned to Haddon and asked, "Are you serious about overthrowing the High Matriarch?"

"Yes, I am. I am convinced she is dabbling in dark magic," said Haddon as he pushed back from the table and stood up. "I will see her overthrown if it is the last thing I do."

Mistress Brena put her hand on his shoulder in sympathy as they left the Chamber together. She had never seen Haddon so upset.

Paelmin overheard the last thing Haddon said and scurried away just before he and Mistress Brena exited the Chamber. He practically ran to his room.

Once there he got out paper, ink and quill and wrote out a long message. He sealed it with wax and pressed his ring into it.

When he was done, he flew from the Wind Dancer's Ledge to the nearest Messenger Station, which happened to be in the Caverns. He calculated the fastest the message could arrive would be in three turns.

"Hello, Councilor Paelmin," said the winged man behind the desk. "How may I serve you?"

"Raynor, I need this message to go to the High Matriarch as soon as possible," said Paelmin. "It must go out immediately."

"That will cost two Gren," said Raynor. "I can send a courier within the hour."

"The sooner, the better," said Paelmin. He handed over the message with the two Gren and then turned on his heel and left the Messenger Station. He thought about the message as he flew back to the Wind Dancers' Ledge.

He was breaking his oath and he knew there would be consequences, but he didn't know exactly what they would be. No one broke an unbreakable oath.

The High Matriarch received the message less than three turns later, just as Paelmin hoped. The messenger service flyers flew around the clock. They flew from station to station and passed the message to the next flyer.

The flyer approached the door to the throne room. "I have an important message to deliver to Her Majesty," he said. He was normally stationed closer to Cliffside but had delivered a message to the station in the south of Lembe. He had been waiting for an opportunity to fly back toward Cliffside Station. So, he had volunteered to take the message directly to the High Matriarch in the hope she would have a return message.

The guards opened the door and ushered him into the throne room. The High Matriarch was not in a good mood.

"What is it?" she asked impatiently. She was busy talking with the Matriarchs and Patriarchs of each of the Eight Realms about the supposed attack by Morren.

The flyer knelt on one knee and said, "I have a very important message for Your Majesty."

"Give it to me then," she said as she snapped her fingers. The messenger stood and handed her the letter. She saw the wax seal and realized it was from her spy on the Wind Council, Councilor Paelmin.

"We will take a break for now," she said. She didn't want to open the message in front of the Matriarchs and Patriarchs. "You will be notified when I wish to continue our discussions." With that, she stepped from her throne and walked to her private quarters behind the throne room. The Matriarchs and Patriarchs left the throne room grumbling at having their important meeting interrupted for a message.

Once she had shut the door, she broke the wax seal and opened the letter. Her expression darkened as she read it. When she was finished reading, she crumbled the letter into a ball and threw it across the room. She was furious. How dare Haddon even dream of removing her from the throne!

Was this his plan all along? Maybe the story about Morren was a ruse to distract her while he plotted with the rest of the Wind Council to replace her. And where were her daughter and her life-mate, that T'Ardis Joran anyway? She would kill them both if she must.

She had received word that they were on their way back to Cliffside. She would capture them there. She would send a cohort of the Wind Guard, not to fight against Morren, but to take all of the Wind Councilors captive too. If Haddon wanted a war, she would give him one. But there would be plenty of time for that.

She would wait and see if Morren really did attack Cliffside. Maybe she would even forge an alliance with him. She would get rid of the Wind Council and hunt down every Wind Dancer in the Realms. For now, she would bide her time and make her plans.

She picked up the wadded letter and smoothed it out. It was evidence of Haddon's crime and the Wind Council's duplicity.

Then she went to her desk to compose a message for Paelmin. She was going to advise him to stay put and keep his eyes and ears open. She had lots of planning to do.

First, she would build up her army. It was fortunate that the Matriarchs and Patriarchs were here in Algren. She had the perfect excuse to demand they send troops. The story about Morren would serve her ultimate purpose.

She finished her message to Paelmin and sealed it with wax. She pressed her seal into the hot wax and blew on it. Then she returned to the throne room.

"Here. Deliver this message directly into the hands of Paelmin and no one else," she said quietly so no one else could hear her. Her ladies in waiting were standing by the throne awaiting her return and she didn't want them to hear.

She suspected one of them was spying for Mother Kerinelle, but she had yet to figure out which one was the spy. She watched to see if one of them left the throne room but was disappointed that they all stayed put.

She handed the messenger the letter and five Gren. "No go with all haste," she said.

"Th...thank you, Your Majesty. It will be just as you instructed," said the flyer. He turned and hurried from the throne room.

"Chamberlain, please summon the Matriarchs and Patriarchs to return to the throne room. We must continue our discussions," said the High Matriarch.

"Yes, Your Majesty," said the chamberlain. He left immediately and soon all the Matriarchs and Patriarchs returned. They did not look happy.

"Now, we were discussing the possible attack of T'Ardis Morrenaire on Cliffside," she said.

"Your Majesty, let me assure you Morren has been dead for over forty cycles," said the Patriarch of Tree Ardis. Loranaire was Joran's father and he had a hard time believing Mother Kerinelle and Father Libranaire's tale that Morren had come back from the dead. Much less did he believe the tale of an undead army.

"I must agree with Loran," said Dendraelle, the Matriarch of Tree Lembe. "It just sounds too incredulous, even for Mother and Father.

"I am inclined to agree with you. Nevertheless, I want each of your Realms to muster your troops and prepare them to go to

Cliffside on a moment's notice," said the High Matriarch. We will wait and see if the attack comes to send the troops in."

The throne room erupted into chaos. The Matriarchs and Patriarchs all began talking at once, each one trying to out-shout the next.

"Your Majesty, what if the attack comes and Morren brings his forces into the Eight Realms?" asked the Patriarch of Soedeen. "Soedeen is the closest Realm to Cliffside. We will be the first attacked."

"If Morren takes Cliffside before we can get troops there, then we will muster our forces in Soedeen," said the High Matriarch. "I do not plan on moving any troops unless, or until, Cliffside is attacked." But the High Matriarch had other plans for the troops. She would use them to remove Mother Kerinelle and Father Libraen, as well as the members of the Wind Council, from office. She planned to replace them with those of her choosing, who were loyal supporters of her dynasty.

"What about stationing some troops at the border crossing in the upper end of the Caverns?" suggested the Patriarch of Kernoeryl.

"And who will send their troops to the Caverns?" asked the High Matriarch.

"I will," said the Soedeen Patriarch, stepping forward and raising a fist. "Better we stop Morren there before he gets to Cliffside."

The High Matriarch tapped her nails on the arm of her throne while she thought about what had been said. Finally, she made a decision.

"Alright, Soedeen will send troops to guard the upper end of the Caverns," she said. "But I want the rest of the Realms to muster their troops and be prepared to fly on a moment's notice."

She turned to the commander of her Wing Guard. "Hurrenaire, you will be in charge of the troops. Report to me when everything is prepared. Unless Morren attacks Cliffside we will not move any troops," she said.

She noticed when Gwendelle, one of her ladies-in-waiting, slipped out of the throne room. Gwendelle hurried to her room and prepared a message for Mother Kerinelle. When she finished the letter she rolled it up and sealed it with wax.

Gwendelle flew to the messenger station and hurried through the door. "Hello, Framen," she said. "I have another letter for my parents."

"How have you been, Gwendelle? Did the High Matriarch give you permission to go visit them yet?" asked Framen.

"I still haven't asked her," she replied. "I'm still waiting for her to be in a good mood."

Framen laughed. "I told you that you'd never ask her then," he said. "She's never in a good mood."

"Well, now she's worried about Cliffside being attacked. But keep that to yourself," she warned.

"Who would be attacking Cliffside?" asked Framen, shocked at this news.

"Some say T'Ardis Morrenaire has returned from the dead and is going to attack Cliffside to get back at Mother Kerinelle and Father Libraen," she said, looking around to make sure no one was listening. "But no one is supposed to know about it except for the Matriarchs and Patriarchs, so please keep it to yourself."

"My lips are sealed," said Framen. "You be careful, Gwendelle. The High Matriarch has spies everywhere. Maybe you shouldn't be telling me these things."

"Don't you have family in Soedeen?" she asked. "Wouldn't you want them to be forewarned? Besides I trust you." She actually knew he would spread the news far and wide, which was just as she wanted. The more people who knew about the attack the better.

"Besides, as soon as the Matriarchs and Patriarchs return to their realms and begin mustering troops, everyone will know," said Gwendelle.

"They are mustering troops?" Framen asked looking alarmed.

"Oh yes, they are discussing it now in the throne room," she said. "I better get back before I am missed. Remember don't say anything yet."

"You stay safe, Gwendelle," said Framen.

"You too, Framen," she said. She flew back to Tree Algren and slipped back into the throne room. She didn't notice the Wind Guard who had been following her.

The High Matriarch was just dismissing the Matriarchs and Patriarchs for the turn. It was almost time for last-meal. Gwendelle had barely made it back in time.

As everyone exited the throne room, the Wing Guard who had been following Gwendelle stepped up and whispered something to the High Matriarch. Her eyes came to rest on Gwendelle and she was frowning.

"Gwendelle, where have you been?" asked the High Matriarch. "You were seen leaving the throne room without my permission."

"I...I wanted to post a letter to my parents before the Messenger Station closed for the turn..."

"And you couldn't wait until tomorrow?" asked the High Matriarch.

"I'm so sorry, Your Majesty," pleaded Gwendelle. "It won't happen again."

"No, it will not," said the High Matriarch. "I suspect you are a spy. Take her to a cell." She snapped her fingers and two Wing Guards stepped up and grabbed Gwendelle by the arms.

Gwendelle struggled and tried to pull away from the two guards. She was able to pull an arm free when she bit the arm of the guard on the right. She pulled a chain from inside her dress. It contained a vial. She pulled the stopper loose with her teeth and emptied the contents into her mouth. She swallowed it all.

"Stop her," screeched the High Matriarch, but it was too late. The poison had already begun to take effect. Gwendelle started convulsing and foaming at the mouth. She would have dropped if not for the two guards holding her up.

They lay her on the throne room floor and she continued to convulse at the High Matriarch's feet until she died. "Well, I know now that she was in fact a spy. Why else would she kill herself?" she asked no one in particular.

"Remove her from my presence," she ordered.

"What should we do with the body?" asked one of the guards.

"Send it to her parents," said the High Matriarch. "Take the body to the Messenger Station and let them pack it up and carry it to her parents. And bring me the proprietor. I want the letter to her parents brought to me at once. I will be in the dining hall." Then she turned and left the throne room

The two Wing Guards dragged the body between them from the throne room and flew with it to the Messenger Station. When Framen saw the body of Gwendelle, he almost fainted. He had just seen her less than an hour ago. He couldn't believe she was dead. The Wing Guards told him that the High Matriarch had said to mail the body to her parents. They allowed Framen to wrap and pack the body in a large box.

"Do you have an address?" asked Framen. It was all he could do not to weep.

"Do you still have the letter she brought earlier to the station?" asked one of the guards. "That letter was supposed to be for her parents. Use the same address. The High Matriarch wants the body sent to them."

"Yes, it's right here," said Framen as he pulled the letter from the box of messages waiting to be delivered throughout the Realms. He wrote the address out as tears fell down his cheeks. If truth be told, he was a bit in love with Gwendelle. But now she was dead. He knew he better not mention a word of what she had told him.

"You are to come with us to Tree Algren for questioning," said one of the soldiers of the Wing Guard.

"But I don't know anything," said Framen as they grabbed him.

"We shall see," said the soldier as a messenger flew into the station.

"You there, see that this box is delivered," said the soldier. "The proprietor is coming with us."

"Yes sir," said the messenger. He didn't know what was in the box, but he would do as he was told and see that it was delivered. He immediately sought a wagon and driver to transport the box. The Wing Guard had given him more than ample pay to get the job done. He would personally go with the driver to deliver the box. He began to suspect something was amiss when three turns later a terrible smell began to emanate from the box.

# ~CHAPTER 14
# AERIELLE

attern flew southward toward the border crossing into the Eight Realms with Aerielle clutched to his chest. He should be there in another octurn. He flew mainly at night, following the river, and rested during the day. Aeri preferred to do most of her sleeping during the day anyway.

It was almost time for the sun to rise. He located a good hiding place in a giant tree near the river. He landed on one of the limbs near the top of the tree and sat down with his back to the trunk.

Spreading his cloak out on the wide limb, he laid Aeri down. He dug in his pack and found the last of his travel bread. He had a few strips of dried meat left, but he decided to save those for later. After eating, he fed Aerielle and laid her back down on his cloak. He covered her up with one of his shirts.

Before he went to sleep he thought about what the witches said to him about making a hard decision concerning Aerielle. He knew what they meant, but he didn't like it. But with Lynette and Joran probably being dead, he had no choice. The last he had seen of them they had been surrounded by undead, fighting for their lives. There was no way they had survived.

As long as Aerielle was with him she was in danger of being caught by the High Matriarch's soldiers. He knew they would still be looking for him, and even though he had grown a full beard and his hair was longer, he didn't want to take any chances.

He had promised Lynette that he would take the baby to safety. But where would that be? Cliffside was going to be under attack soon and he couldn't go there. There was only one place she would be safe from his life-mate's wrath.

An Orphan Tree, where she would be just another, nameless, discarded winglet, was the safest place he could take her. Every realm had at least one Orphan Tree located within its borders. And Mattern knew the perfect Tree.

The High Matriarch had de-winged her chamberlain, Gregton, and he was now serving as an Unseen in one of the Orphan Trees on the outskirts of Soedeen. Mattern would take Aeri there and she would be known as T'Soedeen Aerielle. Each orphan received the name of the realm where the Orphan Tree was located. Then he would go to Cliffside and inform Mother Kerinelle and Father Libraen of what he had done. He knew they would look after Aerielle for him.

Once his course of action had been decided, Mattern checked on Aeri one more time and then dropped off to sleep. He awoke before the moons rose and prepared to leave his hiding place. He thought he heard something.

He stood up and looked down through the lower limbs of the tree he was hiding in. He thought he saw an octet of soldiers setting up camp for the night. He couldn't tell if they were the High Matriarch's soldiers or not. But he was not willing to take a chance. He used the shirt he had covered Aerielle with as a sort of sling to carry her, so that both his arms would be free. He tied her around his chest and closed his cloak over her. He waited until it was completely dark.

Then he leapt into the air and flew toward the river. He prayed that the soldiers would not spot him in the moonlight.

They had built a large campfire, so Mattern hoped their night vision was affected by the firelight.

Mattern continued the journey south and didn't stop again until the sun rose. As far as he could tell, he was only a few turns from the border to the Eight Realms. The border crossing was at the upper entrance to the Caverns next to Cliffside. But Mattern wouldn't stop at Cliffside. Not just yet. He would continue on to Soedeen.

The next few turns were uneventful other than the fact that he had finally run out of food, and the jar containing the Mother's Milk Root Powder was almost empty. He planned to stop in the Caverns and purchase more of both. He would need enough to last another octurn and a half. It would take him that long to get to the Orphan Tree in Soedeen.

It was the beginning of the turn when Mattern arrived at the border checkpoint. The guard waved him on through, not even bothering to question him.

When he flew into the Caverns all the shopkeepers and vendors were scurrying around loading wagons with merchandise. It appeared that they were preparing to evacuate.

Mattern flew to the apothecary shop first. The proprietor greeted him.

"Sorry for the mess. We are packing up to move south. You know about that wizard and his army coming this way, right?" he asked.

"Yes, I know," said Mattern. "When do you think he'll get here?" he asked.

"No one knows for sure. Wing Guards from Cliffside came and warned everyone about it a few turns ago," said the proprietor. "We've been preparing to leave ever since. Now, what can I help you with?"

"I need some Mother's Milk Root Powder," said Mattern.

"I've already loaded it on the wagon. But if you'll wait here I'll go dig it out for you," said the proprietor.

"Thank you," said Mattern.

The proprietor returned after a few moments and set a large jar down on the counter. "How much do you need?" asked the proprietor.

"I'll take all of it," said Mattern. "How much?"

"That'll be five Gren," said the proprietor.

Mattern counted out the coins and plopped them down on the counter. Then he picked up the jar and stuffed it into his backpack. Aeri began to stir and coo.

The proprietor was startled. "Oh, who is that you have there?" he asked.

"My granddaughter," said Mattern. "Thank you." He turned away and left the apothecary shop without another word.

"Uh, thank you," said the proprietor looking after him.

Mattern made his way to a shop that had the sign over the door, "General Merchandise." He went inside and purchased more travel bread, fruit, and tioldoer jerky. When he was satisfied he had enough provisions for the journey to Soedeen he left the Caverns.

He noticed there was quite a bit of activity going on around Cliffside. Parents with children were leaving the limbs of both Sister's Tree and Brother's Tree.

He wondered if all of Cliffside was going to be evacuated. Then he noticed the older students didn't seem to be leaving, just the younger ones. Mattern assumed the older students were going to stay and help defend Cliffside.

Mattern regretted that he couldn't take the time to stop to see Mother Kerinelle and Father Libraen and let them know about the death of Lynette and Joran. But he thought it was better to get Aeri settled as soon as possible. As long as she was with him, she was in danger from the High Matriarch.

He continued flying south for a few more hours. Then he began to feel tired and groggy and decided he would stop for the rest of the turn. A few hours of sleep would be all he needed. He found a suitable tree and settled down to sleep after he fed Aeri. When it grew dark he continued on his journey.

The turns began to blur and before long he arrived in Soedeen. The Orphan's Tree was near the western border of Soedeen. It took another night of flying to arrive, but he finally made it. It was just turning light with sunrise when he landed on the flight platform of Orphan's Tree.

Mattern knocked on the door and one of the Unseen opened it. "May I help you?" the Unseen asked.

"I need to see Gregtonaire. I know he is serving here," said Mattern.

"Yes, he serves here," said the Unseen looking curious. It was rare that anyone came to see one of the Unseen. "Wait here and I will go get him."

"Thank you," said Mattern. From where he stood, he could see into a large dining room. There was a large table where winged children up to eight cycles sat eating. There were no children older than that because the children of the Eight Realms all went to Cliffside from the age of eight.

Mattern watched them sadly. He could imagine Aerielle sitting there with them. It comforted him to know that she would eventually be under the care of Mother Kerinelle and Father Libraenaire. The next eight cycles would not be easy as an orphan, but at least she would be safe from the High Matriarch.

After a few moments Gregton came to where Mattern was waiting by the door. He did not seem to recognize him.

"Sir, may I help you?" he asked. He was dressed in a light blue robe and his hair had all been shaved away. Mattern barely recognized him.

"Gregton, is there a room where we can talk in private?" asked Mattern.

"In private," repeated Gregton. "You wish to speak to me in private?" Gregton thought this was strange. Most people avoided talking at all with an Unseen.

"Yes, please," said Mattern. He opened his cloak and revealed Aerielle sleeping quietly in the sling against his chest.

Gregton said, "Follow me." He turned on his heel and led Mattern to an arched doorway with a set of stairs leading up. They went up the stairs to a room on another limb. "In here." He opened the door to a small office.

Gregton stood aside as Mattern went before him into the room. There was a desk and two armchairs next to a fireplace. A warm fire was going.

"Have a seat, please," said Gregton indicating one of the armchairs. They both sat and Gregton turned to Mattern. "I assume you wish to place a winglet with us."

Mattern opened his cloak and lifted Aeri out of the sling. He laid her on his lap and she cooed at him.

"Yes," he said. "Unfortunately, I do. Gregton, don't you know who I am?"

Gregton looked at him for a few moments. Slowly recognition came over his face. "Your Majesty? Is it really you?" he asked.

"Yes," said Mattern. "I'm afraid so."

"I assume this is your, um, winglet, sir," said Gregton. His face reddened with embarrassment. He thought the Royal Consort had gotten involved with another woman and gotten her pregnant.

"My winglet, no," laughed Mattern. "This is my granddaughter."

"Oh, your granddaughter," said Gregton, realizing his mistake. "I thought...well, um..."

"That's alright," said Mattern. "You see, my daughter and her life-mate are most likely dead. And the High Matriarch must not get her hands on their winglet."

"Oh, I am so sorry, Milord," said Gregton. "What happened?"

"It's a long story," said Mattern. "Do you have time to listen?"

"Yes, Milord, I do," said Gregton.

Mattern told him about his leaving the High Matriarch and his journey to find his daughter. He told him about finding her and the baby on their way out of Halalouma. Then he told him about Morren and the planned attack on Cliffside. Lastly, he told him about his journey back to the Eight Realms and Soedeen, and his decision to place Aeri with Gregton at the Orphan Tree.

It took several hours to tell, and by the time he was finished Aerielle was ready to eat. She began to cry. Mattern picked up his pack and pulled out the jar of Mother's Milk Root powder.

"Would you like me to hold her while you..." Gregton started to say.

Just then someone knocked on the door. Gregton got up and went to the door. He opened it and stepped outside to talk to another Unseen. Then he returned to the armchair and sat down.

Mattern handed Aeri to Gregton and prepared a bottle for her. Then he took her back and began feeding her.

He and Gregton talked while she ate. "I promise to take good care of her for you, Milord," said Gregton. "When it's time, I'll personally take her to Cliffside to begin her training."

"I plan to go to Cliffside to tell Mother Kerinelle and Father Libraen where I have placed her," said Mattern. "They have plenty to worry about right now with the upcoming attack by Morren."

"Sir, we haven't heard anything about it here in Soedeen. Do you think Morren can be stopped at Cliffside?" asked Gregton.

"I honestly don't know," said Mattern.

"If they can't stop him there, will he come into the Eight Realms?" asked Gregton.

"If they can't stop him I'm afraid no one can," said Mattern. "If Morren should attack the Eight Realms, I will return for my granddaughter, that is, assuming the High Matriarch's soldiers have not apprehended me."

"Sir, I hardly recognized you. I don't think you will be recognized by any of her soldiers," said Gregton.

"I hope you are right," said Mattern. Aerielle was finished eating. Mattern put her on his shoulder and burped her. He smelled her downy hair for the last time. He held her tightly while he began to cry.

Gregton knelt before Mattern. He put his hand on his knee and said, "Milord, I promise I won't let anything bad happen to her. I will keep your secret, I swear it."

Mattern stood and passed Aerielle to Gregton. "I trust you with her life," said Mattern. "I must go now." He left the jar of Mother's Milk Root powder and the bottle on the desk."

"Where will you go from here, sir?" asked Gregton.

"As I said, I'll go to Cliffside. But I think I'll spend the night in the inn in Soedeen City," said Mattern. "I've been sleeping in trees or on the ground for quite a while. A real bed would be nice."

"It will only take a few hours for you to get to the City from here," said Gregton. "Just follow the road east."

"Thank you, again, Gregton," said Mattern. He patted Aerielle on the back and kissed her on the head. Then he turned away and went out the door and down the stairs. He made his way quickly to the entrance and left the Orphan Tree.

He flew east, tears streaming down his face. A few hours later he arrived in Soedeen City and found the tree in which the inn was located. He noticed several groups of soldiers in the city, but was able to avoid them.

Unfortunately, there were two soldiers stationed in the inn from the High Matriarch's Wing guard. They were in the tavern part of the inn, sitting in a back corner eating last-meal. Mattern didn't see them at first when he walked into the tavern. But when he finally noticed them it was too late to leave without being suspicious.

He placed his order at the bar. Then he sat at a table near the bar and turned his back to the soldiers.

A serving girl brought out a plate stacked with food and a jug of ale and a cup. She placed everything on the table and said, "Will that be all, sir?"

"Yes, thank you," said Mattern. He poured himself some ale from the jug into the cup and took a long sip. Then he picked up the fork and began shoveling food into his mouth.

One of the soldiers got up and came across the bar. He stood over Mattern, staring down at him. "You don't look like you're from around here," he said.

Mattern just kept eating without looking up. "I said, you don't look like you are from around here," repeated the soldier.

"So," said Mattern around the food in his mouth.

"So, where are you from?" asked the soldier, who appeared to be a captain by the bars on his collar.

"Northern Provinces," responded Mattern. He wiped his mouth on a napkin and looked up into the captain's eyes.

"Northern Provinces, eh," said the captain. "You look familiar. I swear I have seen you somewhere before."

"Ever been in the Provinces?" asked Mattern trying to speak with the accent of the northerners.

"No, I haven't," said the captain. "What brings you to Soedeen?"

"You've heard about the wizard who's going to attack Cliffside?" asked Mattern. He knew he had made a mistake the moment the words left his mouth based on the captain's expression and his next move.

"No one is supposed to know about that," said the captain as his hand moved to his sword.

"Well, everyone in the Provinces knows about it," said Mattern. "I didn't know it was a secret."

"Orders from the High Matriarch," said the captain. "Just keep it to yourself unless you want to be arrested."

"Uh, yes sir," said Mattern as he picked up his cup and refilled it.

The captain stared down at him for a moment longer, "You sure do seem familiar," he said again. Then he turned and went back to sit down with the other Wing Guard. After about an hour they left the tavern.

Mattern had almost finished all of the ale by then. He ordered another jug and continued to drink as other patrons came into the tavern to eat or drink. By the time Mattern was ready for bed, he was quite drunk.

He stumbled his way to the proprietor to retrieve the key to his room. He made his way up the stairs to his room and unlocked the door. He probably shouldn't have drunk so much, but he had wanted to drown his sorrows with ale. He flopped down on the bed and immediately started snoring.

Sometime later in the night, someone kicked down his door. He rolled over onto his back and reached for his sword. Someone shot him with a crossbow bolt. It landed on his left shoulder. He jumped to his feet and pulled the bolt out.

"What the blue blazes is going on," he said as an entire octet of Wing Guards pushed into the room. The captain of the Wing Guard was the same one who had confronted him earlier in the evening.

"I finally remembered where I saw you, Your Majesty," said the captain. He was holding the crossbow. Mattern was bleeding profusely. "You're under arrest by order of the High Matriarch.

Several of the Wing Guards grabbed him and tried to tie his arms behind his back, but he managed to pull loose and grab his sword. He sliced one across the arm and stabbed the other in the stomach. He jumped back as they all drew their swords. He began fighting for all he was worth as they all attacked him.

He was able to kill at least three of them, but he received several bad injuries. If he hadn't been drunk he probably would have killed more of them.

He was not willing to be captured. He knew he would be de-winged at the least, and probably tortured and then killed. He could not allow the High Matriarch to find out about Aerielle. At least she was safe with Gregtonaire at the Orphan Tree.

He fought bravely, but in the end, he succumbed to his wounds. He fell to the floor and the remaining Wing Guards surrounded him. He started laughing. He had beaten the High Matriarch at her game. His precious granddaughter was safe from her clutches. He continued to laugh as he bled out.

"Blast it, we were supposed to take him alive!" shouted the captain as he looked down at Mattern in annoyance.

It was the last thing Mattern heard before he died.

# ~
# CHAPTER 15
# ALLIANCE

The High Matriarch and Finn, her chamberlain, flew quickly through the Caverns on their way to the Northern Provinces. She was on a mission she could trust no one else. She was going to see Morren before he began his attack on Esteryia.

The border guard held up his hand as they neared the guard shack. "Halt," he said. "What is your purpose for going to the Northern Provinces? Don't you know there's an invading army heading south?"

"Yes, we know about it. We are going to see my mother in Esteryia and bring her back to Algren," lied the High Matriarch. She and Finn wore disguises so no one would recognize them. They were dressed as simple folk and had documents supporting their ruse.

"Well, you can pass, but be careful," said the guard. "You see all these people? They are leaving the Provinces for good reason. I would advise you to fetch your mother quickly." He indicated the long line of people heading in the opposite direction.

"Thank you," said Finn. "We will be careful." They walked past the guard shack and then took to the air. They flew north toward Esteryia.

A few turns later they came to the outskirts of the city. People were leaving by droves, trying to escape before Morren attacked. Finn and the High Matriarch made their way through

Esteryia and soon came to a hill looking down on Morren's army.

The High Matriarch walked boldly up to a soldier on the outskirts of the camp with Finn. In his hands, Finn held the flag of the High Matriarch of the Eight Realms on a pole. The High Matriarch wanted there to be no mistaking of her identity now.

"I wish to see your commander, T'Ardis Morrenaire," she said. "Please tell him the High Matriarch has a message for him."

The guard burst out laughing. "Is that so?" he asked. "You don't look much like the High Matriarch."

"We came in disguise. Just take us to him," she demanded. "I assure you he will want to hear what I have to say."

"Alright," said the guard. "But it's your funeral."

He led them down into the camp past row after row of undead warriors. Eventually, they came to Morren's tent. It was a large, red, round affair. There were two guards posted at the entrance, standing at attention. They were members of Morren's regular army.

"This here's the High Matriarch of the Eight Realms," the soldier leading them said sarcastically. "She says she has a message for Morren."

"The High Matriarch, you say?" asked one of the guards. "Well, give me the message and I'll see that Morren gets it."

The High Matriarch had lost her patience by now and pushed the soldier aside. She stepped up to the guard and asked, "Is Morren here or not?"

"Oh, he's here all right," said the guard. "But..."

Before he could say another word the High Matriarch grabbed him by the throat and lifted him with supernatural strength. She threw him across the camp and he smashed into another tent, knocking it down. Her eyes flashed with anger and malice.

The other guard drew his sword, but Finn beat him to it and pressed his sword against the guard's side. "I suggest you move out of the way and let the High Matriarch pass," he said.

The guard looked into the High Matriarch's eyes and put his sword back in its scabbard. He quickly stepped aside and held the tent flap open for the High Matriarch and Finn to pass.

They marched inside and saw a large black orb sitting on a pedestal in the middle of the tent. Standing in front of it with his back to them, Morren spoke, "He said you would be coming. I am glad you are here."

Then he turned around and looked at them. The High Matriarch and Finn both gasped. Morren was hairless and covered in scars. His wings had been burned away. He was the ugliest creature they had ever seen...almost.

Morren stepped aside so that she could see Saarnak in the window of the orb. Saarnak stared back at them malevolently. He was a hideous demon, all red with three horns curling toward the back of his head. He had long fangs hanging down on his chin.

But it was his eyes that were the most startling. They were solid black and it was as if he could see into their very souls. The High Matriarch had met more than her match.

"Ah, you must be Saarnak," she said. "You knew I was coming?"

Saarnak laughed and then grew serious. "Yes, I knew you would not be able to keep away. You are drawn to power...power and dark magic."

"Yes," she said. "I am drawn to you. I admit it."

"What do you want? Why are you here?" asked Saarnak.

"I am here to discuss an alliance between myself and Morren," she replied.

"An alliance? And what would be the basis of this alliance?" asked Saarnak.

"I do not wish to see the Eight Realms destroyed, so this is what I propose," she said. She laid out her plans and Saarnak and Morren listened.

When she was done Saarnak said, "This is a good plan. But are you sure you can get the armies to comply?"

"Leave that to me," she said. "They will do as they are told."

"Then we are agreed," said Morren.

"Yes," she said. "I will leave now..." she started to say.

"Ah, but I require payment from you, T'Algren Devoerelle," interrupted Saarnak, using the High Matriarch's formal name. "I want something in return."

"What is it you require?" she asked. "I have plenty of riches..."

Saarnak laughed. "I have no need of riches," he said.

"Then what..." she started to ask. Saarnak held up his hand and her words were cut off. She put her hands to her throat and tried to scream. A red light began to swirl around her.

She could feel Saarnak's presence in her mind and her being. It was as if every part of her was being stripped away and revealed to him. She felt as if she was losing herself to him, and in a way she was. He squeezed his hand and she arched her back in pain. She had never felt such pain.

The red light slowly dissipated as Saarnak released his fist. She crumpled to the sandy floor gasping. "What did you do to me?" she rasped finally. She slowly got to her feet.

"I have bound you to me...forever. You are now mine," said Saarnak mysteriously. "Now you will return to Algren to set things into motion."

"Yes," she said as she tried to resist him. But she could feel his presence in her mind still.

He laughed at her and said, "You cannot resist me. Your efforts are futile. Like I said, you are now mine. You will do as I say. Now go back to Algren, and you can leave the flag here."

Finn looked at the flag in his hand and then passed it to Morren, who did not look happy.

"So, we are agreed then?" Morren asked. "We have an alliance?"

"Yes," she said. "We have an alliance, blast you." She had given up much more than she bargained for. But at least the Eight Realms would be spared.

Then she turned and left the tent with Finn, who looked at her with fear and trepidation. "Are you alright, Your Majesty?" he asked.

"Yes, I am fine," she snapped and leapt into the air.

They flew back towards the Caverns. An octurn later they were back in Algren. It was nighttime, but the High Matriarch didn't want to retire just yet.

"Finn, you may go to your chambers now," she said. "I will send for you if I need you."

She had work to do, so she went to the rooms beneath Tree Algren. Jathen was there.

"The girl, is she still alive?" she asked.

"Yes, Your Majesty," replied Jathen dry-washing his hands.

She followed Jathen into the cell where a winged girl was stretched out on a stone slab. Her eyes were wide open and she seemed to be in a daze. She was chained to the slab.

"I require some of her blood," she said. She picked up a bowl and a knife from a table against the wall of the cell and brought them to the slab. She made a careful incision on the girl's inner arm and held it over the bowl. Blood dripped into the bowl until it was full.

She took the bowl of blood to another room under the Tree. Carved into the floor was a large, eight-pointed star. She knelt and touched each point with blood from the bowl. Then she stepped into the center and began to chant. Before long a black light began to emanate from the points of the star.

She raised her hands above her head and the black light began to rise and spin around her. Her chanting became louder and louder and the light grew brighter and brighter. It swirled around and around the High Matriarch.

Suddenly she clapped her hands and the light blinked out. "It is done," she said to herself.

She left the chamber and went back up the stairs. She came out of the hidden stairway behind the throne room, which was empty. It was now late into the night as she made her way to her bedroom. She took off her clothes, and falling into bed, she went to sleep. But she had nightmares of Saarnak and tossed and turned and awoke in a sweat.

The sun had just risen in Algren. The High Matriarch got up and sat at her desk to read letters from several Matriarchs and Patriarchs. They had declined her invitation to come to court to discuss the upcoming attack of Morren on Cliffside. She proceeded to write them scathing letters demanding they come to Algren at once.

Oh, they each had a good excuse and they had sent representatives but she had wanted the ruler of each realm to attend the meeting. She was furious they had declined and was planning something nasty to happen to each of them. She had agents and spies in every court of the Eight Realms. In addition, the spell she had used the night before would soon take effect.

She got up from her desk and went to the door. Finn, her chamberlain was standing there about to knock when the door swung open.

"Oh, Finn. What is it? What do you want?" she asked impatiently.

"Your Majesty, there is a word of the Royal Consort. He has been found in Soedeen according to the Wing Guard stationed there," said Finn. They brought him here and sent this message to you..."

"Give it to me then," she said as she snatched the message from his hands. She read the message and her face darkened. "Tell them to bring him to the throne room immediately."

She turned on her heel and stalked to the throne room. She climbed up on her throne and sat impatiently waiting for her orders to be obeyed.

Before long the Wing Guard from Soedeen flew into the throne room carrying the body of Mattern between them. They lay the body down before the throne and stepped back. The courtiers and ladies-in-waiting gasped when they saw the body.

"Who is responsible?" asked the High Matriarch. "Who killed the Royal Consort?"

"Um, that is not known at this time. We found his body in the alley behind the inn in Sodeen," lied the captain. The members of the Wing Guard who were responsible for Mattern's death had agreed to keep the truth hidden. They were deathly afraid of what the High Matriarch might do to them for killing the Royal Consort.

She got up from her throne and walked down the steps to examine the body. He looked older with a full beard and his clothes were ordinary and soiled. She could see several wounds from what seemed to be crossbow-bolt holes in his flesh as well as cuts from swords. His body was in bad shape.

"And you found nothing on him? No messages or anything?" she asked. She put her handkerchief to her face.

"It appears that he was the victim of a robbery as his body was found with no Gren or anything else of value," said the captain. "There were no messages on his person either."

"When was he found?" she asked. The body was already beginning to smell.

"We found his body two turns ago and we immediately returned to Algren with it, Your Majesty," replied the captain. "We have flown almost non-stop since we found him."

The High Matriarch walked back up the steps to her throne and sat down. "We must find these robbers," she said. "You will return to Soedeen and find out who did this," she said, although she had a good idea who had really killed her mate. But she didn't want to confront the perpetrators just yet so she went along with the story.

"Do not return without the guilty parties," she said adamantly. "Someone must pay for this crime." She was secretly pleased that Mattern was dead, but she put on a good show for the Matriarchs and Patriarchs in court. She would play the widow and milk it for all it was worth. She would even put on mourning clothes and mourn the appropriate amount of turns.

"We must build a funeral pyre at once," she said piously. "Finn, see to it."

"Your Majesty, there are no Wind Dancers to perform the ceremony. They have all been called to Cliffside," protested Finn.

She slammed her fist down on the arm of her throne. "I said you are to see to it, Finn. I will not repeat myself. We don't need any Wind Dancers. I will perform the ceremony myself. Now remove the body and make preparations for the ceremony."

There were numerous gasps from the courtiers. Only Wind Dancers performed the funeral ceremony in the Eight Realms. The High Matriarch was breaking with a tradition that was as old as the wind.

The Wing Guard bent and picked up the body. Then they flew from the throne room to Military Tree where the body was placed in a cell until the pyre could be built. Finn went with them. He requisitioned several soldiers to bathe and prepare the body. They weren't Wind Dancers but they would get the job done.

Finn flew back to Tree Algren to get a suitable outfit for the Royal Consort. By the time he returned to Military Tree, Mattern's body had been stripped and the soldiers were bathing him. When they were done they placed the outfit Finn had selected on the body.

"He looks regal, doesn't he," said one of the soldiers. They all stood around the body in respect.

"I liked the Royal Consort," said another soldier.

"Yeah, I did too," said the first soldier. "He was always kind to me."

"Well, don't just stand around," snapped Finn. "Get to work building the funeral pyre."

"Where should we build it?" asked the soldier.

"Build it in the square of the city, below Tree Algren," said Finn. "Send word when you are done."

The soldiers set to work and it was late in the turn when they were finished. By now, word of the Royal Consort's death had spread throughout Algren City. Hundred of citizens surrounded the square awaiting the burning of the pyre.

Several captains of the Wing Guard brought the body out of the cell and flew with it to the pyre. They laid the body out on the wood and draped his cloak over the body. Several citizens walked up and laid flowers on Mattern's chest.

By the time Finn flew back to the throne room to tell the High Matriarch that everything was ready, the sun was setting. She walked to the flight platform overlooking the funeral pyre. Several citizens gave a half-hearted cheer.

The High Matriarch lifted both her arms to get everyone's attention. She began to speak, "Citizens of Algren, this is a sad turn. The Royal Consort was found murdered in Soedeen two turns ago by my Wing Guard stationed there. He was apparently robbed. This will not go unpunished. They are returning to Soedeen to find and apprehend the robbers. But now we are gathered to say farewell to T'Ardis Matternaire, my mate and Royal Consort."

She aimed her hand at the pyre, said a quick spell, and the pyre burst into flames. The citizens all gasped. A Wind Dancer was supposed to perform this ceremony. It was unheard of for any other person to light the pyre.

Then she began to chant the words of the traditional Wind Dancers' funeral ceremony, "Flame to the Wind, Wind to the Sky, Sky to the Heavens. Born of the Ashes, Death to Life, Ash in the Wind, Ash in the Wind." She chanted over and over as the pyre burned. Then she lowered her hands and turned on her heel and went back inside the castle in Tree Algren.

The citizens assumed she was overcome with grief, but in fact, she was eager to get back to her planning and scheming. She went back to her bedroom and back to what she had been working on at the beginning of the turn.

She had been working on a letter to be delivered to Morren. Ever since she and Finn had returned from meeting with him in Esteryia she had become more and more convinced that Saarnak could not be trusted. She wanted to find out how Morren felt about the possibility of forging an alliance with her apart from Saarnak. She was afraid of the demon and wanted to be free of him. The new alliance would serve a two-fold purpose. It would ensure that there would be no more trouble from Cliffside and hopefully, they could find a way to be rid of Saarnak.

But she needed to meet with Morren alone and she thought she knew of a blood spell that would enable her to do so secretly. She was going to send him a copy of the spell so that they could meet at a specific destination, away from prying eyes. She sincerely hoped he would be willing to betray the demon Saarnak.

# ~ CHAPTER 16
# PERMISSION

Mother Kerin and Father Libraen both leapt to their feet at stared at Lynette and Joran as they rose from the floor. They were shocked to see them suddenly appear in their office.

Joran repeated Lynette's warning, "Morren plans to attack Cliffside in three octurns. And has an army of undead as well as regular army."

"Three octurns," said Libraen. "Are you certain of this?"

"Is my father here," asked Lynette hopefully. She was more concerned with the location of her baby and father than she was with the coming attack.

Kerin came around the desk and put her arm around Lynette's shoulder. "No, we haven't seen him," she said. "I thought he was probably with you. Was he coming here?"

"Yes, he was supposed to bring our daughter here," said Lynette plaintively.

"Why don't we go into the salon and sit down," said Kerin. "We can talk in there. She guided Lynette into the other room. Joran and Libraen followed.

Lynette and Joran sat on the couch, the same couch they had sat on so long ago for a scolding from Mother and Father, before they ran away from Cliffside. It had been less than a cycle ago but it seemed like eons.

They had found the ancient mythical city of Halalouma, and had met Ooloo and the others from the Northern Plateaus. Lynette had had their baby. And they had been attacked by Morren and sent to the world of dreams by Ooloo. Now they had come full circle. They were back at Cliffside where it had all begun.

"Now, tell us everything that has happened since you ran away," said Mother Kerinelle.

The words poured forth and they took turns telling the tale. By the time they were finished, the sun had set and the moons had risen.

"So, you are life-mated and you have a baby," said Mother Kerinelle. "We learned as much from Hanoera's message. Do you think she and Kevar are still alive?"

"I don't know," said Joran. "The last we saw of them they were surrounded by undead. Kevar was down and Hanoera was fighting over him. They could have been taken captive, I suppose."

"Oh, I hope they are still alive," said Lynette. "But, has anyone else from our group made their way here? I didn't see what happened to Tavat and the warriors from the North. Ooloo was captured by Morren with some kind of powerful energy net. Then we were transported to the world of dreams."

"No, no one else has come. And we received the message from Swen over an octurn ago," said Libraen.

"Mother, Father, are you making preparations to stay and fight or are you planning on evacuating Cliffside?" asked Joran.

"The younger students through the fourth level are already leaving. The rest of the students have been given a choice of whether to stay or to go," said Kerinelle. "I'm proud to say that most of them wanted to stay to defend Cliffside.

"We cannot abandon Cliffside," said Libraen. "Children, for thousands of years, have been brought here for education and training, and to be prepared for the Wind Trials. The three Trees of Cliffside are the oldest on Eruna. We cannot allow Morren to destroy the school."

"I'm glad you're going to stand and fight," said Joran.

"You must come with us to see the Wind Council. It is time to go against tradition," said Kerinelle.

"What do you mean, Mother," asked Lynette.

"She means to teach the students that stay here how to use their magic to help us defend the school," said Libraen.

"The Wind Council refused our first request. Hopefully with your testimony, and the fact that Morren will be here in three octurns, they will listen to reason," said Kerinelle.

Lynette looked at Joran and said, "Three octurns is not much time. We could help teach the students. We learned how to access our magic in the world of dreams and have learned so much."

"That's good," said Father Libraen. "That will help."

"If you two are ready we should make haste and go talk to the Wind Council. Once they learn the threat is eminent and Morren will be upon us soon. Surely, they will listen to reason," said Kerinelle.

"We are ready," said Joran. He and Lynette followed Libraen and Kerinelle out onto the flight platform outside their office.

"We will go directly up the mountain instead of going through the Caverns. The downdrafts shouldn't give you any trouble. The wind has been surprisingly cooperative lately, as if it's holding its breath, waiting for Morren.

They all leapt into the air and flew up the cliff toward the Wind Dancer's Ledge. The guards at the door opened it immediately for them.

"We need to see the Council again, immediately," said Libraen.

By now the chamberlain was used to calling the Wind Council to assemble on such short notice. He turned on his heel and practically ran to ring the bell to call them. Libraen, Kerinelle, Lynette, and Joran went directly to the Council Chamber.

Before long the Council members began to make their way into the Chamber. They went to their seats and sat down. They did not look happy.

"You have called us to assembly again so I can only assume you have more news," said Wind Master Haddon.

"Yes, and you aren't going to like it," said Libraen. "Morren will be here in three octurns." The members of the council all began to speak at once. This seemed to be a habit for them.

"Please be quiet," said Master Haddon.

"How can you be certain of the timeframe?" asked Wind Mistress Glenbole.

"Because Erboer has fallen and Esteryia is next," said Kerinelle. "It will take at most three octurns for Morren to make his way to Cliffside."

"Who told you Erboer had fallen?" asked Council member Paelmin. "We haven't heard anything yet."

"Well you wouldn't have," said Kerinelle. "It just happened."

"Then how did you hear about it so quickly? asked Paelmin.

"Before we go any further, let me introduce T'Ardis Joranaire and his life-mate T'Algren Lynettelle," said Kerinelle. She hoped what they had to say would bare more weight if she used their formal names.

"Ah, the parents," said Master Haddon. He started to say more, but Libraen interrupted him.

"Let them tell their tale," said Father Libraen.

Joran stepped up to the podium and began to speak. "I don't know how much you know, but there is a young winglet named Ooloo Noo"Loon from the north..."

"Yes, yes, we know about her," said Master Haddon. Mistress Grenbole put a hand on his arm. "Let them tell it their way," she said gently.

"Morren attacked us shortly after we exited Halalouma over four octurns ago," said Joran. "He has an army of undead as well as a regular army. Ooloo transported us to the world of dreams in the midst of the battle. She was captured by Morren but was able to save us."

"Transported?" asked Mistress Grenbole. "You had a dream?"

"No," said Lynette. "We were transported there bodily...um. fully."

"What Lynette means is that we actually went there," explained Joran. "And we met the guardians of the world of dreams."

"That's preposterous," shouted Paelmin as he jumped to his feet. Other Council members started arguing with one another.

"Quiet!" boomed Master Haddon. "I will have order in the Chamber!"

Everyone quieted down and Paelmin sat. But he continued to glare at Joran and Lynette. "Let them continue then," said Paelmin. "This just gets better and better."

"Be quiet, Paelmin. No more interruptions, please," said Master Haddon.

"Anyway, the guardians taught us to access our magic..."

"What? But you are not Wind Dancers," interrupted Mistress Grenbole.

"No ma'am, but nonetheless we have learned how to fight with magic," said Lynette impatiently. She was beginning to get fed up with all the petulant Council members."

"May they continue?" asked Kerinelle.

"Yes, let's hear the rest of what they have to say," said Master Haddon.

"Anyway," Joran continued. "Ooloo would come visit us in her dreams and so we learned that the attack on Cliffside would occur in three octurns. We asked the guardians to send us to Cliffside, which they did."

"And we brought them to report to you," said Libraen. "I think we need to readdress the question of teaching the older students to use their magic."

"Yes, tradition has now been broken," added Kerinelle. "There is no longer any reason for you to forbid it."

The entire Wind Council was silent for once. They all looked troubled. "What you say is true," said Mistress Grenbole. "I think we should put it to a vote."

"Wait a minute," said Paelmin. "We need to discuss this."

"We have already discussed it," said Master Haddon. "I think, with the attack coming in three octurns there won't be enough time anyway."

"I disagree," said Libraen. "I think you are underestimating our students."

"You have to at least give us a chance. You cannot just sit there and let Cliffside be destroyed," insisted Kerinelle.

"We have no intention of just sitting here and letting that happen," said Master Haddon. "We can help you teach the students..."

"But there has been no vote," objected Paelmin.

"Fine, those who agree to allow the upper-level students to be taught how to defend their school with magic say "aye." They went around the table and just about everyone gave their assent. Paelmin said "Nay," which was no surprise to anyone.

Libraen and Kerinelle breathed a sigh of relief. "Thank you," said Libraen. "You won't regret it."

"Now, we will come to Cliffside as soon as the sun rises to get started," said Master Haddon. "I expect every one of the Wind Council Members to do their part. Wind Dancers from the Eight Realms have been summoned. They can help teach the students also as soon as they arrive. I will leave it to you two to decide who teaches what when they get here."

"We want to do our part also," said Lynette. "The guardians of the world of dreams taught us quite a few spells and techniques of offense as well as defense."

"Alright," said Master Haddon. "You may help. Did you learn anything about healing?"

"Only the basics," said Joran. "There wasn't time for more."

"Then when you aren't teaching you will be learning about healing from Mistress Grenbole," said Master Haddon. "There is sure to be a need."

"Yes, there will," said Mistress Grenbole.

"If there is nothing further, you may be excused. We will stay and discuss who is going to teach what. May T'Airiat be with you all," said Master Haddon.

"And with you," said Libraen.

Libraen, Kerinelle, Lynette and Joran left the Council Chamber and walked out of the building. They walked down the stairs as they talked.

"That went well," said Libraen.

"Better than I thought it would," said Kerinelle.

"Do you think they are afraid?" asked Lynette.

"I imagine so," said Father Libraen. "I know I am." He laughed but there was no mirth in it.

"I am too," said Kerinelle. "We all should be afraid."

By the time they returned to Cliffside it was time for last-meal. "We still have a lot to talk about," said Kerinelle. "Why don't you take last-meal with us in our salon?"

"Thank you, Mother, that would be nice," said Lynette.

They walked into the salon from the landing platform and sat down. Kerinelle picked up a bell and rang for Nona. She told her that the four of them were going to eat in the salon and in almost no time platters of food were brought and they were eating.

"You said that you learned offensive techniques as well as defensive from the guardians. Can you be more specific?" asked Father Libraen.

"Well," said Joran after he swallowed the bite of food he had just stuffed into his mouth, "they taught us a way that they think will be useful in killing the undead."

"Yes," said Lynette. She put her fork down. "They taught us how to make bolts of lightning. The only way to kill an undead warrior is to stab him in the heart. That puts a stop to them for good. Lightening explodes the heart. The guardians believe it would be very effective."

"Yes, I imagine it would be," agreed Kerinelle. "What about defensive techniques."

Joran spoke again, "We learned how to make shields of all four of the elements. But the most effective, I think is a shield of compressed air. Compressed air also makes a good offensive weapon." He rubbed his chest where he had been hit with air. It was still a little sore.

"So, do you have an element that you prefer to work with?" asked Libraen.

"I prefer fire," said Lynette. "But I seem to be equally proficient in all elements."

"Me too," said Joran. "I mean about being proficient in them all. I like to use air, though. It can pack quite a wallop."

Libraen laughed. "Yes, it can he said."

"Well you obviously have no trouble centering your focus on your magic if you can use all four elements," said Kerinelle. "I think that is what you should start out teaching the students. Libraen, do you think they should work with the eighth-level students?"

"Yes, and when they have a grasp on it, they can move on to offensive techniques. We'll work with the younger students. I'm sure Master Haddon will agree, but we'll have to ask him in the morning," said Libraen.

Lynette yawned. "Excuse me, it has been a long day."

Mother Kerinelle smiled. "Since you are life-mated you will stay in one of the guest quarters. I imagine you would prefer that than to sleep in your separate trees in your old rooms," she said.

"Thank you," said Lynette blushing. "That would be nice."

"Yes, thank you," agreed Joran. He stood up and pulled Lynette to her feet.

Kerinelle rang her little bell again as she and Libraen stood. Nona quickly came into the salon.

"Nona, please take these two to one of the guest quarters," she said. "One of the nicer ones."

"Thank you, Mother," said Lynette again.

"Sleep well. We have much work to do over the next three octurns," said Libraen.

"Yes, we do," agreed Kerinelle. "We'll wake you an hour before sunrise. We need to take advantage of the sunlight. We will work as long as there is light and then some."

Joran and Lynette followed Nona to the guest quarters. It was luxurious, even nicer than their quarters in the world of dreams. Nona bid them goodnight and then shut the door.

Lynette went into the bathroom and she was pleased to see a large tub there. It was at least as big as the one in Halalouma in the world of dreams.

"Joran," she called. "You should see this tub. I wonder if there's hot water?"

"Why wouldn't there be?" he asked. He turned a knob, and sure enough, there was hot water. He let it run until the tub was full of water.

They threw their clothes off and got in the tub. They stayed there for the better part of an hour. They found towels on a rack next to the tub and used them to dry off.

Lynette walked into the bedroom naked and plopped down on the bed. "Joran, do you think Mother and Father meant what they said about being afraid?" she asked.

"I don't know. I've never thought of them being afraid of anything," said Joran as he joined her on the bed. "But, I think you should be very afraid of me." He began tickling her and she started squealing. Before long the tickling and squealing stopped and they began to kiss. They ended up in each other's arms and made passionate love. Morren and the undead were forgotten for a time.

If only they had their daughter with them. Where could her father and her daughter be, wondered Lynette. They should have been in Cliffside by now.

True to her word, Mother Kerinelle woke them about an hour before sunrise. They decided to all eat first-meal in the dining hall with the students. Mother and Father had an announcement they wanted to make.

"If I may have your attention," shouted Father Libraen, trying to get the attention of all the students. He banged his knife on his cup until everyone was quiet.

"As you already know T'Ardis Morren is going to attack Cliffside. We now know that he will arrive, at the most, in three octurns," he said.

The dining hall erupted. Libraen banged on his cup again. He shouted, "Quiet, please. Be quiet."

An eighth-level student stood up. "Father, what are we going to do? The Wind Dancers still aren't here," he said. "Will they arrive in time?"

"Whether they do or not, each of you is going to be taught how to access your magic," said Libraen. The dining hall erupted again, this time all the students talking excitedly at once. The students were hopping up and down and cheering.

Libraen let it go on for a while. Then he banged on his cup again and asked for quiet. Eventually, the students settled down.

Just then Master Haddon and the members of the Wind Council landed on the flight platform outside the dining hall. They walked into the dining hall and stood in a line across the front of the table where Libraen, Kerinelle, Joran and Lynette sat.

"I see you have informed the students of our decision to let them study magic," said Master Haddon. "We could hear them cheering as we flew down from Wind Dancers' Ledge."

"Yes, we have," said Libraen.

"I'll take over from here," said Haddon. Libraen sat back down. He had a sour expression on his face though. It was just like Haddon to take over. Every student knew who he was, that he was the highest-ranking Wind Dancer in the Eight Realms.

"You all know who we are, but I'll introduce each of the members of the Wind Council. This is Wind Mistress Grenbole to my left..."

After he had introduced them all he proceeded to tell the students who would be teaching what aspect of magic.

"We will start by teaching you how to focus and find your center. We will work on this until it is time for mid-meal. Those of you who are successful will move on to the next lesson...accessing your magic. Those of you who are unsuccessful will assist the healers. Everyone will have a job. Any questions?"

None of the students was brave enough to ask Master Haddon a question. He divided the students between the Council members, and Lynette, Joran, Kerinelle, and Libraen. When he was done the students were led to various classrooms to begin their training.

In all, there were over a thousand students that passed the first test. Only forty-five students didn't make it. They went with Mistress Grenbole to learn how to be medics.

"It will be your job to help heal anyone who is injured. And let me assure you, there will be injuries."

A few of the younger students started crying. Mistress Grenbole looked at them with no pity. "It will do no good to cry. Your job will be as important as those who are fighting for the School, maybe more important," she said. "Now stop crying at once. Let us begin."

# CHAPTER 17
# EXODUS

Tavat rose from washing his hands in the river and smelled the wind. "I smell smoke," he said to Lare. "And it's not from our campfire." The sun was just beginning to rise.

"Where do you think it is coming from?" asked Lare. He sniffed the air and could barely smell the smoke. He squatted and filled his canteen with water from the river.

"I do not know for sure, but I think it is coming from the north. Maybe it's even from as far away as Erboer," said Tavat. "If it is from Erboer, then we don't have much time. We must leave immediately and head straight to Cliffside. I will tell the priest."

"I will get the others ready to go," said Lare. He went to where the Malakand were sleeping by the fire. He woke Gormon first, then Bicken and Fessa. They turned yellow with fright when he told them about the smoke. They put the campfire out and began making the preparations to leave. Lare saddled Nart.

Tavat flew to the temple and knocked on the door. Jamen opened the door and asked him to come in.

"May I help you?" he asked.

"I must speak with the priest immediately," said Tavat.

Jamen led him to the priest's office. The door was open so they walked on in. Gannaire had been expecting him.

"You smell the smoke, don't you?" he asked.

"Yes, I do," answered Tavat. "It is a bad omen. Morren is on his way here sooner than we thought. We must leave. Come with us, you and Jamen."

"I must warn the others. I will advise that they evacuate Esteryia as soon as possible," said Gannaire.

"But hasn't the Mayor already warned the people?" asked Tavat.

"I'm sure he has begun to warn them, but there are a few which I'm sure haven't been reached," said Gannaire. He was thinking of Selene and Merrium. He rose from his chair and put on his robe.

He walked to the flight platform with Tavat. "I must go warn someone now. If you are still here when I return, we will go with you. If not, we will still make our way to Cliffside with all haste and try to catch up with you." He flew off toward Selene and Merrium's tree.

When he arrived, he found the two sisters had loaded up a small wagon. With Merrium being blind it was the best way for them to travel.

"Yes, Merrium has been smelling smoke. Is it Morren, do you think?" asked Selene as she put several packets of powders, herbs, and other concoctions into her backpack.

"He is coming this way, according to the Mayor," said Merrium. "You came to warn us, didn't you?"

"Yes, I didn't think the Mayor would send someone out here to warn you," said Gannaire.

"Oh, he didn't," laughed Merrium.

"Oh," said Gannaire. "Where will you go?"

"We will head to Cliffside," said Selene. "That is where the battle will be decided. We will lend what aid we can."

"I was going to suggest that you go to Cliffside. I'm...ah, sure your skills will be welcome."

Selene laughed, "Yes, I'm sure they will."

"Well, if there is nothing I can do to help you, I will be going," said Gannaire

"Thank you for coming to warn us," said Selene.

"Yes, thank you," said Merrium.

By the time Gannaire returned to the temple, Tavat, Lare, and the Malakand were just getting ready to leave. Jamen brought out two backpacks full of clothes, travel bread and other foodstuff, books, and scrolls. He gave one of the packs to Gannaire.

"We need to stop in Esteryia to tell the Mayor of our suspicions. He should prepare to make his way to Cliffside. The whole town should evacuate," said Gannaire.

Tavat, Jamen, and Gannaire leapt into the air and flew toward the road while Lare rode Nart and the Malakand ran behind him. Wug sat on Lare's shoulder. Before long they were in town. Lare left the group to do some shopping.

In Esteryia, both winged and wingless people were scurrying everywhere, preparing to flee from the coming danger. The Mayor was busy in his office, gathering documents and other important papers to take south when Tavat and Gannaire arrived.

"We smelled smoke and came to warn you..." Gannaire started to say.

"Yes, yes, we have had reports that Erboer has fallen and that Morren will be here sooner than we thought," said the Mayor. Cyntha came into the room looking frightened.

"I don't know what to pack, Lund," she said, flustered.

"My dear, let the servants pack. Just worry about yourself," said the Mayor. They had several wingless menservants and maids who were busy loading a large wagon with boxes, bags, and barrels of their belongings.

"Lund, I will see you in Cliffside, I suppose?" asked Gannaire.

"No, we are going on to Algren. My life-mate has family there and we will stay with them," said Lund.

"But what about the Wing Guard?" asked Gannaire. "They will be needed for the battle."

"Yes, they have been ordered to go to Cliffside. We will take a few with us as guards for our journey to Algren," said Lund. "But the rest will join up with the Wing Guard detachment at Cliffside."

"Well, I will leave you to your preparations then," said Gannaire.

Lare decided to purchase a small wagon for him and the Malakand to ride in. He paid triple what it was worth, but he was glad to get it. He pulled Nart's saddle off and hooked him up to pull it. They threw their packs and the saddle in the back of the wagon. The Malakand climbed into the wagon on top of the packs, and Lare stepped up to sit on the narrow seat. Tavat and Gannaire nodded their approval.

"We will make better time with the wagon," said Tavat. "Are you ready?"

"Yes," said Lare. He shook the reins and Nart took off running. It was as if the garing knew there was danger coming. Tavat, Gannaire, and Jamen flew above the wagon.

There were many other wagons and wingless people on the road, as well as flyers making their way south. It was a mass exodus from Esteryia and the surrounding villages. The smell of smoke was growing stronger. The fear was almost palpable.

They journeyed to the next village. No one there seemed to know what was going on with all the people and wagons passing through. Once they heard that Morren was on the way with an army of undead all bedlam broke loose.

Gannaire wanted to stay and talk to the village elders, but soon realized there was nothing he could do or say that would change anything. They were busy anyway with their own preparations.

By the time the moons set Tavat called a halt for the night. Lare was relieved that Nart was going to get a rest. The garing had faithfully pulled the wagon the whole turn without complaint.

They got off the road and pulled the wagon near the river. Lare unhooked Nart from the wagon. The Malakand hopped down and began making camp while Gannaire and Jamen gathered wood for a fire.

Tavat built the fire and Gannaire channeled a flame to start it. Fessa pulled out her pot and began boiling some roots she had left from her pack. She also cut up some of the dried meat she had saved. With some of the travel bread and fruit they had purchased, they had a satisfying meal.

Tavat and Gannaire sat talking while the others settled down to go to sleep. Other travelers had also stopped for the night and their fires dotted the landscape up and down the riverside.

"I will keep watch first," said Tavat. "I'll wake you when I grow tired."

"You really think it is necessary?" asked Gannaire.

"Yes, I do. We don't know who we can trust," said Tavat as he nocked and arrow just in case. "People are desperate in times like these."

"Yes, I suppose you are right," said Gannaire as he lay down on his bedroll.

"I'll take a second watch," said Lare."

"No, that is alright," said Gannaire. "I'll do it."

"But you don't have a weapon," said Lare.

Gannaire raised his eyebrows and grinned. "Son, I am a Wind Dancer. I am a weapon. I won't have any problems protecting our little group," he said.

"Oh, I forgot," said Lare sheepishly.

"For that matter, so is Jathen," added Gannaire.

"So, you are both Wind Dancers and can use magic?" asked Lare.

"Yes, we are, but every Wind Dancer is not equal. Some have more magic than others," said Gannaire. "I am particularly gifted in the use of fire and water, while Jamen is somewhat gifted in the use of water."

"Tavat has told me about his granddaughter, Ooloo. He says she is extremely gifted in magic," said Lare. "He says she is Ans'Isna, whatever that means."

"Yes, he has told me about her," said Gannaire. "From what he says, she is gifted in all the elements of magic."

"Unfortunately, she was captured by Morren," said Lare.

"Yes, that is unfortunate," said Gannaire. "I wonder what Morren wants with her?"

"I don't know. Wasn't Morren also a Wind Dancer at one time?" asked Lare.

Gannaire sighed, "Yes, he was. He delved into dark magic and it was assumed he was killed by a spell that was too powerful for him," he said. "Apparently, we all assumed wrongly. I was a seventh-level student at Cliffside when he went missing."

"What exactly is dark magic," asked Lare.

"Dark magic involves the use of blood in a spell, or when trying to control another person against his or her will. Both practices are forbidden by the Wind Council," answered Gannaire. "We had better get some rest now."

Lare rolled over and went to sleep almost immediately, but Gannaire found it hard to stop thinking about Morren. He remembered how talented Morren had been. He had also been a good friend of Kerinelle's and Libraen's.

Their friendship had seemed to wane after Libraen and Kerin were life-mated. Rumor had it that he was in love with Kerin, but it had been Libraen who had undergone the Desideratum with her. Morren had been unable to get over it. Then he had elicited their help with the spell that backfired. It was said that he had tricked them into helping him with a blood spell, unknown to the two of them. The whole affair had almost prevented them from becoming Mother and Father, leaders of Cliffside. It would have if they had known the spell Morren used was a blood spell. But they were innocent in that respect and so they ended up at Cliffside after all.

Gannaire hoped they knew by now that Morren was on the way to exact revenge. He wondered what they planned, whether to make a stand or evacuate. If he knew Mother and Father they would stay and fight.

Finally dropping into a deep sleep, it wasn't long before Tavat gently tapped him on the shoulder. He awoke with a start and sat up. Tavat held his finger to his lips, signaling him to be quiet. He had put the fire out and the only light was that of the two moons.

"Someone is trying to sneak into our camp," he whispered quietly. "They are coming from the west, near the road. I have been watching them as they creep through the grass."

"What do you think they want?" asked Gannaire quietly.

"Nothing good. They probably want to steal our wagon or our supplies," whispered Tavat. "It is not too long before sunrise so I think I will wake the others so we can go ahead and get started."

He woke Lare and the three Malakand. Gannaire woke Jamen. They all moved quietly about the camp under the moonlight packing up. Lare harnessed Nart to the wagon and the Malakand climbed in. He walked beside Nart rather than riding on the narrow seat.

Tavat, Gannaire, and Jamen also walked as they approached where Tavat had seen someone in the grass. Tavat held up his hand to signal them to stop.

"Come out now and you won't get hurt," said Tavat loudly.

He heard whispering. He repeated, "Come out of the grass now. That is your last warning."

A wingless man and woman stood slowly with their hands up. They looked frightened. They held no weapons, which Tavat assumed they had dropped in the grass along with their packs.

"Why were you sneaking into our camp," demanded Tavat.

"We were just going to the river," said the woman. "And we didn't want to wake you." The man touched her arm to silence her.

"We were just being careful," said the man. "We saw you with your bow and arrow and we didn't want any trouble."

"Get your belongings and go to the river then," said Gannaire. "We are leaving."

"Can we go with you," pleaded the woman. "There's safety in numbers."

"No, we have enough in our group," said Tavat. "No, move on."

They picked up their packs. The man picked up a small crossbow. Gannaire held up his hands just in case.

"You're Wind Dancers?" asked the man.

"Some of us are. I suggest you be careful with that crossbow unless you want it burned," said Gannaire.

"I know you," said the woman. "You're that priest from the temple in Esteryia."

"Yes, I am. Now do as you were told and kindly move on," said Gannaire. The two of them slowly walked past the group and made their way to the river. The Malakand peeked at them over the edge of the wagon. Lare stepped up on the wagon and sat down. He clucked his tongue and Nart moved off toward the road with Jamen and Gannaire. Tavat stood and watched the man and woman for a while then turned and walked to the road where the rest of the group was slowly moving forward.

The sky was just beginning to lighten as Tavat, Gannaire, and Jamen took to the air. Lare shook the reins and Nart took off running, keeping pace with the flyers. There were only a few others on the road and a few flyers in the air.

When the sun was high in the sky they pulled off the road to stop for a while to rest and to eat. They had a quick meal of travel bread and fruit and then set off again. This time they didn't stop until long after the moons had risen.

They all felt an urgency to get to Cliffside as soon as possible. But the flyers were exhausted and so was Nart. They pulled off the road and made camp by the river again. This time Lare took the first watch. Gannaire relieved him after a while. The night was not disturbed this time and when Tavat awoke early, before sunrise, they set out again.

They continued on with the journey for almost two octurns. When they arrived at the checkpoint to enter the Cavern, Gannaire was elected to do the talking. But the guard just waved them on through without a challenge.

When they entered the Cavern, they were surprised to see that it was practically empty. Very few stores or stalls were occupied by vendors or buyers. Those who were there were packing up their merchandise preparing to leave. Wagonloads of goods were being carted down the mountain through the Cavern.

"This can only mean one thing," said Gannaire. "They know about Morren already."

"The messenger arrived then," said Tavat. He told them about Swen whom they had run into as soon as they had exited the tunnel to Halalouma.

They stopped and Lare said, "This is where we part ways. I must continue on to Algren, where my parents live."

"What about the Ferndorens? Won't they still be looking for you?" asked Tavat.

"Probably, but with Fessa's help, I look entirely different. My own mother wouldn't know me," laughed Lare.

Tavat stepped up to him and clasped him by the upper arm. "I thank you for your help. I owe you my life," said Tavat

"Yes, thank you," said Gormon. "Tavat would have died if you did not help us."

Lare bowed to Fessa and Bicken and shook their scaled hands. Then he shook hands with Gormon. Lastly, he turned to Gannaire and Jamen and clasped each of their arms in farewell.

Everyone retrieved their packs from the back of the wagon as Lare unhooked Nart and saddled him. He waved at the group as they moved on down the pass.

As they wound their way through the Cavern, Tavat told Gannaire about Lynette and Joran and their baby. He also told him about Mattern running into them in the tunnel leading from Halalouma, and his escape when Morren attacked them.

They arrived at the lower end of the Caverns. They came out of the opening and saw the three giant trees of the Cliffside. They were breathtaking, being the largest and oldest trees on Eruna.

"We should go to Central Tree," said Gannaire. "That is where Mother Kerinelle and Father Libraen have their offices. Jamen you stay with the Malakand. Find us somewhere to stay and then meet us at the base of Central Tree at the end of the turn."

Tavat and Gannaire flew toward Central Tree. Below in the square, there were students practicing magic. They were using each element as a weapon. They threw water and fire at targets. Some of them were practicing lifting and tossing large boulders across the grounds.

"There are some of the Wind Council members down there with the students. They are teaching them magic," said Gannaire. "I can hardly believe it. Magic has always been taught at Wind Dancers Ledge, after a pupil has passed the Wind Trials."

Tavat suddenly said, "I see Lynette and Joran working with some of the students." They were using air to throw spears at fantastic speed into dummies. "I should go speak to them."

"No, I need you to go talk to Mother Kerinelle and Father Libraen with me. You need to meet them," said Gannaire.

"Yes, I need their help to save Ooloo," said Tavat.

"Yes, well, let's see what they have to say," said Gannaire.

They landed on the flight platform outside Mother and Father's offices and walked across the limb the door. There were two Wing Guards posted at the door.

"We need to speak with Mother and Father immediately," said Gannaire. "It is an urgent matter concerning the wizard Morren and his plans to attack Cliffside." One of the guards opened the door and ushered them inside.

Mother and Father were sitting at their desks pouring over books and scrolls. There were other books and scrolls strewn about the room. Gannaire could only imagine they were looking for a way to defeat Morren."

Father looked up first and said, "Gannaire, is that you?"

"Yes, it is I, and this is Tavat from the Northern Plateaus," said Gannaire.

Father moved from behind his desk as Mother Kerinelle looked up. "We have heard all about Tavat and his remarkable granddaughter Ooloo," she said.

"You have heard of Ooloo?" asked Tavat.

"Yes, Lynette and Joran arrived over two octurns ago and told us how you met up in Halalouma. They also warned us about Morren's plans to attack Cliffside," said Father. "Won't you have a seat? There is much we need to discuss." He led them to a side room containing a couch and two armchairs in front of a fireplace. Wood was laid out for a fire and Mother waved her hand over it as Tavat and Gannaire sat down on the couch. The fire came to life and Mother sat in one of the armchairs while Father sat in the other.

"Now, please call us Kerin and Libraen. We don't stand on formality anymore, considering..." said Father Libraen.

Kerin picked up a bell and shook it. Nona came into the room from a side door and said, "You rang, Mother?"

"Yes, please bring some keris for us and our guests," said Kerin. "Oh, and some of those cookies Father likes."

"Yes, ma'am," said Nona as she exited the room. She returned a short while later with the keris and the cookies. She sat the tray down on the table in front of Tavat and Gannaire. Kerin poured the keris and passed the cup and saucer to them. They had hardly stopped talking since they had sat down.

Tavat told them about Ooloo being captured. Lynette and Joran had not seen what happened to her since she sent them to the world of dreams.

"I need your help to get her back from Morren," said Tavat.

"Of course, we will do everything within our power to get her back to you safely. But our main concern is to defeat Morren," said Libraen.

# CHAPTER 18
# JENEN

Lare rode out of the Caverns on Nart as fast as he could go. Avoiding the main roads, he rode on until late into the night by the light of the two moons. It would still be an octurn before he made it home to Tree Ferndoren in Algren. First, he had to ride through the Realms of Soedeen, then Kernoeryl, and finally into Algren. He had to cross the Algren River, which divided the Eight Realms into four Realms each. Tree Ferndoren was a minor Tree in the western portion of Algren near Felder's Field and Lake Ferndoren.

It had been over a cycle since he had accidentally killed Master Ferndoren. His father had helped him escape, and now he was coming home from the Northern Provinces where he had been hiding out.

He had grown taller, and he had a full beard and longer hair now. And the Malakand female, Fessa, had helped him permanently color his skin darker with some concoction she had made from a plant. He thought even his parents would not recognize him, much less the Ferndoren Wing Guards or soldiers of the High Matriarch.

Besides, they had probably given up on finding him since it had been so long. Ferndoren Wing Guards had apprehended him in Erboer, but he had managed to escape and had immediately headed south with Tavat and the Malakand. For all the soldiers knew, he was still in the Northern Provinces somewhere. He didn't think they would be looking for him in Algren.

Several turns later he stopped by the Algren River in Kernoeryl and unsaddled Nart. He tied him to a small tree by the river where there were plenty of river grasses for Nart to eat. He decided not to build a fire because it might attract unwanted visitors. Eating some travel bread, he settled down for the rest of the night. He lay back on his saddle and soon went to sleep.

He had an uneventful night and woke shortly after the sun rose. After saddling Nart he headed south along the river to the crossing into Algren. There were other people on the road, some on foot and others on wagons or riding garing. Border guards were there and he already had a story prepared.

"Halt," shouted the guard and holding a hand up when Lare rode Nart up to the guard shack. "State your business."

"I'm from the Northern Provinces and I've come to set up a trade for my master with Tree Ferndoren," said Lare.

"What kind of trade," asked the guard.

"We have wood and they make finished products...furniture and such," answered Lare. "My master wishes to trade his wood for their furniture."

"Where are your papers?" asked the guard.

"I was robbed in Soedeen. They took my pack with everything in it," said Lare. "Fortunately, I had my master's money in my boot and they didn't get that. I had to replace my pack and buy more supplies in Kernoeryl."

"Do you know who it was that robbed you?" asked the guard.

"Just some other Grubs, sir," answered Lare. "They took everything, even my bow, and quiver. I had to replace it all."

"That's tough luck," said the guard sympathetically. "You can pass. Just try to avoid getting robbed again. You should be okay as long as you stay on the road going toward Algren City. Tree Ferndoren is not too far from the main road. Move on." He waved Lare through the checkpoint.

Lare rode past the guard shack and smiled. That had been easier than he thought it would be. He made good time and stopped in central Algren not far from the road just before sundown. He had another uneventful evening and rose early with the sun. By the end of the turn, he arrived at Tree Ferndoren.

He rode up to Tree Ferndoren and around the roots until he came to the house where he hoped his parents still lived.

The sun was just setting but he could see that the place looked a little run down. The fence was down in some places. He put Nart in the little barn and unsaddled him. He tossed the saddle over the fence and checked the trough to see that there was plenty of water in it. Then he walked to the back door of the house.

He knocked on the door until someone answered it. An old woman opened the door and said, "Yes, can I help you?" She looked older and frailer than Lare remembered. There were dark circles under her eyes.

"Ma?" said Lare. "It's me, Lare. I'm back...from the Northern Provinces."

The woman put her hand to her throat in alarm. "Lare?" she asked. "Is it really you?" She grabbed one of his arms and pulled him into the house.

"What are you doing here?"

She stepped outside and looked around to see if anyone had seen him. Then she slammed the door and threw her arms around Lare. She started crying.

"Lare? Look at you, a full beard and a head taller, and you're so dark," said Aina. "We hoped you had gotten away. We were so happy when some traders brought news about you. That must have been almost a cycle ago. How have you been son?"

"I've been alright. Where's Pa? Isn't he back from work yet?" he asked.

"Oh, you must be hungry. There's plenty of time for questions. Are you hungry Lare? It's about time for last-meal. Just let me set the table," she chattered away.

He grabbed her by the shoulders and she began to cry again. "Ma, where is Pa? He should be home from work by now," he said adamantly.

"Oh Lare, they came and took him shortly after Eigurn," she said.

"Who took him? The Ferndoren Guard?" he asked.

"Yes," she sobbed. "When they couldn't find you they took him for questioning..."

"Where did they take him?" he asked, gently shaking her.

"They took him to the cells under the Tree, and...and..." she broke down sobbing again.

Lare put his arms around his mother and hugged her to his chest. "What happened?" he asked, fearing he already knew the answer.

"They tortured him, Lare, but he never told them anything. First, they broke all his fingers," she said. "Then when he still didn't talk, they broke his legs. But he never said where you were."

"Then what happened?" he asked, tears streaming down his face.

"They let him go. I brought him home, but infection set in. I tried to save him, but he died just after mid-cycle," she said. "I think he just gave up. He could no longer play the bolairea, you see. Oh Lare, I'm so sorry."

"You have nothing to be sorry about, Ma. I'm the one who is sorry," said Lare. "I never should have left." He paced back and forth, fuming. "It's all my fault. I never should have left."

"No, no...you can't blame yourself," she said. "The Ferndorens are to blame.

"Blast the Ferndorens," said Lare vehemently.

He led his mother to the kitchen table and they both sat down. He took both of her small, frail hands in his big, rough hands as she continued to cry. Sorrow had made her so frail. They both sat there crying. Eventually, they stopped.

"You must be hungry," she said suddenly. She used her apron to wipe her tear-stained face. "It's time for last-meal." She got up from the table and went to the fireplace. She hung a pot over the fire. "Let me just warm this over."

"Well, I could eat," said Lare.

"You always could eat, any time of the turn," she sniffed. She set plates, cups, and utensils on the table and before long they were eating.

"Tell me everything that has happened to you since you left," said Aina.

Lare talked for hours and before long it was late into the night. He told his mother about Morren and the coming war with Cliffside, and about his friendship with Tavat and the Malakand. Finally, he asked the question that had been burning in his heart.

"How is Jen?" he asked.

Aina wouldn't look at him at first. She got up from the table and took the dishes to the sink. He began to fear the worst.

"Ma, she's not dead too..."

She turned around and looked at him. "No, no, nothing like that," she said.

Lare got up from the kitchen table and went over to his mother.He took her by the shoulders. "Then what, Ma? What has happened to Jenen?" he asked.

"Oh Lare, I'm so sorry. Jenen is married," she answered as she looked into his eyes sadly.

Lare felt that he couldn't breathe. The shock of losing his father had broken his heart, and now finding out that Jenen was married opened the wound all over again. He stumbled back over to the table and plopped down in a chair. He laid his head down on the table, but he couldn't cry...not anymore. He was so weary.

"Whom did she marry?" he finally asked. "It wasn't Bose was it?" Bose was his best friend, so in a way it would have been alright if Jenen had married Bose.

"No, it wasn't Bose," said Aina. "It was a boy from Tree Costera. Norn is his name. His sister Nalla and Jenen became friends and then Norn and Jenen began to spend a lot of time together. They've only been married a few octurns."

"Nalla. I remember meeting her at the dance at Felder's Field," said Lare. He rubbed his face.

"Lare, Jenen thought you were gone for good," said Aina.

"I came back for her," said Lare. "I was going to secretly give her the betrothal chain and ask her to wait for me until after the war with Morren. Then I was going to take her to the Northern Provinces with me..."

"Oh son, I'm so sorry," she said and sat down next to him at the table. She placed her hand on his clenched fists, which were clasped tightly in front of him. Finally, he relaxed.

"Do you want your betrothal chain back?" he asked. "I've got no use for it now." He pulled the chain out of his backpack and held it up to her.

"No, son. You keep it," she said. "You will meet another girl one day. Then you'll need it." She pushed his hand away and patted it.

"I need to see her," he said.

"Do you think that's a good idea?" asked Aina.

"I have to, Ma," he answered. "Does she live at Tree Costera?"

"Yes, they have a little place between the north and northeastern roots. Bose knows where it is," said Aina.

"Then I'll go see Bose before the sun rises and get him to show me where she lives," he said.

"Then where will you go? You can't stay here," said Aina.

He thought for a moment. "I'll go to Cliffside. I'll help fight Morren and then go back to the Northern Provinces. You could go with me. I could come back and get you after the war," he said.

"No, Lare. Thank you...but, no. This is my home. I wouldn't know what to do with myself in the North."

"How are you making a living here?" he asked.

"Oh, Rena got me some work making bread for some of the lesser families of Tree Ferndoren.," she said. "I do alright." Rena was Bose's mother and she worked for several families in Tree Ferndoren, supplying them with bread and other baked goods.

"I've still got some Gren," he said as he pulled out his money pouch and tried to give her some.

"No, I don't need it, Lare," she insisted. "You keep it to make a new start-up North."

"Are you sure, Ma?" he asked. "I've got plenty. I've hardly spent any of it since I left. All I've really bought is a saddle for Nart."

"I'm sure," she said. She patted his hands reassuringly. "Are you sure you have to leave in the morning?"

"Yes, I'm putting you in danger by being here," he said.

"I doubt anyone will recognize you. You look like you're from one of the desert tribes from the Western Wastelands," she said laughing. "I just wish we had more time."

"Me too," said Lare. "But I need to leave well before sunrise."

"Could we talk a little more? Tell me more about all the people you've met," she said. "I'll put on a pot of keris." She got up from the table and went back to the fireplace to put the kettle on. "You know, Bose got married last cycle."

"What? Bose got married? Who would have him?" he asked, but he had a pretty good idea. "Who did he marry?"

"Why, Nalla, of course," she said. "They live with Rena. They seem to be quite happy."

"Well, how about that," laughed Lare.

They talked for a few more hours. Lare yawned several times and so did Aina.

Eventually, she said, "I guess we should get some rest if you are going to leave before sunrise. Your room is just as you left it."

"Thanks, Ma," said Lare, yawning again. "I'll see you in a few hours." He stumbled sleepily off to his old room and plopped down on the bed. He didn't even bother to take his boots off. He was asleep almost instantly.

Aina followed him a few moments later. She stood in the doorway watching him. She went into the bedroom and pulled his boots off. Then she got out a quilt and threw it over him. By then he was snoring peacefully.

She went back out to the kitchen table and poured herself another cup of keris. There would be no sleeping for her tonight. She sat quietly drinking keris until it was time to wake Lare. She cooked breakfast and then went to wake him.

She went into his room and gently shook is shoulder. He awakened with a groan and sat up.

"Something smells good," he said.

"Your breakfast is ready," said Aina as she wiped her hands on her apron and smiled. "It's almost like old times." Then she turned and went back into the kitchen before Lare could see her sad expression.

"Thanks, Ma, I'll be right out." Lare put his boots on and got up off the bed. He went into the kitchen and sat down at the table.

His mother poured him a cup of keris and then set a plate of food before him. She sat down across from him to watch him eat.

"Aren't you going to eat?" he asked.

"Oh, I already ate," she said. "Do you want some more griddle cakes?"

"Yes, please," he said. He ate two more helpings of griddle cakes and drank three cups of keris before he was done. He enjoyed the meal immensely. He knew it would probably be the last-meal he would ever eat in his home.

He hated to leave his mother, but it was time to go. He went to the barn and saddled Nart.

His mother came out to see him off. She handed him some travel bread, still warm from the oven, wrapped in a clean dishtowel. He put the bread in his backpack and hung the backpack from his saddle. Then he turned to his mother and put his arms around her. She started crying again.

"Ma, I gotta go now," he said. "I'll try to send word to you after the war and when I get settled." He squeezed her tightly one more time and then turned away and mounted Nart.

"Goodbye, son, I love you," she said. She held her apron wadded up in her hands.

"Goodbye, Ma. I love you too," he said.

He turned Nart and rode off to Bose's house. It only took him a few minutes to get there. When he went around back to tie up Nart, he noticed a garing there, tied to the fence. The two garing sniffed at each other, but that was all. They should be okay together.

He tied Nart to the fence next to the other garing and walked around to the front of the house. He knocked on the rough wooden door. Several minutes passed. He knocked again finally someone cracked the door.

Bose stood there holding a knife in one hand and a lantern in the other, peering out at him. "What do you want?" he asked. "The sun is not even up. Don't you know what time it is, stranger?"

"I'm no stranger, Bose. It's me...Lare," said Lare.

"Nah...nah...it can't be," said Bose as he opened the door all the way. He stood there staring at Lare. "Is it really you, Lare?"

"Yep, it's me," said Lare. "Back from the North."

"Well, come in, come in. Don't just stand there," said Bose. He ushered Lare into the house and shut the door. "Nalla, come out here. It's Lare, my old friend."

A young woman came out of Bose's bedroom wrapping a robe around her very pregnant frame. She smiled shyly at Lare. "I remember your name, from the dance," she said. "But you look different with the beard and the tan. I wouldn't recognize you except for the eyes and the smile."

"I remember you too, Nalla," said Lare. "But you've changed too." He looked at her large waist. "My mother forgot to mention that."

She laughed and patted her belly, "Yes, but soon I'll get my figure back."

Bose went to stand beside her. He put his arm around her and grinned. He looked extremely pleased with himself.

Just then Rena, Bose's mother came out of the other bedroom and said, "I thought I heard Lare's voice," she said sleepily. "Oh my, who is this?"

She stared at Lare for a moment, "It is you. I knew I heard, Lare," she said smiling. She walked over to Lare and gave him a big hug. "Have you seen your mother yet?"

"Yes, ma'am," said Lare. "I just came from there. She told me about Pa and everything. She told me Bose was married, but not about the baby." He grinned at Rena. She smiled back at him.

"Yes, a few octurns from now I'll be a grandmother," said Rena happily.

"Oh, I don't think it will be that long," said Nalla. "At least, I hope not." She stretched and put her hands on her back. Then she and Bose walked over to the kitchen table. Bose pulled out a chair for her and she sat down with difficulty.

"Sit, please," said Rena to Lare. "I'll make pot of keris."

"No, thank you. I need to talk to Bose...um, in private," said Lare.

"Oh...oh, alright," said Rena. "Nalla, why don't we go back to bed? It's too early for me and I know you need to prop up your feet."

She walked over, helped Nalla get up from the chair, and walked her back to bedroom. She propped several pillows up at the foot of the bed and Nalla placed her swollen ankles on them. Rena shut the door and the two women started talking.

Meanwhile, Lare and Bose sat at the table to talk. "What's up, Lare?" asked Bose. "What do you want to talk about?"

"I want you to show me where Jenen lives," said Lare. "I want to see her."

Bose rubbed the back of his neck and looked at Lare with his eyebrows raised. "You know she is married now," he said. "It's only been three octurns since the wedding."

"Yes, I know. Ma told me. I have to see her Bose, to see that she's alright...and happy. Then I'll go away again," said Lare. "Are you gonna help me or not?"

"Well, I don't know," said Bose shaking his head. "Their place is over at Tree Costera."

"I know," said Lare. He got up from the table and began to pace back and forth. "I just want to say hello. I'm going to Cliffside to help the Wind Dancers fight against an evil wizard named Morren. I may even die, Bose. I don't want to die without seeing Jenen one more time."

"I heard some talk, but I thought it was just rumor," said Bose. "So, it's true then?"

"Yes, it is true. Now are you going to help me or not?" asked Lare impatiently.

"Yes, yes, I'll help you, but I don't think Norn is going to like it," protested Bose.

"I'll wait until he leaves and goes to work," assured Lare. "He doesn't have to know I was ever there."

"Well the sun will be up soon," said Bose looking out the window. "We better leave if we're going to be there to see that Norn goes to work."

Bose got up and went to the bedroom to tell his wife and mother that he was going to be gone for a couple of hours. He didn't tell them where he was going and they didn't ask.

"Be careful, Bose," said his wife.

Lare and Bose walked out the door and around the house to where the garing were tied to the fence. "So, when did you get a garing?" asked Lare. He picked up his saddle.

"It was a wedding present from Nalla's father," said Bose. "I think he felt sorry for me. And, Nalla gave me the saddle."

"Well, she's a fine garing. What did you name her?" asked Lare as he saddled Nart. He could see that the garing was female.

"Persa, I named her Persa," said Bose. "If you hadn't disappeared I could have mated her with Nart. He put the saddle on the garing and tightened the cinches. Then he mounted and they were ready to go.

They took off at a trot in the direction of Tree Costa. "So, why did you disappear?" asked Bose after a few minutes. "You didn't even say goodbye."

Lare told him about the accident and about what he and his father had done with the body. "I couldn't say goodbye to anyone," said Lare. "I had to get away before Master Ferndoren was missed."

"So that was why the Ferndorens took your father," said Bose, understanding at last why Earel had been tortured. "I'm really sorry that he died, Lare, real sorry. It was awful what they did to him."

Lare winced and looked away. "I know. Ma told me about his hands and all," he said.

They continued on in silence for a while "Look if you want to send letters to my house for your mother, I'd see that she gets them," said Bose trying to think of a way he could help his friend.

"That would be great," said Lare. "I'll use the name Bram Vendal. In fact, that's going to be my name from now on. As far as the Ferndorens are concerned Lare Bren is dead."

They soon came to Tree Costera, and circled around to the northern and northeastern roots where Jenen and Norn lived. Dismounting from their garing, they tied the animals to a small tree in the woods away from the cottage and walked toward it. But they stayed in the woods as they drew near.

They found a good hiding spot from which to watch the cottage and settled down to wait. By now, the sun had risen and before long, they were getting anxious.

After several more minutes, Norn exited the cottage and walked around to the back of the cottage. He came back around to the front again leading a male garing.

Jenen came out the door, handed him a sack, which was most likely his lunch, and kissed him. Then he mounted the garing and took off down the road. Jenen stood watching him for a few minutes.

Lare and Bose stood up from their hiding place and walked towards her. She looked alarmed at first and said, "Wha...what do you want?" Then she noticed one of the men was Bose.

"Bose, I swear, you scared the living lights out of me," she scolded and punched Bose in the arm. Then she noticed the stranger with him. "Who is this?" He looked familiar but she couldn't place where she had seen him.

"It's me, Jen. It's Lare," he said.

She stepped back from them and shook her head. "It can't be..." she started to say. But then she looked into his blue eyes and she knew. It was Lare Jensen.

"Oh Lare, we thought you were dead," she cried. "I'm so sorry..." then she started crying.

"You don't have anything to worry about," said Lare soothingly.

"Um, I'll go now," said Bose uncomfortably. He held out his hand to Lare. They shook hands at first, and then they hugged each other and patted each other on the back.

"Take care, Bose," said Lare. "And check on my mother for me from time to time. I don't think I will be back this way any time soon."

"I will, Lare...er, I mean Bram," said Bose, using his new name. "You take care. I'll be looking for your letters."

"Thanks, Bose. Goodbye," said Lare as Bose walked into the woods where they had tied the garing.

Lare turned back to Jenen. Tears were streaming down her face. She swiped at her face with her apron and finally stopped crying.

"Won't you come in, Lare?" she asked and looked around. "Someone might see you, not that they would recognize you." She gave a little laugh and led him into the cottage.

"Have a seat at the table while I put the kettle on," she said. She hung the kettle over the fire and then sat down across from Lare. "I think you owe me an explanation," she said finally.

"Yes, I certainly do," agreed Lare. He told her about why he'd had to go away and about all the adventures he had had since leaving as they drank cup after cup of keris. Hours passed and Lare realized it was time for him to leave.

"Jen, I just want to know if you are happy," said Lare.

"Yes, I am happy," said Jenen. "After you left I didn't think I'd ever be happy again, but then Norn started courting me, and then..." she left the sentence hanging.

"Do you love him, Jen? Is he good to you?" asked Lare.

"Yes, to both questions," she said smiling. "We are going to start a family next cycle," she said. Lare looked uncomfortable so she changed the subject.

She laid her hand on Lare's big hands. "I am so sorry about your father," she said.

"Thank you, I am too," he said, his face darkening.

"What are you going to do now?" she asked. "Where will you go?"

"From here I'm going to Cliffside. I'm going to help the Wind Dancers defeat the wizard and his army of undead soldiers," he said.

"So, the rumors are true?" she asked. "No one is supposed to talk about it, by order of the High Matriarch."

"Yes, it's true. I have just enough time to get to Cliffside before he attacks," he said. "I'd better be going..."

They both stood and Lare held out his hand. But Jenen ignored it and threw her arms around him. She hugged him fiercely and he hugged her back. He breathed in the smell of her hair for the last time. She pulled back from him, stood on her tiptoes and kissed his cheek.

They both had tears in their eyes when they parted. He turned on his heel and walked out the door. He made his way quickly to the woods where he had tied Nart. He untied and mounted him.

He rode long into the night planning how he was going to hunt down and kill every Ferndoren Wing Guard he could find, starting with the one who had tortured his father. It hurt too much to think about Jenen.

# CHAPTER 19
# PLANS

Swen and two members of the Wing Guard from Cliffside crept slowly through the grass so as not to be seen by Morren's soldiers. They had been sent to spy out Morren's armies and get a closer estimate as to when the attack on Cliffside might occur.

They were on a hill above Esteryia looking down on the destruction wrought by Morren and his dragon. Large portions of the tree city were on fire and many of the citizens had been rounded up and forced into servitude or made into undead. The rest were killed.

Swen and his men also estimated troop strength and observed tactics. Soon it would be time to return to Cliffside and make their report. But first, they had to get close enough to check on the young winglet, Ooloo whom Morren had captured. Mother Kerinelle and Father Libraen had promised her grandfather, Tavat, that they would bring word of her condition.

They froze as two guards walked past their position. Fortunately, they were not spotted. Swen decided it would be best if the two other men stayed back while he crept forward to check on Ooloo.

He slowly made his way down the hill toward the wagon where she was kept when she wasn't training with Morren or riding the big, black dragon into battle with him. It was almost time for sunset and Swen was hoping to use the cover of darkness to slip into the camp and try to get close enough to the wagon without being detected.It was supposed to be a dark night due to the cycle of the moons. It was now or never if Swen was going to talk to Ooloo.

He stood and slipped into the camp. He sprinted past tents and campfires, just outside the light, where members of Morren's regular army sat eating, smoking, or sharpening their weapons. Soon he made his way to Ooloo's wagon and peered between the bars of the small window.

"Ooloo...can you hear me?" he whispered.

"Who's there?" she asked. She stood and looked out the window. She was careful not to touch it.

"My name is Swen and I am from Cliffside," he said. "If I can get the door open I can get you out of here."

"You can't help me," she said forlornly. "Morren keeps me chained and the door and windows are spelled. I can't touch them without great pain. You need to get out of here before you are caught."

"Your grandfather, Tavat, is at Cliffside and is worried about you," he said.

"My grandfather is alive, then?" she asked.

"Yes, he is and he is going to get you back somehow," said Swen.

A group of soldiers came in their direction. Swen quickly crawled under the wagon until they passed. When they were gone he crawled back up to the window.

"Ooloo...is there anything you can tell me that would help us defeat Morren or his armies?" asked Swen.

"You can only defeat the undead by stabbing them in the heart. I suppose you could destroy them by burning them to a crisp, just as long as you destroy their hearts..." she said.

"What about Morren? How can he be defeated?"

"Morren? He can only be defeated by magic," she said. "I am going to kill him and the demon who has been helping him the first chance I get."

"What demon?" he asked.

"Saarnak is the demon's name," she replied. "I am going to kill them both."

"Are you sure you can't escape somehow?" Swen asked.

"Yes, I am sure," she said. "Go now. Tell my grandfather that I am as well as can be expected. The warriors who came with us are captives too, except for Batab. She has been made...undead."

"What about Hanoera and Kevar?" he asked.

"I do not know for sure, but they are probably undead too," she said sadly.

"Have courage, Ooloo. Mother Kerinelle and Father Libraen will help you escape somehow," said Swen reassuringly. "And I'm sure they will find a way to save your warrior friends and Hanoera and Kevar. Stay strong. May the Winds bless you, Ooloo."

Then he slipped away into the darkness as she watched from the small window. He made his way back to his men. They crept farther back up the hill and flew away toward Cliffside. It would take almost an octurn for them to return, even though they would fly almost around the clock.

After Swen left, Ooloo sat down on her pallet in the wagon and cried in frustration. Before long Morren came to the wagon and opened the door.

He stepped inside and unlocked the chain holding her to the floor. Then he took off her collar and bracelets and led her out of the wagon, all without saying a word.

"What do you want now?" she asked defiantly.

"It's time for your training," said Morren.

Ooloo sighed and asked, "So what is it you think you can teach me now? I've already learned how to use all of the elements. What else is there?"

"Now I am going to teach you how to use combinations of the elements," said Morren.

"What do you mean?" asked Ooloo curiously, in spite of herself.

"Well, for example, you can freeze water with air, like this," he responded. He pulled moisture from the air and then froze it into spears of ice. He heaved a spear at one of the undead soldiers. It caught the soldier in the heart and he dropped to the ground. As he fell, he screamed and a red light came out of his mouth and then dissipated.

Ooloo was not impressed. "What about this..." she asked. She conjured a bolt of lightning and threw it at Morren. Before it could get to him he threw up a barrier. She continued to throw bolt after bolt at him, screaming in fury.

"Stop it, Ooloo, or I will hurt your friends," he said. "When will you learn you cannot defeat me?"

She stopped and stared at him. "I thought you left them back at the fortress," she said.

"You thought wrong," he said smugly. "Come with me." He grabbed her by the arm and walked her across the campground toward the burning city. They came to a large barred wagon, and inside it sat five of the warriors who had accompanied her and Tavat from the Northern Plateaus.

Morren raised his hand and Conoc began convulsing in pain. "Ans'Isna, do not cooperate with this devil, no matter what," said Kivik. "Conoc is a strong warrior and he is prepared to die."

Morren squeezed his hand and Conoc began to choke. He started turning blue and Ooloo knew it was only a matter of time before he died. She could not allow this. She would not be responsible for another's death. She still remembered and felt responsible for what Morren had done to Batab.

"But he is killing Conoc," said Ooloo, tears streaming down her face. "Stop, Morren, please. I won't do it again, I promise."

Morren unclenched his fist and Conoc stopped convulsing and gasped. He put his hands to his throat and took several deep breaths. "Ooloo, do not cooperate with this devil, even if he kills every one of us," said Conoc once he could speak. "You must resist him."

"I can't just let you die or become undead like Batab," she sobbed.

"Enough," said Morren. "There is someone else I want you to see." He led her to his tent and pulled back the flap. He pushed her into the tent and she fell to her knees.

There in the center of the tent was a pedestal with the familiar large black orb sitting on it. Morren waved his hand over the orb and a small window opened on it.

Saarnak smiled down at Ooloo who was still on her knees. "You," she said. "I thought we left you behind and I wouldn't have to see your ugly face for awhile."

"Saarnak laughed and said, "Still defiant, I see. Morren, she is almost ready. I sense the power in her. It won't be long now."

"What won't be long?" asked Ooloo. "What are you talking about?"

"You are going to help Morren with a task," said Saarnak.

"I will never help Morren with any task," said Ooloo. "I will die first."

"No, you won't," assured Saarnak. "I will not allow it. And you will have no choice but to help me. You will see." Then he laughed again.

Ooloo got to her feet and turned her back on Saarnak. "I want to leave," she said.

"Now we must get back to your lessons," said Morren. He grabbed Ooloo by the arm again and marched her back across the camp.

Morren continued with her training late into the night. He forced her to try multiple combinations of elements over and over. By the time Ooloo was returned to her wagon she was exhausted. She laid on her pallet with the collar around her neck, chained to the floor of the wagon. The hated bracelets were back on her wrists. She finally dropped into a dreamless sleep.

***

Mother Kerinelle was sitting in her office when Nona knocked on the door. She put down the document she was studying and said, "Come in."

Nona came into the office and handed her a note. Kerinelle opened it and read it immediately. It was marked "Urgent." Her expression darkened perceptively.

"Who gave you this message?" she asked.

"A messenger from the Messenger Station...I think it was Dorianaire," said Nona. "He wanted to deliver it to you directly, but I assured him that I would hand deliver it to you myself. He just left. Do you need to speak to him? I might be able to stop him."

"No, but I will have to leave for a bit. It seems I have a large, mysterious package at the Messenger Station. They want me to come and claim it personally," said Kerinelle. "This is very unusual."

She got up from her desk and went to find Libraenaire. She practically ran into his manservant, Cullen, just outside the office. He was coming to find her with a message from Libraen.

"Father Libraenaire is in the Great Library, in the ancient manuscripts section, and needs to see you immediately," said Cullen.

"Well, I need to see him," said Kerinelle. "Can you please tell him to meet me at the flight platform just outside the Great Library? It is urgent."

"Yes, Mother," said Cullen, who turned to do her bidding.

Kerinelle got to the platform before Libraen and paced back and forth impatiently. She had a very bad feeling about the message she had received.

Libraenaire came out to the platform. "What is so urgent, my dear?" he asked. "Cullen was adamant that you needed to see me immediately."

"I've received a message from the Messenger Station," she said. "It seems that Gwendelle has sent me a large package. For some reason they want me to claim it personally."

"Isn't she your agent, one of the High Matriarch's ladies-in-waiting?" he asked. "What could she possibly be sending you? Don't you think this a little suspicious?"

"Yes, she is and yes I think it is suspicious. I have a very bad feeling..." said Kerinelle. "I want you to come with me to the Station to have a look at this package."

She leapt into the air and Libraen leapt after her. They both flew in the direction of the Messenger Station where the package was located.

They went through the door and they immediately knew there was a problem. There was a terrible smell emanating from the station's back section, where all the packages were delivered.

"Oh, Great Wind!" said Kerinelle. "That is clearly the smell of death."

"Yes, it is," said Libraenaire.

The Station Manager, Norven, came out of the back with a handkerchief over his nose. He looked ill.

In addition to working as a Station Manager, he also worked for Mother and Father, routing specially marked or coded messages and packages to them. But this package was different.

"Mother, Father, I knew immediately that I could not deliver this package to Cliffside," he said. "Come with me."

He turned and led them to the back section. He pointed to a large wooden box sitting on the floor. "This is it," said Norven. He stepped back to let them get a closer look.

"Open it," said Kerinelle.

"Mother, are you sure?" Norven asked.

"Yes, she is sure," answered Father Libranaire, stony-faced.

Norven picked up a hammer and began pulling nails. When he was done he lifted the lid. In the box was the now bloated body of Gwendelle.

Mother and Father each covered their noses with a hand and stepped back. Norven hurriedly ran to the front door and proceeded to retch.

"She has gone too far," said Kerinelle, seething.

Libraen didn't need to ask whom she was talking about. He knew she meant the High Matriarch.

"We will deal with the High Matriarch accordingly when the crisis with Morren is over," said Libraen. He put his arm around Kerinelle's shoulder and led her out of the station.

"Norven, please reseal the box and deliver it to the bottom of Central Tree immediately. We are going to prepare a funeral pyre for her. We intend to give her the honor she is due," said Kerinelle.

Norven had stopped throwing up and wiped his mouth with his handkerchief. He returned to the back of the shop and resealed the box as Mother and Father flew back to Central Tree.

It was almost sunset before the funeral pyre was ready. Several Wind Dancers gently lifted Glendelle's body from the opened box and placed her on the pyre.

Kerinelle turned and looked at the students and Wind Dancers who were gathered to honor Glendelle. There was much she wanted to say, but she kept it brief.

"T'Rostyr Glendelle was one of my agents," she said, knowing that the admission would somehow reach the ears of the High Matriarch. "That is the reason she is dead. She served me well and I promise her death will be avenged. That is all I can tell you for your own safety."

Kerinelle channeled a flame and set the pyre on fire. As the wood went up in flames all the students and Wind Dancers began to chant in unison.

"Flame to the Wind, Wind to the Sky, Sky to the Heavens. Born of the Ashes, Death to Life, Ash in the Wind, Ash in the Wind," they chanted over and over.

Everyone stayed, honoring Glendelle, until nothing but ash was left. Then the ever-present wind of Eruna blew the ashes to the heavens.

The following turn Master Haddon and Wind Mistress Brena sat in the salon in Central Tree with Mother Kerinelle and Father Libraen. They had just finished mid-meal and were discussing the upcoming battle with Morren. They had been feverishly preparing ever since word came that they only had three octurns before he attacked.

Wind Dancers from all over the Eight Realms had been arriving at Cliffside in a steady stream. The students at Cliffside had been learning how to fight with their magical skills.

The Wind Dancers joined Lynette, Joran, and the members of the Wind Council in teaching the students. A few minor accidents had occurred, but the injured parties had been healed and they had gone back to training almost immediately.

Tavat had been busy supervising the making of bows, arrows, and spears. Gannaire taught several of the students how to rune and spell the weapons so they would be more effective in taking out the undead. The only way to stop an undead soldier was to shoot or stab him in the heart. Tavat also trained as many students as he could in how to effectively use the bow and the spears.

Those at Cliffside were doing everything they could to prepare for Morren's attack. They sincerely hoped it would be enough to defeat him.

Mother Kerinelle had sent the commander of the Wing Guard, Swen, to scout out where Morren was currently located. Swen had just returned and was giving them his report.

"I went as far as the southern outskirts of Esteryia. The whole city seemed to burning and Morren and his forces were still heading this way. I estimate that he will be here in an octurn unless he stops for some reason," he reported.

"Were you able to make contact with the winglet, Ooloo?" asked Mother Kerinelle.

"Yes, I was," said Swen. "When she is not being trained by the wizard she is kept locked up in a wagon. He makes her wear a collar and chain, and some kind of bracelets that prevent her from using her powers when she is not being trained."

"She is being trained?" asked Wind Master Haddon incredulously.

"Yes," said Swen. "As far as I could tell Morren is training her in the use of the four elements. He also makes her ride with him on his dragon sometimes as he burns down the giant trees. Almost all the trees in Esteryia have been burned."

"Great Wind," said Mother Kerinelle. "It's worse than we thought. That poor winglet, we must do everything we can to get her away from him."

"What of the citizens of Esteryia?" asked Wind Mistress Brena.

"Some of them have agreed to serve Morren. Those who refused are being turned into the undead or killed," said Swen.

"Yes, it is much worse than we thought," said Father Libraen. "We have to get Ooloo away from Morren before he completely destroys her."

"What about the destruction of Erboer and Esteryia?" asked Master Haddon.

"Aren't you concerned?"

"Of course we are," said Kerinelle. "But there is little we can do about it now. We must continue to prepare as best we can."

"How are the students doing in their lessons?" asked Libraen.

"They have exceeded all of our expectations," said Master Haddon. "I am extremely impressed with Lynette's and Joran's abilities as teachers. And we are fortunate that so many Wind Dancers have answered the call to come to our aide. Overall, I would say we are almost prepared for the attack."

"How are Lynette and Joran holding up?" asked Kerinelle. "There has been no sign of Mattern and their winglet."

"They are both worried sick, but that is not preventing them from doing their best to prepare the students for the upcoming battle," said Mistress Brena. "I cannot imagine what they must be going through."

Tavat came into the salon then. He was out of breath. He had been running ever since he heard that Swen had returned from his scouting mission. He had wanted to go on the mission with Swen, but Libraen and Kerinelle had talked him out if it. He would have gotten himself killed trying to rescue Ooloo.

"How is Ooloo?" he gasped between breaths. "Is she alright?"

"Yes, she is alive and well," answered Libraen.

"But what is happening to her?" Tavat asked. "What does the wizard want with her?"

"She is being trained," answered Swen without thinking. He realized his mistake when he saw Libraen's face.

"She is being trained in the use of her magic," amended Libraen as he glared at Swen.

"Where is she being held?" asked Tavat.

Swen repeated what he had told the others. Tavat was furious that she was being treated so callously.

"I will kill this Morren when I get the chance," said Tavat through gritted teeth.

"You will have to stand in line," said Swen. "Your granddaughter said she is going to kill him and the demon, Saarnak. And I believe her."

"Then may the Great Wind give her the strength," said Tavat. "For if she doesn't kill them, I will."

"Tavat, we will do what we can to rescue her," assured Kerinelle. "But it will have to be at the right time."

"For now, we must discuss our plans to defeat Morren," said Master Haddon. "I think it would be best if we set a trap for him in the Caverns. He must pass through them to get to Cliffside."

"Yes, if we can stop him there then maybe we can save Cliffside," agreed Kerinelle. "What do you think Libraen?"

"I think we need to prepare defenses at both the Caverns and Cliffside," said Libraen. "What is it you propose, Haddon?"

"When Morren leads his armies into the Caverns we will be ready to throw everything we have at him," said Master Haddon. "We can attack with magic and with physical weapons. We can station Wind Dancers in the shops and side caves, and then spring the trap on Morren and his armies."

"We can take down the undead army and regular army there, and save the students for the defense of the Trees of Cliffside," said Kerinelle.

"Exactly," said Haddon. "If we can stop Morren in the Caverns, then we need not endanger the students."

"I like this plan," said Kerinelle. "The safety of the students is important, but they may not appreciate being excluded. They have been preparing for octurns now and are willing to do whatever it takes to defeat Morren."

"I have a feeling that they will have plenty of opportunity to put their newfound powers to use," said Mistress Brena. "I don't think Morren is going to be so easy to defeat."

Master Haddon sighed, "I don't either, but I think we can at least weaken him and his forces."

"As you are aware, I have been training many of the older students in the use of the bow," said Tavat. "Gannaire has runed and spelled the arrows to strike true. They will be of great use in defeating the undead."

"We should include Gannaire, Lynette and Joran in these discussions," said Libraen. "I'll send Cullen to fetch them." He stepped outside the salon for a few moments and sent Cullen on the errand.

It wasn't long before the three of them arrived. They were in the dining hall when Cullen found them. They had been talking with the students and Wind Dancers about the upcoming battle.

"One thing we haven't discussed is the High Matriarch's plans," said Master Haddon after Gannaire, Joran, and Lynette showed up. "As you know she had me tortured when I reported the upcoming attack by Morren. Surely by now, she believes me."

"I'm sure she has heard the reports from Erboer and Esteryia," said Kerinelle.

"She sent for all the Matriarchs and Patriarchs of the Eight Realms," said Master Haddon. "She ordered that they muster troops."

"That could be in our favor," said Libraen.

"That remains to be seen," said Kerinelle. "She could be mustering them to join with Morren's forces. The last message from Glendelle indicated that was a possibility."

"Great Wind preserves us if that is the case," said Mistress Brenna.

# CHAPTER 20
# DRAGONS

Lynette and Joran sat in the salon in Central Tree with Mother Kerinelle, Father Libraen, Master Haddon, and Mistress Brena. Lynette and Joran were talking about their time in the world of dreams.

"We learned something very interesting about the Malakand," said Joran. "And we were wondering if you knew about it."

"What is it?" asked Kerinelle. "What did you learn?"

"Did you know that the Malakand were once dragons several thousands of cycles ago?" asked Lynette.

Libraen and Master Haddon looked at one another. Master Haddon nodded his head as if making up his mind about something.

"Yes, we know about it," he said. "It is thought to be nothing more than a myth, though. There are some ancient manuscripts and documents about it in the Great Library. Nothing has ever been proved, one way or another."

"Tell us what you learned," said Mistress Brena.

"The dragons were a lot vicious and blood-thirsty. They controlled the skies and the winged and wingless were in danger of being wiped out," said Lynette. "That is why Halalouma is underground. The Wind Dancers of that time moved the earth and formed the giant underground cave in which the city now resides."

"But something had to be done about the dragons, so a great device was built in Halalouma that could change the dragons and make them peaceful," said Joran.

"So, a great device was built by the Wind Dancers and when it was activated, it did, in fact, change the dragons," said Lynette taking up the story. "That is where all the Malakand come from."

"But some were thrown into a void-like space and were changed into demons," said Joran. "We learned that Saarnak was once the leader of the dragons and was changed into the demon he is now."

"We had an idea," said Lynette. "Maybe there is a way to change the three Malakand that came here to Cliffside with Tavat back into dragons."

"But what of the blood-thirsty nature of dragons?" asked Kerinelle. "We have enough to worry about with the coming attack."

"Yes, what's to say these Malakand won't become vicious as dragons," said Mistress Brena.

"These Malakand have peaceful natures," insisted Lynette. "They are our friends. We believe they would be a great asset in the defense of Cliffside."

"Wouldn't there be a way to change the Malakand back to dragons?" asked Joran. "Surely the Wind Dancers would have had a spell or something, some way to return the Malakand to their natural form."

"Yes," said Libraen excitedly. "They probably did. I think I may have come across something about it in my ramblings in the Great Library. I will go search the ancient documents about the dragons and see what I can find."

"But do you want to take the risk of changing these three Malakand back to dragons?" asked Kerinelle.

"I think at this point we don't have a lot of choice," said Libraen. "Let me see what I can find out before we make a final decision." He got up and left the salon and went to the Great Library.

After many hours of searching and reading, Libraen finally found what he was looking for—a spell to reverse the effect of the ancient spell that turned the Malakand into dragons.

By the time he returned to the salon, Lynette and Joran had long since gone back to the practice field and resumed their training with the students.

Libraen held in his arms the ancient manuscript containing the spell. He spread it out on his desk in their office. He and Kerinelle looked over it with Master Haddon and Mistress Brena to familiarize themselves with it.

It would require many Wind Dancers to reverse the spell, and fortunately, almost every Wind Dancer in the Eight Realms had gathered to help in the defense of Cliffside.

But first, they would need to talk to the three Malakand. They called a meeting with Tavat, Lynette, and Joran to see what they thought about it before talking with the Malakand.

"Tavat, you know the Malakand better than anyone here," said Kerinelle. "We would like to know your opinion concerning their willingness to be changed back into dragons."

They told Tavat about the ancient Wind Dancers and the spell that changed the dragons into Malakand. Tavat was shocked that the Malakand's ancestors had been the dragons of the ancient world. His people, the Clans of the Northern

Plateaus, had stories and legends about the dragons of the ancient world.

"I do not know how the Malakand will feel about being changed," said Tavat. "I feel that Gormon and Fessa will probably agree, but I am not sure about Bicken. You had best ask them. I will go and find them and bring them to you." Tavat left the office and flew to the blacksmith's shop where they were helping to make arrows.

"Gormon, Fessa, and Bicken, Mother Kerinelle and Father Libraen wish to see you," said Tavat.

"What for they wish to see us?" asked Gormon.

"They want to ask for your help," said Tavat. "Just come with me and they will explain everything."

Tavat led them to the lift and took the Malakand up to the flight platform outside Kerinelle's and Libraen's office. They walked inside and saw that Lynette and Joran were there with Kerinelle, Libraen, Master Haddon, and Mistress Brena.

"Let's go to the salon," said Kerinelle smiling. "It is much more comfortable than this office."

Everyone followed her into the salon and once they were all seated he asked Lynette to tell them what she learned in the world of dreams concerning the Malakand.

"Gormon, I don't know how to tell you this, so I'll just spit it out. The Malakand were once dragons, thousands of cycles ago," said Lynette. "The dragons were a violent race who attacked both the winged and the wingless mercilessly. They were in danger of wiping them out."

"Dragons?" asked Gormon, shocked. "We were dragons? But what happened?"

Bicken didn't seem to be surprised, but Fessa was just as shocked as Gormon.

She looked at Bicken and put her hands on her hips.

"Bicken, you don't look surprised," commented Libraen.

Bicken hung his head and then looked up at Libraen. "This I know," he said.

"My father tells me, and his father tells him, and his father tells him, way back. That is why I know the way to Halalouma. Is all big secret."

Fessa chattered noisily at Bicken and they argued for a few moments. Then she turned her back to him in anger. She was mad at him for not telling her of their ancestors' past.

"We were once dragons," said Fessa in amazement.

"Your ancestors were," said Kerinelle. "Wouldn't you like to be dragons again? Libraen has found the spell that would make it possible."

"Yes, I would," said Gormon almost immediately. He looked at Bicken and spoke in chatters and chirps explaining what Kerinelle and Libraen had told them.

"I hear what they say," said Bicken frowning. "I thinking about it." He stood and began pacing back and forth across the salon with his hands clasped behind his scaly back.

Fessa chattered at him angrily. He stopped pacing and sat back down beside her. He tried to pat her reassuringly on the knee, but she pulled away from him.

"We wants to be dragons too," she said, glaring at Bicken. He was always so contrary, but she was going to brook no nonsense from him with something as important as this.

"What we needs to do?" asked Bicken, sighing. Sometimes Fessa could be so unreasonable.

"You don't need to do anything," said Libraen. "We will call you when we have gathered everyone and everything we need for the spell."

The Malakand, Lynette, Joran, and Tavat were excused and went back to their tasks preparing for the attack from Morren.

"Perhaps we should confer with the rest of the Wind Council," said Master Haddon. "Mistress Brena and I will go meet with them and explain what it is we want to do."

"Do you think they will object?" asked Kerinelle.

"Some will, some won't," answered Mistress Brena. "You know how they can be. But with something this important, what Master Haddon and I think will make all the difference. I don't think we will have any trouble convincing them. You aren't having second thoughts, are you?"

"No, I think we should go ahead with our plans as soon as possible," said Kerinelle.

Master Haddon and Mistress Brena left the salon and flew to gather the Wind Council. After meeting with them and explaining the plan, almost all of them agreed. They flew back to the salon and told Libraen and Kerinelle that the Wind Council had agreed with the plan.

Libraen walked out to the flight platform and called a meeting of all the Wind Dancers and students gathered in the field below the three Trees of Cliffside. When he had everyone's attention, he told them of their plan to change the Malakand into dragons. He explained what they would do and summoned the Malakand. He instructed them to stand in the center of the field.

Then he told the Wind Dancers and students to form concentric circles around them, in row after row of circles, with the Wind Council members forming the first circle.

Libraen taught them the words of the spell. He lifted his hands and began to chant. Everyone began to chant with him. The wind picked up and swirled around the three Malakand who looked scared. They were all bright yellow.

Suddenly the Malakand began to grow. Their bodies stretched out and their tails grew longer. Their heads became larger, with rows of viciously sharp teeth. Wings began to sprout and grow on each of their backs. The wind continued to swirl around the now changing Malakand.

The concentric circles of Wind Dancers and students were forced to back up as the Malakand grew into dragons. They were ten wingspans from the tip of their snouts to the tip of their tails. They were enormous, and they were beautiful. Their scales were multifaceted and a rainbow of colors. And they were no longer afraid. They were a beautiful shade of green. Fessa, being female, still had a row of spines on top of her head.

Each of the dragons began to roar with joy and the sound was deafening. Now was the time to find out if they were going to be a threat.

"Gormon, can you hear me," asked Libraen.

The dragon that was formally Gormon turned and looked down at Libraen. He lowered his head until his eyes were even with where Libraen stood on the flight platform. He looked him in the eye and Libraen could see that Gormon had the same temperament.

Gormon laughed and said, "Yes, I can hear you. You need not even speak. I can hear your thoughts," he said perfectly. Gone was the halting speech of the former Malakand. "You need not worry either. We are with you and will help you defend Cliffside from Morren and his army of undead."

Libraen sighed in relief. "What about Fessa and Bicken?" he asked.

"We are with you also," said Fessa. She looked at Bicken and nudged him with her snout.

"Yes, we are all with you and will help defend Cliffside," agreed Bicken. "We are no danger to you."

"Thank you. Why don't you test out your new wings," Libraen suggested.

"Yes," said Gormon. "Let's fly!" He spread his wings and leapt into the air. Fessa and Bicken soon followed him. They flew round and round above the field, roaring. Soon they flew up to the Wind Dancer's Ledge and landed to look out across the Eight Realms.

Then they leapt off the Ledge, swooped down to the three Trees of Cliffside. Each landed on one of the three Trees. They roared in delight. Then they flew down and landed back on the field where the Wind Dancers and students stood in awe. The majesty of the dragons held everyone transfixed.

Master Haddon and Mistress Brena flew up to the flight platform and joined Libraen and Kerinelle. They excused everyone else and discussed tactics with the dragons until time for last-meal.

"One other thing," said Gormon with the equivalent of a dragon smile. "We will need something to eat. What do you suggest?"

"Ah, yes," said Libraen. "We have a large herd of tioldoer at the edge of the camp. You are welcome to take what you need. Or you can go hunting the wild tioldoer."

"Hunting sounds good to me," said Bicken. Gormon turned to look at him.

"Yes, we will go hunting then," agreed Gormon. The three dragons leapt into the air and flew away to hunt. They each returned with a fat tioldoer and settled down to eat them almost whole.

When they were done the sun was beginning to set. The dragons curled their tails around their bodies and settled down to sleep in the field beneath the three Trees.

Before they went to sleep, Tavat came to talk with them. "I am proud of you," he said. He walked around admiring them. "I am also glad you are on our side."

Gormon laughed. "Yes, I can hear your thoughts, Tavat. We are still the same Malakand mentally, or I should say, we have the same temperaments. We are still your friends."

"Yes, we are just bigger and smarter than before, and we have wings," said Fessa happily. "It is wonderful to fly, Tavat."

"Yes, it is," he agreed. "What about you, Bicken? Are you happy to be a dragon?"

"Humph," said Bicken. "It is nice to fly and I must say, I did enjoy hunting the tioldoer, feeling the wind in my wings..."

"Yes, he is happy," interrupted Fessa as she nudged Bicken with her big head.

"Well, I will go now, and let you get some sleep," said Tavat. "I'm sure there will be more planning to do."

Gormon spread his mouth wide and yawned. A big flame erupted out of his mouth and nostrils. "Oh, excuse me," he said somewhat surprised.

"Do that again," said Fessa excitedly.

Gormon opened he mouth and shot a spear of flame into the air. Then Fessa and Bicken tried it and also blew flame out of their mouths.

Tavat laughed with delight. "Just be careful not to set the trees on fire," he said. "Your flames will be valuable when the fighting begins."

The dragons finally settled down and went to sleep. Tavat spread his bedroll out next to them, but far enough away that they couldn't roll over on him. He still felt protective of them. After all, they had saved his life and he owed them a debt, which he doubted he could ever repay.

***

Lare had been riding in a haze of heartache and disappointment almost non-stop for an octurn. He had barely eaten anything, and now that he was almost to his destination, he realized he was hungry. He took this as a good sign. At least he felt something.

As he rode into Cliffside, he was amazed to see hundreds of tents lined up in military fashion. He saw Wind Dancers and students performing magical spells, shooting at targets with bows and crossbows, and practicing with swords and knives.

He didn't know what good he would do in the fight with Morren, but he was willing to use his fighting skills in the defense of Cliffside. There was even a unit of wingless soldiers practicing on the field before the Trees of Cliffside.

Lare spotted Tavat and wondered where the Malakand was. Tavat was in front of the blacksmith's shop making arrows.

Gannaire was there with some Wind Dancers. They were carving runes on, and spelling, the arrows.

When Tavat looked up, he saw Lare dismounting from Nart. He went up to Lare and clasped him by the forearm.

"It is good to see you, my friend," said Tavat. "I thought you had gone home and we would never see you again."

Lare sighed and hung his head. "My girl got married in my absence. There is nothing there for me anymore," said Lare. "So, I thought I would come here and offer what help I could against Morren. But it looks like preparations are well underway."

"Yes, but we can use every able body we can get for the coming battle. You need to meet Mother Kerinelle and Father Libraen. I'm sure they will have a use for you," said Tavat.

Lare tied Nart to a fencepost in front of the blacksmith's shop and checked the trough to see that there was plenty of water in it. Then he unsaddled him and tossed the saddle over the fence. He slung his pack onto his back.

"Will Nart be all right if I leave him here?" he asked.

"Yes, we could ask the Malakand to keep an eye on him, but I don't think anyone will bother him," said Tavat laughing.

Just then the dragons flew over the field and Lare ducked. "Great Winds!" he exclaimed. "Where did they come from?"

Gormon, Fessa, and Bicken, landed in the field and trudged ponderously over to the blacksmith's shop to greet Lare.

"Hello, Lare," thundered Gormon.

"How do you know who I am?" He looked at the three dragons somewhat fearfully. For some reason Tavat was laughing. "What is going on? What is so funny?"

Tavat stopped laughing and wheezed, "Lare, don't you recognize the Malakand?"

"What? Where…" said Lare as he looked around for them.

"Here we are," said Fessa. "We have been changed to dragons."

"What? How…" stuttered Lare. He couldn't believe it. "What happened?"

They told him about the ancient dragons and how they had been changed, and about the spell that had changed the three of them into dragons.

"I can hear your thoughts. Yes, it is really we. We are now dragons. And no, we won't eat you," laughed Fessa.

"Then you must be Bicken," said Lare to the dragon that had yet to speak.

"Yes, I am Bicken," he said as he lay down and curled his tail around his large body. "And we have just returned from hunting." He smacked his lips.

"Hunting?" asked Lare.

"Yes," said Gormon. "We enjoy hunting the wild tioldoer. But soon we will be hunting the undead." He roared and blew a flame to show off to Lare.

"Well, all of you are certainly impressive," said Lare. He was still a bit uneasy around them.

"Come, I'll take you to meet Mother Kerinelle and Father Libraen," said Tavat. They will know how best to use you in the battle."

Tavat walked with Lare to the lift for Central Tree. Although Tavat could have flown to the flight platform outside their office he rode the lift up with Lare out of politeness.

"How was your family," asked Tavat.

"My father is dead," said Lare. "He was tortured by the Ferndorens, the family that has been looking for me."

"I am sorry, my friend," said Tavat. He put his hand on Lare's shoulder in sympathy. "What of your mother?"

"She is well," said Lare. "I wanted her to come with me but she would not leave her home. I suppose she is safer there."

They arrived at the platform and walked off the lift toward the office. Tavat knocked on the door and Cullen opened it.

"May I help you?" asked Cullen.

"We need to see Mother Kerinelle and Father Libraen," said Tavat. "I have brought someone who is willing to fight to protect Cliffside."

Cullen opened the door wider and stepped aside so that Tavat and Lare could pass. "Right this way," said Cullen. He led them to the salon where Mother and Father were talking with Master Haddon and Mistress Brena.

"Ah, Tavat," said Father Libraen. "I see you have brought someone. Please have a seat." He indicated the sofa next to the fireplace.

Tavat introduced Lare to everyone. Then he and Lare sat on the sofa across from Kerinelle and Libraen.

"Lare helped me when I was wounded. I would have died without his help," said Tavat. "But I have brought him to you because he wants to help Cliffside now. I told him you would know how best he could help."

Libraen looked at Lare strangely. "He is perfect," he said. "Kerin, what do you think? Do you think he is the one?"

Kerinelle looked at Lare and then got up to go stand in front of him. "You know I had a vision about you," she said finally.

"Me? You had a vision of me?" asked Lare incredulously. "But I'm a nobody."

Kerinelle put her hand on Lare's head and shut her eyes. "Yes...yes, you have absolutely no magic," she said. "You are rare. Everyone has some magic, even the wingless. The winged have more magic, of course, as they are the ones who can become Wind Dancers. But the wingless have at least a spark of magic even if they don't realize it. But you are completely devoid of any magic whatsoever."

"I...I am?" asked Lare. "And that is a good thing?"

"Yes, it is a good thing as far as Tavat's granddaughter is concerned. You will be able to get past the spells Morren uses to keep her confined," said Libraen.

"Ooloo can be rescued then?" asked Tavat looking hopeful.

"I am saying that Lare will be able to get past the spells Morren put on Ooloo's wagon. He is probably the only person who can. Anyone with even a spark of magic would be affected by the spells," said Kerinelle.

"Then we should go rescue her immediately," said Tavat as he jumped to his feet.

"No, not yet, Tavat. You heard what Swen said about her captivity. There is more to it than just getting past the spells," said Master Haddon. "Timing is important. Besides, our first concern is protecting Cliffside from Morren's attack."

Tavat sat back down dejectedly. "How will we know when the time is right?" he asked.

"It will have to be when Morren is preoccupied with his attack," said Libraen. "That could be any turn now. We have spies stationed just past the upper opening of the Caverns. We will know soon when Morren will be here."

"Well, it cannot come soon enough for me," said Tavat. "For then Lare and I can go rescue Ooloo."

# CHAPTER 21
# ATTACK

The three dragons soon discovered that they had another gift. They discovered that they could turn invisible as well as breathe fire. With this new talent, they could sneak up on Morren and his armies and never be seen. They also discovered that they could communicate with others mentally as well as vocally.

They had just returned to Cliffside from hunting and eating their first-meal of the turn. Libraen and Kerinelle walked out onto the flight platform to speak with them.

"Gormon, we want you and Fessa and Bicken to fly through the Caverns into the Northern Provinces and scout out where Morren is currently camped. We also want you to estimate the troop strength of the undead as well as the regular army. Then return here as soon as possible," said Libraen. "But do not engage the enemy."

"When do you want us to leave," asked Gormon.

"The sooner the better," replied Kerinelle. "We need to get a definite idea of when Morren is going to attack. We need to prepare a surprise for him in the Caverns."

"We will leave now then," said Gormon. "How is Wug?" He missed the little creature.

"Wug is fine," laughed Kerinelle. "He is a handful, though."

"Are you sure you do not want us to attack Morren?" asked Bicken impatiently.

"Yes, we are sure," said Libraen. "Just stay invisible and scout out his strength."

"We will see you soon then," said Fessa. The three dragons leapt into the air and flew to the Caverns. They had to enter one at a time due to their size. They flew one after the other through the Caverns and came out at the upper end. Then they flew into the Northern Provinces, but not before turning invisible.

They only had to fly about half a turn before they spotted the enemy. They were shocked to see the hoards of regular troops and the thousands of undead soldiers.

Morren rode on his big, black dragon, circling over his armies. The dragon began to sniff and stare around wildly. Gormon realized that the black dragon might be sensing their presence.

"We had better get out of here," he communicated to Fessa and Bicken mentally. "I'm not sure, but I think Morren's dragon can sense our presence." He turned and flew back toward the Eight Realms. Fessa and Bicken followed close behind.

They returned after about half a turn and flew back through the Caverns just before dark. Libraen and Kerinelle rushed out to the flight platform to talk with them.

"What did you find?" asked Kerinelle.

"Morren is only a turn from the Caverns," said Gormon.

"What about his troop numbers?" asked Libraen "How many has he gathered?"

"He has at least two thousand regular troops and about an equal number of undead," said Fessa. "He also has a sizable army of about two hundred wingless soldiers with him also."

"One other thing," said Gormon. "I think that Morren's dragon sensed our presence. But I couldn't be sure. We didn't hang around to find out, but flew immediately back."

Bicken spoke up just then, "You don't have much time. Whatever you are planning to do, I suggest that you prepare for the attack to come by first light, if not sooner."

"Thank you, we will get in position just after last-meal" said Libraen. "Have you eaten yet?"

"No, we flew directly back," said Gormon.

"Feel free to take what you need from the herd of tioldoer," said Libraen. "You need to stay close. After you eat you will need to get into position in the Caverns to spring the trap we discussed."

The dragons flew over the herd of tioldoer and each grabbed one. After they had eaten, they flew back to the Caverns and got into position. They each perched on separate ledges overlooking the winding road that ran around the edges of the Caverns. Members of the Wind Council also positioned themselves in the Caverns, along with several hundred Wind Dancers.

The plan was to prevent Morren and his hoards from coming through the Caverns. If they could be stopped there then Cliffside would be safe. Boulders had been moved to the lower entrance, creating a bottleneck that only a few at a time could pass through.

Tavat, Swen, and Lare positioned themselves outside the Caverns near the upper entrance. Tavat would fire a flaming arrow as soon as they spotted Morren's forces. They would stay hidden until he and the enemy were passed. Then they would make their way to the wagon where Ooloo was held and try to free her.

If she were riding the black dragon with Morren, then they would still go to Morren's camp and hide. They would wait until Ooloo was once again confined to the wagon and would free her if possible. Tavat also intended to kill Morren if the opportunity presented itself.

Joran and Lynette hid near the upper exit of the Caverns to await the coming attack. They talked quietly as they waited.

"Are you afraid?" asked Lynette.

"Of course. But I'm not going to let that stop me from doing whatever is necessary to prevent Morren and his armies from getting through the Caverns."

"In a way, I am glad Father and Aerielle are not here. I wonder, though, where they are," Lynette said sadly.

"Don't worry. We will find them after we have defeated the enemy," said Joran. "Your father will take good care of our daughter."

Libraen and Kerinelle had positioned themselves near the middle of the Caverns so they could have an overall view of the coming battle. They talked about the accident that led them to believe Morren was dead. They wondered how he had survived and was now coming to exact his revenge. The sun had set by the time everyone was in position and ready to spring the trap.

The dragons and Wind Dancers didn't have long to wait. A few hours before sunrise, Tavat saw the undead soldiers flying toward the Caverns. He fired the warning arrow and Joran spotted it. Joran blew the horn letting everyone know the attack was imminent. Cliffside's forces were well hidden and everyone waited until the Caverns were almost full of enemy soldiers.

Then Joran blew the horn again and the Wind Dancers came out of hiding and sprung the trap. Hundreds of crossbow bolts and magically runed arrows flew into the undead, striking them in their hearts in a carefully planned crossfire.

Many of the undead fell to the ground, arrows or crossbow bolts sticking out of their chests. Then the second part of the trap was sprung as the dragons came out of hiding.

A magical wall of flame bore down on the enemy just as the regular troops flew into the Caverns. The flames took out almost half of them. They fell to the floor of the Caverns, and their wings burned to stubs. There they died quickly. The rest who escaped the flames continued to fly toward the lower entrance of the Caverns. Last to enter the Caverns were the foot soldiers.

"We need to stop the remaining troops," shouted Joren over the sounds of fighting. He and Lynette came out from behind the boulders where they were stationed near the upper entrance and flew after the enemy.

"There are just too many of them," said Lynette as she and Joran threw lightning bolts at the enemy.

Joran blew the horn a third time and the Wind Dancers attacked the remaining troops with magic. They smashed them with boulders and continued to throw fireballs and lightning bolts at them.

The enemy broke ranks and flew toward the lower entrance of the Caverns. The Wind Dancers engaged the enemy wherever they could, using magic as well as swords and other weapons in the fight.

But some of the troops still made it down to the lower end of the Caverns. While some fought, the rest moved boulders and widened the opening. The undead and regular soldiers who got through the entrance began to attack the students who were protecting Cliffside.

The students threw everything they had at them and more of Morren's troops were destroyed. But they kept coming. Cliffside's forces were still vastly outnumbered.

At last, Morren swooped into the Caverns on Death and began to take out some of the Wind Dancers and Wind Council members who had gathered there to fight. His power was incredible. He must have had a shield up because lightning bolts and fireballs just bounced off him. His shield was impenetrable.

Libraen and Kerinelle decided to pull their forces back to the lower end of the Caverns as Gormon, Fessa, and Bicken attacked Death. Gormon latched onto Death's neck as Fessa and Bicken each attacked a wing, tearing chunks of flesh away. Death tried to wrench away, but they renewed their efforts, roaring and growling. They had to be careful though because Ooloo was sitting on Death in front of Morren. She looked miserable.

Ooloo had finally made it to Cliffside, but the circumstances were not as she had imagined. If only she could get free of Morren. She watched as he attacked the Wind Dancers and Council members, who continued to throw fireballs and lightning bolts at him to prevent him from getting to the lower end of the Caverns.

As the students defended Cliffside they suddenly noticed another large army flying toward them from the west. These troops wore the livery of the High Matriarch. The students were relieved, thinking they were there to help until the troops also began to attack them. Now they were fighting two foes.

"Great Wind," said Kerinelle. "The High Matriarch has betrayed us. Blast her black heart."

Libraen quickly flew over the forces and magnified his voice so they all could hear him. He had to put a stop to the slaughter of his students.

"You must not do this," he shouted. "These students are the sons and daughters of the Eight Realms. The High Matriarch has betrayed us all by forging an alliance with Morren. Help us defeat his forces. If Cliffside falls then the whole Eight Realms will fall. For the love of the Winds, you must turn and help us defeat the real enemy."

Some of the High Matriarch's soldiers stopped attacking the students and instead began protecting them. Others began to fight against Morren's troops, both regulars and undead. It was hard to tell who was fighting for whom. Some of the troops of the High Matriarch continued attacking the students and Wind Dancers, but many of them switched sides.

Meanwhile, in the Caverns, Morren's dragon was being attacked and his wings were torn to shreds by the teeth and claws of Gormon, Fessa, and Bicken. Gormon was bleeding where Death's teeth had torn a chunk from his left wing. Fessa and Bicken also had wounds inflicted by the big dragon's claws and teeth. Nevertheless, Morren flew back toward the upper Caverns to escape the three dragons. As he flew he healed his dragon as best he could, but there would be scars.

Ooloo was barely able to hang on as the dragon as Death swerved to avoid another bite from Gormon. Ooloo suddenly fell off. But she was wearing the collar that chained her to the collar around Death's neck. She dangled from the chain, her legs swinging wildly while she grasped and tore at the collar around her neck. She felt that she was going to choke to death as she struggled and gasped for air.

Morren reached down and pulled her back up to sit in front of him on the dragon. Gormon and the others snapped and bit at Morren but they could not get through his shield.

Gormon tried repeatedly to attack Morren but his shield held fast. He even tried to snatch Ooloo away from him but he was unsuccessful. She was now enclosed in Morren's protective shield also.

Morren flew back to the upper entrance and blew it up with a blast of power as he flew out of it. It began to cave in. Rocks and boulders rained down on the three dragons and the Wind Dancers who were still fighting in the Caverns. They all quickly flew out of the lower entrance to escape being crushed by the falling boulders.

"Come on," shouted Joran. "We have to get out of here."

"Right behind you," said Lynette as she followed Joran out of the Caverns.

Gormon. Fessa and Bicken tried to follow Morren, but the upper end of the Caverns was sealed. They finally had to exit the Caverns at the lower end.

The dragons attacked the remaining enemy troops going through the opening, blowing flames and burning them down. They chased them out of the Caverns and toward Cliffside, continuing to attack. But they had to be careful not to hurt any of the students fighting to protect the school. They used their teeth and claws to take out as many enemy soldiers as possible.

Kerinelle fought with magic as well as a sword. She was surrounded by several of Morren's regular troops and was about to be overcome by them. Gormon swooped out of the sky and snatched two of the enemy up with his claws and bit their heads off. Kerinelle dispatched the remaining two soldiers with her runed sword. She was bleeding from a wound in her side but she kept fighting, stopping only long enough to allow one of the healers to minister to her. Then she turned to help one of the students as they fought off the enemy.

Libraen fought a few feet away, throwing fireballs and bolts of lightning at the enemy. He was with a group of students in front of Central Tree who were preventing the enemy from taking over the Tree. Other students were busy protecting the other two Trees.

Meanwhile, Tavat, Swen, and Lare made their way into Morren's camp. The only ones left in the camp were the men and women who served the soldiers.

They slipped by tent after tent until they stealthily made their way to Ooloo's wagon. There was no mistaking it because it was the only wagon in the camp. They discovered she wasn't there so they found hiding places behind stacks of supplies and settled down to wait until she was returned to her wagon. When they had left the fight, Morren's dragon had been under attack by Gormon, Fessa, and Bicken. They didn't know how long they would have to wait, but they suspected it wouldn't be long from the looks of the big dragon.

Still, back at Cliffside, the students and Wind Dancers were harried by Morren's troops. They fought on until long after sunrise. Finally, as more and more of the High Matriarch's troops switched sides, Libraen saw that they were beginning to make headway. The turning point came when the last of the undead soldiers were taken out. Now they just had to defeat the remaining enemy troops and the soldiers of the High Matriarch who continued to attack Cliffside.

There were plenty of wounded on both sides and the healers were kept busy the entire fight. Slowly, the remaining troops were almost defeated, mainly due to the three dragons. Without them, Cliffside would have been defeated.

As more and more of the regular troops were defeated as well, many of them threw down their weapons and surrendered. Soon, the rest of the enemy soldiers were defeated by the brave students and Wind Dancers of Cliffside.

As the sun began to rise high in the sky the battle wound down. Forces from each side were exhausted. Father Libraenaire flew over the battlefield and observed as the students and Wind Dancers rounded up the last of the enemy troops. He instructed the students to stack the bodies of the dead and undead into a giant funeral pyre and then he magically set it ablaze.

Meanwhile, Morren barely made it back to his camp. Death was still terribly wounded. His wings were partially shredded and blood seeped from numerous bite wounds and claw marks. Morren chanted and completed healing him before the big dragon succumbed to his wounds.

Morren had deserted his troops, but he had one more trick up his sleeve. He dismounted Death and dragged Ooloo off the dragon with him. He unhooked her chain from the dragon and made his way to the large round tent where the pedestal and black orb were kept, dragging Ooloo all the way. She kicked and screamed and tried to pull away from him, but it was useless. She couldn't use her magic because she still wore the nullifying bracelets.

"I have a surprise for you," Morren said as he led Ooloo by the chain. He pulled back the folds of the tent and jerked the chain, making Ooloo follow him into the tent. She fought him the whole way.

Once they were both inside the tent, he removed the chain and collar from around her neck, but he left the bracelets on her wrists. She knew he wanted her to ask what the surprise was, but she wouldn't give him the satisfaction. She followed him in stony silence, her head hanging down and her fists clenched to her sides. She was looking for an opportunity to strike him down.

But when she looked up, Ooloo saw an old winged man chained to the pedestal, his arms stretched around it. He was gagged and had been severely beaten about the face. She recognized him anyway.

"Paap," she screamed and attempted to run across the tent to him. Morren grabbed her by the shoulder before she could go two steps. Saarnak laughed from the window in the black orb.

"You see, Ooloo, we will have your cooperation," said Saarnak. He closed his fist and squeezed, just as he had done to Ooloo, and Tavat convulsed and seemed to be choking. Ooloo could not stand it.

"Stop it," she screamed, tears streaming down her face. "Stop hurting him."

But Saarnak did not stop. He held his fist for several more seconds to make a point. Tavat's face began turning blue.

"Make him stop," Ooloo appealed to Morren. "Please, make him stop." She pulled on one of Morren's sleeves. Finally, Saarnak stopped.

"Oh, Paap, I'm so sorry," cried Ooloo. Saarnak laughed again.

"If you help us, I will let him live," he said. "If you refuse, then..." he squeezed his fist closed again and Tavat convulsed and screamed around the gag.

"Stop, stop, I'll help you," Ooloo said. "Blast you, I'll help you!" She glared at Saarnak. "What must I do?" Saarnak released his fist again and Tavat slumped between the chains holding him up.

Morren turned to her and said, "You simply have to hold my hands and lend me your power." He removed the cuffs from her wrists and held his hands out to her. He stared at her expectantly.

She thought for a moment to attack Morren now, but she knew Saarnak would kill Paap before she could do anything. She resignedly placed her hands in Morren's. He began to chant in a strange, dark language. As he chanted the window in the black orb began to enlarge.

Ooloo felt power draining from her. The window expanded beyond the orb and became a large opening. When the opening was large enough, Saarnak stepped through. Behind him came demon after demon and pushing through the tent opening.

Ooloo tried to let go, but Morren would not release her hands. He continued to chant and the window ceased to grow. The pedestal and the black orb stood in an open doorway now. The portal was the size of a large double door standing in the middle of the tent, and more and more demons continued to pour through. All of them were winged and some had horns while some did not, but they were all terrifyingly ugly and malevolent.

Finally, Morren stopped chanting and released her hands. She immediately ran to Tavat and removed the gag. She was horrified to see that the winged man chained to the pedestal was not her Paap at all. He was the same size and age, but he was definitely not Paap. Morren and Saarnak had tricked her and had conjured Tavat's appearance onto the wingman chained to the pedestal.

"What have I done?" wailed Ooloo. "Where is my grandfather? What have you done with him?" she asked.

"I have no idea where your grandfather is," said Saarnak. He laughed wickedly. I saw him in your mind, so it was easy to make this man look like him.

Ooloo immediately threw a ball of fire at the demon lord, but he easily deflected it with a wave of his hand. In return, he conjured a net of energy and threw it at Ooloo. She dodged it, which surprised both Morren and Saarnak.

"Enough of this," said Saarnak and held out his fist again and squeezed. Ooloo tried to fight against the power but she was weakened from opening the portal. Ooloo collapsed in pain and felt she was choking.

Morren conjured another net of power and tossed it over Ooloo as she was distracted by Saarnak's attack. The net tightened around her, and the more she struggled, the tighter the net became, just as before. And just as before she realized the futility of fighting against it. She became still and quiet.

Saarnak released his fist and Ooloo gasped with relief. Morren walked over to her and waved away the net. Before she could move he clapped the cuffs back on her wrists.

"Get up," he said. "Time to go back to your wagon."

Ooloo slowly rose to her feet. "You got what you wanted. Why do you need me now?" she asked.

"Oh, I don't need you now, but I might in the future. With your power I can open a portal to anywhere," laughed Saarnak. "Now be a good little winglet and go back to your wagon."

He reached over and patted her on the head. Ooloo jerked away from him and glared angrily. Morren dragged her out of the tent by her arm. Demons were still pouring through the portal as she looked over her shoulder. There must be hundreds of them by now. And she was responsible for releasing them into Eruna. They flew after Saarnak toward the Caverns. The blocked entrance would not be a problem for Saarnak. He would reopen the entrance and fly through the Caverns to attack Cliffside.

As the demons flew away, Morren led Ooloo back to her wagon and shoved her through the open door. She collapsed to the floor of the wagon. At least Paap was not really harmed. Morren and Saarnak had tricked her. But what had she done? She lay down and began to weep uncontrollably.

Morren went back to where Death lay and contemplated mounting him. He knew he should head back to Cliffside but first, he wanted to check on the portal he and Ooloo had opened.

He returned to the tent, poured himself some wine, and stared through the portal gazing at the void he had escaped from so long ago. He drank all the wine in one gulp and threw the goblet into the void. He swore to himself he would never go back, regardless of what Saarnak wanted. Then he turned on his heel and left the tent. He mounted his dragon and flew off quickly toward Cliffiside.

By now, Saarnak and all the demons had left the camp on their way to Cliffside to attack the school and gain victory once and for all. Ooloo could no longer hear their snarls and war cries. It was then that she thought she heard Paap's voice.

"Ooloo, I am here, winglet," he said. "Stop crying now. I am going to get you out of here."

"Paap, is it really you?" she asked. She was not going to fall for Saarnak's tricks again.

"Yes, Ooloo. Swen brought me and a friend who will free you from this wagon," said Tavat.

Ooloo stood up and looked out the small window. She could barely see anything through the window, but she was able to see that it was really her Paap this time.

"The door to the wagon is spelled," she said forlornly. "No one can open it or touch it."

"I have brought someone who can," assured Tavat. "His name is Lare and the magic will not affect him. Trust me, little one."

Lare sneaked over to the door and began picking the lock. Before long Ooloo heard a satisfying "snick" as the lock popped open. Then Lare opened the door and climbed into the wagon.

"I cannot go through the door," said Ooloo sadly.

"I know," said Lare kindly, "That is why I am going to carry you through the door."

"Can you remove these bracelets first, please?" she asked hopefully.

Lare pulled off the first one, then the other, bracelet. Ooloo rubbed her wrists in relief.

"I am ready," she said.

Lare picked her up and leapt through the open door with her in his arms. Ooloo felt only a moment of pain as they passed the threshold.

"Give her to me, quickly now," said Tavat. He took Ooloo from Lare and hugged her to his chest.

"Oh Paap, I have done something terrible," she cried. "I have released a terrible army of demons into Eruna."

"Hush now, little one, we saw them as they flew toward the Caverns and Cliffside. We will be careful to avoid them. But we must leave this place at once. We will go north, away from the demons and Cliffside."

"NO! We must go help in the fight against the demons. I have not traveled all the way across Eruna to turn back now!" insisted Ooloo.

"But Ooloo, I just got you back..." Tavat started to protest.

"She is right," said Swen as he put his hand on Tavat's arm. "We must go back and help protect Cliffside."

"I'm going back too," said Lare. "We can't let the demons destroy Cliffside or the Eight Realms. We must help in the fight."

"We need to free the other warriors," said Ooloo. "They were captured when I was taken prisoner by Morren. They are being held in a large tent on the other side of the camp."

"They are still alive?" asked Tavat. He knew she referred to the warriors who had accompanied them on their trek across Eruna. He was surprised Morren had not killed them all.

"All are alive except Batab," said Ooloo. "Morren turned her into one of his undead warriors. I hope to find some way to free her and the other undead warriors and turn them back to normal. But first I want to make Morren pay for what he has done."

"Where is Morren now?" asked Tavat. "I will kill him for you." He did not want his granddaughter to bear the burden of killing someone, even someone as evil as Morren.

"He should be in the circular red tent in the middle of the camp unless he has returned to Cliffside," said Ooloo. "He is very powerful, Paap, but I think I can penetrate any protective shield he may try to use. Then you can attack him. We will need to surprise him with our attack, though. I have an idea. I'll show you where the others are kept first." They made their way across the camp to the large tent where the warriors were kept. They were sitting on the floor of the tent chained together. Lare and the others freed them from their confinement.

After greeting and hugging one another they made their way cautiously to the red tent. But they were disappointed to find that Morren was not there and his dragon was gone. He had apparently returned to Cliffside.

"Paap, there is a terrible demon named Saarnak who wants to take over all of Eruna. We cannot allow this to happen. We must go back to Cliffside and help defeat him," pleaded Ooloo.

Tavat hung his head in resolve. "You are right. We must go back," he said resignedly. He didn't like it, but it was the right thing to do. Saarnak must be defeated.

www.ingramcontent.com/pod-product-compliance
Lightning Source LLC
LaVergne TN
LVHW040523190325
806010LV00001B/2